Stickerhand

Moss Croft

ISBN: 9798389252875

The Novels of Moss Croft

Stickerhand

The Flophouse Years

Crack Up or Play It Cool

God Help the Connipians

Rucksack Jumper

Boscombe

Raspberry Jam

Ghost in the Stables

About the Author

Moss Croft is a pen name. Doesn't give much away, does it? If he went to Cambridge, you can bet it was to the Travelodge, not the fancy university they have there.

Contents

Disclaimer

This is a work of fiction and resemblance to real persons or events is the result of unforeseen coincidence.

Chapter One

In and Out of Bins

1.

The doctor wears a summer dress. A rich cream adorned with heads of wheat all of which are the colour mauve. The thinnest black lines bring out the design, arrest the eye. Classy. The wearer is trying very hard to make small-talk with the staff, two experienced nurses and a student who sit in on her ward round. All but the student wear jeans, only the doctor makes the effort. Varina is here too. She wears better than jeans—a skirt of sorts, long, denim, and a sweater for which the day is far too warm— she looks a bit of a state but social workers sometimes do. And there is a junior doctor in here. Smart as the consultant; this one's a bloke. A charcoal suit, thinnest of pinstripes upon it. Bright blue tie. Not upstaging the consultant doctor, not at all. And it's a full house, the room packed out. One spare chair for the patient; each seen in turn, called off the ward proper.

Caitlin Kavanagh is the doctor's name. All the nurses say Doctor Kav-an-agh, draw out her name. She speaks slowly and they mirror her laboured speech pattern. It isn't a diabolical power which she has, being a figure of authority is enough. Works on the ward. It is as if the stripe on the shoulder has cast a spell. Patient-wise, she decides who stays or goes, what medication they swallow while they are here. With the staff it is simply the meter of speech which she exerts her control over. When she leaves the ward, they revert back to normal. Full pelt for the more excitable nurses. For Casey, the young student.

'The weather is far too nice to be stuck in here all day,' says Caitlin Kavanagh.

'We asked the patients if they wanted to sit in the courtyard,' says Sandra Widdecombe, ward sister. 'It's lovely and sunny, you'd think they would. None of them were interested. Not one.'

'It's a shame,' says the doctor. She glances around the room to see if anyone else wants to contribute their thoughts on the matter. 'Of course, those taking tricyclics can burn very easily.' Her gaze falls on Dr Okafor, the junior doctor doing his six months in psychiatry. The GP training scheme. He simply nods. Dr Kavanagh's small talk is an acquired taste. Technical.

'You'd think sunshine might do them more good than all the meds do,' continues Sandra.

Dr Kavanagh gives this comment a stern look. Doctors, generally, are big fans of medication. This one loves the stuff.

On hearing a commotion outside the door of the room, all quieten and look around. A loud patient is on the approaches. A male nurse, attired in jeans and a T-shirt—most staff dress as the patients do on this ward—puts his head around the door. 'Rice is restless,' he tells those gathered.

The junior doctor gives him a thumbs-up. 'Two minutes.' The inserted head withdraws, the door closes.

'Rice is restless. What a cryptic comment that is,' says Caitlin.

'Latest admission, Dr Kavanagh,' says Ahmed. Dr Ahmed Okafor.

'Rice. We've admitted a Mr Rice, have we?'

'No.'

As she is staring at him, trying to read his face, Dr Okafor suppresses a small grin. Might be giving her his most inscrutable look. Sandra Widdecombe, intervenes, answers the riddle. 'Rice Bradford. Rice is his Christian name. It was after midnight when he came on the ward. Last hospitalised two years ago. Not on this ward.'

'But it was in The Princess Margaret?'

'Oh yes, Dr Kavanagh.' Kav-an-agh, she says, speaking very slowly. Nothing said can be missed in these ward rounds. The content might be wise but to the casual ear they speak to each other like imbeciles. 'We've asked retrieval...' Re-triev-al. '...to bring the old file up. It has already gone into archive—to the basement—but I expect they'll find it.'

'Two minutes, Dr Okafor. Would you fill me in about the man's admission before he comes in. Is he going to plead for his release?'

'Yes, Doctor. I don't know how he is this morning. Very, very labile last night. High. Hyper. And he was most delusional. I think it is schizoaffective disorder which he suffers from. I expect that he is not taking his medication, we haven't got his blood results back yet. It is his first relapse in two years.' The junior doctor's reply is comprehensive and spoken surprisingly quickly. He must have missed the memo.

'The first that has come to our attention, certainly. Which doctor saw him before?' she asks.

The junior doctor studies his notes before replying. 'Dr Chowdhury.'

Caitlin Kavanagh nods purposefully. Old Doctor Chowdhury has retired, Rice Bradford will be her patient now. 'Why was he admitted at that time? It was after midnight, Sandra just said?'

'Stark naked in Brislington. The police picked him up on the street. You see, Dr Kavanagh, he seemed completely unaware of the fact. When I pointed it out—that he was not wearing any clothes at all—he was very surprised. A most hyper mental state. Up like a kite in the sky when I admitted him.'

'Good grief. Will he be clothed when he comes in here? There are ladies present.'

Most in the room chuckle. Sandra, the ward sister, nods at the doctor. 'Very cooperative. Does as he's told and that includes putting his clothes on. Keeping them on. Very cooperative.' The doctor looks at her searchingly. 'Talks twaddle,' adds Sandra. 'Night staff said that he kept asking for his trumpet.'

The student nurse, a fair-haired girl called Casey, laughs out loud. When no one joins in, she cannot stop. Turns it into a cough. The junior doctor talks over her noisy expulsions. 'Rice Bradford, forty-seven years of age, gave us an address in the Greater Manchester area. The hospital database has a different address for him. One just a mile from Brislington High Street. Quite close to where the police picked him up. We have to confirm which is correct, my educated guess, Dr Kavanagh, is that it will be Brislington. The next-of-kin on our records is also local...'

'Yes, yes, Ahmed. Symptoms, please? We want him in here in a moment. We mustn't tell him to wait two minutes and then get him agitated by having the poor fellow wait longer and longer.'

'Quite tricky to say, Doctor. He was causing a disturbance by being naked, more than by his actions. He was approaching strangers and asking about his trumpet...' The coughing girl gives another little splutter. '...even the police said he was polite about it. He gave his name and date-of-birth accurately. When I was admitting him, I asked him a simple cognitive question. Who is the current prime minister? That one.' Dr Okafor pauses, looks once around the room. Eye contact for all who will. 'He said it was Harold Wilson. I think he must have seen my look of surprise, because he tried to correct himself. "Silly of me. Resigned. It's Callaghan." Those were his words. I think those old timers both came before Maggie Thatcher. Long before I came to this country...'

'April, nineteen seventy-six,' says Varina Pope, the psychiatric social worker. She is a regular sitter-in to these ward rounds. A better contributor than most of the nervous nurses. 'That was when Callaghan replaced Wilson. Twenty-one years ago. And he thinks it's just happened.'

'Very good, Varina,' says the presiding doctor. 'Spoken like a pub quizzer. Am I right?'

The room contemplates the new admission's time-shift, how the man with the funny name—Rice—could get so simple a question so spectacularly wrong. Rectified the first error with a second guess that is really no nearer to the right answer.

After a few seconds silence, Caitlin Kavanagh asks it again. 'Are you a pub quizzer, Varina?'

'Good heavens, I am not. I was qualifying around then. A social work student at the University of Birmingham. We all think politics matters in our formative years, don't we? I know I did.'

The doctor nods. 'I think he is here,' she says. The previous noise outside the door is making itself heard again. A loud northern accent. Ken Tinsmith, the male nurse, puts his head around the meeting room door for the second time of the morning.

'Bring Mr Rice in,' says Caitlin Kavanagh, her Irish brogue turning the name from Rice to Royce.

The nurse at the door begins to shake his head. 'Mr Bradford...'

The doctor immediately corrects herself; head down into her notes and straight back up again. '...Rice Bradford. I'm so sorry.'

* * *

'She's a doctor? A doctor-doctor, not just learning, like you?'

Rice Bradford is speaking at a greater volume and a faster speed than anyone else in the room. He lounges back in the seat reserved for the patient at this ward round, hands behind his balding head. Ken Tinsmith sits beside him, just to ensure that there are sufficient males on hand. A rowdy patient gets special attention. No one is heavy-handed: Rice is new and unpredictable; the staff team has yet to learn how he might behave in a given situation. A little muscle at the ready is the safest bet. Ken does not join the ward round as a participant, pays attention only to Rice, observing his body language. Not necessarily attending the words of the consultant. Watching Rice from the next chair along. Looking intently at the man's side profile. Dr Kavanagh has done all the talking up to this point. She has a soothing voice. Speaks slowly, softly. Patients more aggressive than Rice Bradford frequently enter this ward. Things never kick off. Almost never. Drawn-out speech works a treat.

'He's the one learning to be a doctor, not me,' says Ken, pointing towards Ahmed Okafor.

'I am a doctor,' says the smartly-dressed man. 'And we are all learning, are we not? I am a doctor. Dr Okafor.'

'And you're a trick-cyclist already, young lady? Well done. What is your name again?'

'Dr Kavanagh.' Kav-an-agh.

'Your first name? I can hardly call you Dr Kavanagh if we're on a date, can I?'

'This is not a date, Rice. This is my ward round.'

The man laughs, shows the assembled professionals a couple of gaps in his teeth. 'I know we're not on a date. You can do better than me, can't you, doctor? You don't mind me kidding around, do you?' The speed of Rice Bradford's delivery outpaces the doctors by a distance. He has yet to catch the bug.

'Rice, I need to assess how we can help you,' says Dr Kavanagh. The man stares back at her, shows no understanding of such a need. 'It is a very unusual Christian name, isn't it? Rice.'

'An unusual name. It could be that I'm an unusual bloke. Seems likely.' As he speaks, he beams at the ladies in the small crowded room. 'Mr Unusual, you can call me. Or Rice, seeing as how we're on a date...' He winks at the young student nurse sitting on the floor. Ken Tinsmith took her chair because she is the youngest in this crowded room. Knees drawn up, holding her skirt down so it covers them best it can. '...or not on a date. Have it your way.'

Dr Kavanagh has her hands together, making a steeple, elbows on her own knees, nodding as the man speaks. This room has heard it all. The pressure of speech—the speed with which the patient hurtles words from his brain into the moving of air particles—is part of a flailing attempt to prove sanity. The impossible conundrum. Once they've been declared crazy, a patient's subsequent request for a cup of tea can sound like a symptom. And Rice Bradford is fooling no one.

'Is it a Chinese name?' asks Dr Okafor.

'Oh, now then, that's a bit racialist, isn't it?' says Rice. An unexpected accusation, flung without rancour at the only black person in the room. It is also true that Rice looks not remotely Chinese, speaks with a broad northern accent. 'I'm British. You can call me Fish-and-Chips if you like, Rice just happens to be my name.'

The consultant psychiatrist makes a small hand gesture, imploring Dr Okafor, her mentee, to allow the patient to continue. Not to argue the silly point. Her head gives a barely discernible shake. No one in their right mind would accuse Dr Okafor of being a racist, seems to be its intent.

Rice looks directly at the student nurse, the girl hugging her knees on the floor across from him. 'What's your name, love?' he asks.

She glances at Sandra the ward sister before saying, 'Casey. I'm Casey.'

'Very nice. And I'm Rice. Do you think mine is a funny name, Casey?'

'Not funny. It's a rare one.'

'I suppose it is. I'll tell you the story. My dad chose it but he messed up, if you know what I mean.' He says this in quick bursts of speech, loud reports with a pause between each phrase. At a volume to entertain the room and the corridor beyond. 'Do you know what I mean?'

Casey shakes her head. The social worker is sitting behind her—Varina Pope—'Tell us, Rice,' she murmurs.

'There you go, Casey,' says Rice, 'your mum wants to know. Keener than you, I think. Probably on account of being nearer my age.'

Varina laughs at that. 'I'm eager to learn why your dad called you Rice,' says Varina. 'And I'm the hospital social worker, not young Casey's mum.'

'You don't need a social worker,' says Rice, staring at the girl sitting on the floor. 'Keep her as a mum. More useful by a long chalk. That's been my experience, sweetheart.'

Everyone in the room is tittering. It's hardly stand-up but patients on a high are good value. Voice what no one else will.

'When I was a new born—aged nothing, out in the world but only a day or two old, my birth still to be registered—all the family had gathered around,' booms Rice, his northern accent seeming to swell with pride. 'My mother and father and aunties and uncles, they were all saying different names. Brian and Desmond and what have you. Couldn't agree between themselves what was the bestest name for the tiny little baby. Which was me, don't forget. So, by and by, they decided to write them all down and pull just one out of a hat. My dad couldn't spell; he could hardly read nor write. Tram driver, he was. Didn't need reading and writing for his job. Not much of a job if you think on it, you can't steer it anywhere, what with it being wedged into its tracks. But that's a story for an evening when the powers gone off.'

Varina is listening closely, Dr Kavanagh too, while many in the room are laughing—not openly—amused by the self-important delivery.

'He, my father, I remind you, said to all the assembled family— mostly from my mother's side—"How do you spell Eric?" and they all joined in shouting out the letters. He didn't put them down in the right order, you see. Heard them shout the letters out but didn't write them in the proper order. And then my mum only went and picked his paper out of the hat. Rice, that was the word he had written. Right letters, wrong order. Could happen to anyone. And that—Casey and Casey's mum, doctors and nurses, dentists and plumbers too, if you've any in here—is why I'm Rice Bradford. I don't even look like an Eric, do I?'

'For real?' says Casey.

'Oh, I am very, very real,' says Rice. The doctor is shaking her head at the student nurse, her contribution greater than that which anyone so junior usually makes. 'Unless I'm not real, doctor,' adds Rice, turning to the consultant psychiatrist. 'You're in charge, might know better.'

'Thank you, Mr Bradford. And now may I ask one or two questions, please?'

Rice nods his head, makes an exaggerated open-palmed hand gesture. Shows he is all hers.

'Yesterday evening you were picked up on the street by the police. Do you remember that?'

'Of course I remember that. It isn't the sort of thing that happens to a bloke every day, you know.'

'But it has happened before? That you've been picked up by the police.'

'Yes. Only when I've forgotten my clothes. Another doctor, not you, one like you—older, another trick cyclist, they're the only ones who ever examine me—he said there was a name for it. Said I've got a certain condition. He knew the name.'

'A name for taking off your clothes, Mr Bradford?'

'Yes, doctor. I forget what it was.'

'Unfortunate. I should have liked to have heard it.'

'Agitation of the underpants, I expect,' says Rice.

Casey laughs out loud and Varina puts her face in her hands to stifle something similar.

'I should write the textbooks, shouldn't I, love?' he says, peering down at the student nurse, who again tugs her skirt across her knees.

'Mr Bradford,' says Dr Kavanagh, speaking at a quarter of the speed with which the large man expels his words. 'I understand you were looking for a trumpet?'

Rice's broad smile drops off his face. A gentle thud as it hits the often-shampooed carpet. 'I think that must have been the other fella,' says Rice quietly, far more slowly. The pressure in his earlier speech has evaporated. 'The other fella wants the trumpet, doctor. I can't hold a tune.'

'And who is that, Rice? Who is this other man? The man who wants the trumpet.'

'A-ha, that would be telling. The secrets from the other side of the tracks are to be kept exactly there.' His quickness of verbal step has tap-danced straight back into the room. 'A drum is the only instrument for Rice Bradford. Have you seen those Japanese drums, Dr Kavanagh, seen and heard, seven or eight banging in unison. That's what I'm going to play when I'm out of here. Done with the nuthouse and back in the big game.'

'Have you played the drums before?'

'No, not me, not him. But when I'm out of here. Ha-ha. Drummer-boy Rice it will be. Boom boom. You'd like that, wouldn't you, young Casebook?'

'My name's Casey,' says the pretty girl he keeps staring at.

'Now, Rice, can you listen to me a moment,' says Doctor Kavanagh.

The man is not listening at all. He looks from face to face; a sickly smile each time around for young Casey Taylor. Then he puts a big sweaty palm on the top of Ken Tinsmith's head, holds it in position. Grins at the faces in the room which watch him. Not an act of violence; most certainly an invasion of personal space. A grubby hand firmly atop the male nurse's hair. He wiggles it, rubs it slowly. 'Don't look so worried, Mr Sunshine,' says Rice.

The two older female nurses giggle a little at this. Both the doctor and junior doctor look concerned.

'Remove your hand please,' says Ken.

Rice does this immediately. 'You have nice hair,' he tells his minder. 'Very nice hair. Cut by professionals; I know about these things.'

The nurses snigger, Ken's hair a grown-out crewcut.

'Rice,' the doctor tries again, 'do you recall Dr Okafor talking to you last night, when you first came here?'

'I do. I remember everything you know?' He taps his left index finger on the side of his nose.

'He asked you who the prime minister was. Do you remember what you told him?'

'I do.' Rice looks at Dr Okafor, stares into his face for ten seconds. 'Do you not remember what I said, young man? Jim Callaghan. Tell me who's in charge of your country and we'll both be the wiser.'

Dr Okafor, sucks in air, takes a moment before saying, 'This is my country, Mr Bradford. I am a British citizen now.'

'Then you really should know who the prime minister is without having to ask the likes of me, shouldn't you?'

The junior doctor bristles. Others look aside. It was quick-witted, if impolitic.

'Very good,' says Dr Kavanagh. 'And what year is it, Rice? What year do you think it is now?'

'Oh, I don't know the answer to that one. I don't follow politics.'

Rice Bradford can time a joke. Do it very well when he's in this elevated mental state. The ward sister, Sandra Widdecombe wasn't wrong when she said that he talked twaddle. Rice does it in spades. Funny, pacey twaddle.

* * *

After Rice has gone back onto the ward—Ken Tinsmith too—Caitlin Kavanagh begins to discuss the new patient's presentation with Dr Okafor. 'Rice would make an interesting case study,' she says.

'Very schizoaffective, I thought,' says Ahmed Okafor.

'His loss of twenty years is most unusual though. We see it far more often in gerontology than in schizophrenia,' says Caitlin.

'It wasn't absolute, was it?' interjects the social worker, Varina Pope.

They all dwell upon this. When asked on admission—and again in this ward round—Rice Bradford offered James Callaghan as answer to the who-is-the-prime-minister question beloved of psychiatrists nationwide. When she, Varina, said, 'Do you know who Tony Blair is, Rice?' the man had turned on her. He used a tone of voice as if she was stupid. Smiling, keeping up his good humour but putting down her enquiry. 'Of course, I know all about young Tony,' he said. 'I voted for him. He won. He's the prime minister...' And as his answer tapered away, he saw for himself how ineptly he had answered this question at the first two times of asking. When Dr Okafor followed this up to clarify his living arrangements, his home address, he gave the same one that appears on the hospital database. A local address in Brislington, Bristol, although he had given a road name in Greater

Manchester—one which fits his broad accent and might have been his when Wilson and Callaghan occupied number ten—the night before.

'Some funny things going on in his brainbox, aren't there?' observes Caitlin Kavanagh for the room. It is the bottom line in her assessment at every ward round.

'Do we trust him to stay?' asks Varina. She is the worst-dressed in a scruffy room. An old denim skirt that doesn't date back to Callaghan's premiership, just looks as if it might. Her hair is short—some grey, some not—her comb has become a stranger. The doctors alone have made an effort. Nurses and social workers go a bit native on the psychiatric wing. All but Casey have done exactly that today.

'Did you want him on section?' Ahmed Okafor asks.

'No.' Varina laughs to herself, looks at Dr Kavanagh, the one with the biggest vote in this decision. 'I never want any of them put on a section, it just has to be done now and then. If Rice tries to walk out in the buff again, we should detain him, shouldn't we? But what if he chooses to leave the hospital fully clothed.'

'I see your point,' says Doctor Kavanagh. 'He seems compliant enough. Loud and a little argumentative—high as a kite actually—but never unfriendly.'

'He wanted me out of the country,' observes Ahmed.

'Yes and no, Dr Okafor,' Caitlin tells him. 'I would suggest that he's simply typical working class. Insensitive to your situation. His tone was never offensive, even if you found the words to be.'

'A lot talked like him twenty years ago,' says Varina.

The junior doctor nods. The British doctor of Nigerian origin.

'I'm not minded to section him while he's behaving,' says Dr Kavanagh.

'I need to find out if his home is going to be supportive whenever the time is right,' says Varina. 'Should I talk it over with him later today. Try to gauge if he really is for staying, like he says he is?'

'Yes, do that. It was curious. He told us there was nothing wrong with him...' The doctor puts a dismissive palm across her eyes as she continues. '...he simply forgot to put his clothes on last night, got Dr Okafor's quiz question wrong. And then when I said he needed to stay, he said, "You're the doctor." Agreed to it as if

I'd offered him a cup of tea.'

'He's a nice man,' says the ward sister, Sandra Widdecombe. 'Nice man, nutty as a fruitcake.' The doctors termed it schizoaffective, hers is layman's language.

* * *

The lounge on Mendip Ward is a large rectangle, a jumble of armless angular blue sofa's, all illuminated by strip-lighting from its low ceiling. The monotonous off-white perlite tiles that a tall man can touch with raised arms. This day-room is completely devoid of natural light. There are six open exits from the lounge, two on each of the long walls, one on the short ones. Not doors, large openings. They all lead onto the corridor which surrounds the lounge. Off the corridor are the bedrooms—plus the nurses' station—each enjoying a window to the outside world, as the lounge does not. One side looks down on the staff car park; one to a building of similar stature which houses the student nurses; one faces the narrow side road that runs beside the hospital, bin lorries reverse down it to the site's refuse collection point; and one proudly faces the entrance, the busy main road. Rice's room faces the nurses building.

On leaving the ward round he went briefly back to his tiny bedroom. Tried to open the window, bring air into the stifling space. Two and a half inches were all he managed, a restrictor upon it. Mendip Ward is on the second floor and there is strictly no jumping. When he looked down, he saw two girls—student nurses though he hasn't figured that out yet—sunning themselves to the front of their accommodation block. They live on site, have no other place to be when off-duty, unless they journey to their parental homes. Rice enjoyed the view. One girl sitting upright on her towel, mostly just the top of her head visible to him; the other lying down, sunbathing in shorts and a small bra or bikini top. A lot of white skin on display. Rice decided he ought to look away. Old enough to be their father. And he'd been ogling the young girl in the doctor's room. The one on the floor who kept covering up her knees. Pretty face too, teeth looked straighter than anybody's used to be when he was the Casey-girl's age. It's normal enough—what men do—looking at girls. But more than one a day might be greedy.

He's left the little bedroom now, taken himself to the lounge. A man in a state of euphoria needs company. Other patients are sitting on many of the sofas. A woman older than him and a girl in her twenties are at opposite ends of one. He places himself between them.

'I'm Rice,' he states to no one and both of them.

'Rice pudding,' says the older woman. 'Are you rice pudding?'

'Aye, I might be that. They serve a lot of rice pudding in these bins and it could be I've turned into one.'

The younger girl is not looking at Rice, she has both hands on her bare knees, looking at the nurses' station, although there's no one there. Just a locked-up drugs' trolley, chained to the central heating pipes, standing next to the empty desk in that corner of the ward.

'What's your name?' asks Rice.

'I don't like you saying that?' she tells him.

'It's my name, Rice. The rice pudding is just daft talk, she started it.' He gestures the older lady.

'I'm called Cheryl, right, and it's the other thing I don't like. We're in a hospital.'

'I know we're in a hospital,' says Rice, then he barks a little laugh, 'although I don't see anybody having an operation. Do you? It's not a normal hospital, not one where they let you leave on a pair of crutches.'

'It's a hospital, not a bin!' Cheryl shouts at him, a contrast to Rice who has remained calm. Spoken more softly than he did at the ward round.

'It's a loony bin for loonies, it's just that they always put the wrong ones inside. Always have. There are as many who are crackers on the outside as there are in here. I should know, I've been in a few.'

'Shut up,' says Cheryl. She rises from the sofa, pulls her short skirt down as far as she can tug it. 'Stop looking!' she shouts over her shoulder as she walks to the nurses' station.

A nurse on duty, who was standing by the far wall, and may have been listening, walks across and puts a proprietorial arm over her shoulders. 'All right, Cheryl. Rice is new, don't pay him any mind.'

Rice hears, turns his head. He wasn't asking for her vote, just having a conversation. Does it matter whether he calls it a loony bin or a mental hospital? It won't change what goes on inside. The nurse who dismissed his talk, who told the girl to pay it no mind, has a beautiful face. She's light haired, not blonde exactly, the lightest possible brown. Rice supposes she is only trying to settle Cheryl, not dismissing his thoughts about the most apt name for places like these. He's not talked to her yet. Not found out. And Cheryl might be of the sort who really needs the loony bin. They can be the most militant.

'Were you ever in Partington?' asks the older lady sitting beside him.

'No. It's closed down, hasn't it? Reckon I've missed out on that one. What's your name?'

She tells him it is Rose, shares details of her depression and her corresponding addictions. There are seldom secrets between patients on a psychiatric ward.

'You must be well bunged-up!' he announces with a spluttering laugh. Within her confession, she advised that she was drinking bottle after bottle of kaolin and morph before this recent admission onto Mendip Ward. The lady looks affronted by his laughter. It is a diarrhoea relief that she has become addicted to, its tiny morphine content of little effect unless taken by the bucketload. 'Well bunged-up,' he repeats through tears of laughter.

Eventually the woman relents, concedes it is a funny thing to take too much of. 'They'll let me out once I've had a decent shit. They'll keep you locked away until your hair grows back.'

Rice smiles at her, puts the palm of a hairy hand upon his bald pate. Then he pulls it back down again. 'I'm not a dingbat, Rose, but I know someone who is.' She stares at him, waiting for an explanation. 'I just know,' he reiterates, taps a finger on the side of his nose. Doesn't expand the thought further.

The nurse who comforted Cheryl comes across to them. Rice looks up from his seated position into her face. Something in the delicacy of her perfect face soothes him, makes him feel pleased to be here. As the nurse is starting to open her mouth, he says, 'How can we help you? Happy to be of service.'

'I came to say it's lunchtime. You'll be wanting to make your way to the refectory. Do you know where it is?'

'I'll show him,' says Rose.

'You're Fiona, I believe,' says Rice to the nurse. 'We've not been introduced; however, I am a clairvoyant. With my special powers, I am able to divine the names of the beautiful of this Earth.'

'You don't know anything,' says Rose. 'It says her name on that badge.' She points to the nurse's blouse. Fiona Palmer: bold lettering on a sky-blue background, NHS logo.

'And you're Rice. I've been hearing a lot about you.'

He laughs loudly, nodding his head. 'I expect you're terrified I'm going to take my clobber off and show you all my tackle, not that I will, Nurse Fiona. That was last night's show. A mistake. I've turned a corner.'

The nurse has gone a little red, if this was what she was thinking, she doubtless had no expectation the man would blab for the ward to hear.

'Ha-hey,' says Rice, looking into her blushing face. 'You show me yours, I'll show you mine. Ha-hey!'

'Take him to the refectory, please,' says Fiona to Rose.

* * *

In the early afternoon Varina Pope comes back onto the ward. She hopes for a one-to-one conversation with Rice, wants to get to know him. Begin to work out a plan, how the assorted professionals might arrest the cycle of admission and readmission which sounds to be Rice's lot. Stopping a man from taking off his clothes might need a good one.

Rice and Cheryl have long made up. They're back on the sofa, minus the constipated kaolin and morph addict. Rice is telling the girl she has nice eyes, a nice forehead. She seems surprisingly at ease, smiles at the compliments. This morning's tension has fled.

'Hello Rice, do you remember me from the ward round?'

'Why does everyone ask, "Do you remember this," and "Do you remember that," like being in the Princess Margaret means you must have gone doolally. You're that young nurse's mum, and when you're not doing that, you're a social thingy. I know about them, visit people like us in their houses and flats.'

'I'm a social worker, Rice, just that, and I've been assigned to your case. To help you while you're in hospital and when you move out if there are things you need then. Can we talk?'

'Well...' He glances at his new patient-friend, gives her a wink. '...we were planning a wedding but it's going to have to wait, isn't it?' Then he says loudly but specifically to Cheryl. 'I like social workers. They don't inject you up the bottom like all the nurses do.'

Cheryl goes into a laughing fit. She's been laughing at his talk of bins and nuthouses for the last half hour.

'Will it take long?' asks Rice.

'No. Yes or no, really. I need to find out more about you.'

'You won't be torturing it out of me, will you?' Then he rubs his big hand on the top of his head, taps it lightly with his knuckles. 'I've forgotten your name, social worker. You're not Dr Okafor, he's the other sex and a different colour.'

'It's Varina, Varina Pope.'

'Miss Pope, please meet Cheryl of Mendip, my future wife.'

The young patient laughs again and then pulls her loose hair across her face. 'He's just being daft,' she says. 'It's probably best that you keep him in here.'

Casey Taylor trots in from the corridor and makes straight for the three talking together. 'Miss Pope,' she says, voice quaking slightly. 'Dr Kavanagh is on the phone from outpatients. She has another patient who needs you. You've got to fill in the forms to section her.' Then Casey glances sideways at Rice and Cheryl. 'It's awful but it's got to be done.'

Varina looks at young Casey before speaking. The student nurse has been on the ward barely a month, lives on site like most of them. She seems keen to listen to patients, a smile for everyone. Nice face and a lot to learn. 'I have to do no such thing, Casey. I hope that Caitlin has requested I come to make an assessment. If she feels an outpatient may require involuntary admission then I am to offer a view. Help determine if this is, or is not, the course of action we shall ultimately follow. That's what she wanted to say, whichever form of words she used.' Varina turns to Rice. 'I'm sorry, do you mind if I attend to this other matter? It may be tomorrow afternoon before I can get back on the ward—these things take some time—speak with you again then.'

Rice gives the social worker a small salute. 'Tomorrow,

tomorrow,' he says.

'Thank you,' says Varina, as she walks quickly in the direction of outpatients. To where Caitlin Kavanagh hopes to utilise her powers as an approved social worker.

'Sorry about the wedding joke,' Rice tells Cheryl. 'I think the social worker has an eye on me—singling me out like that—I didn't want her getting ideas.'

2.

When Casey Taylor arrives on the ward at five minutes before nine on the following morning, it is in uproar. An overnight admission—a large man, unknown to any of the staff on duty—is the cause. He has turned most of the sofas in the lounge upside down. Chairs lie prostrate. A wad of loose-leaf paper dispersed across the floor, four or five coffee mugs too. One broken, the large man having stamped on it; may have been oblivious to his own destructive action. He is shouting, 'Paul Norton! Paul Norton!' over and over again. Occasionally spicing it up. 'Paul fucking Norton!' Not too often, every eighth or tenth oration. Once a minute.

'We've sent for on-call,' Cindy Walsh, today's nurse-in-charge, tells the young student. Casey looks into the lounge warily. The man is the height of a basketball player, pale white skin, not necessarily a shooter of hoops. His voice is almost hoarse and still he rasps his repetitive mantra forcefully. 'Don't worry, Casey, they'll give him a sedative.' It doesn't reassure, she looks back into her colleague's face—Cindy's face—fear visible upon her own. 'It's not like this every day,' says the nurse-in-charge.

Rice comes up behind the two girls. 'Looks like a great show today.'

Casey narrows her eyes at him, the patient who jokes about everything and anything. His own misfortunes and those of others. 'He needs help,' she tells him. 'That's why they are all in here. They need help.'

'Then I'd best give it a go,' says Rice. He cups his hand over his mouth, shouts at the big rabble rouser. 'Paul, Paul! Give over!'

The new patient looks up immediately. 'I can't. I've taken some

I-don't-know-whats. Taken a fistful of them. I can't.'

'Look at what you've done in here?' says Rice. He has entered the lounge, gone to stand amid the sofa carnage, beside the man everyone else on Mendip Ward fears. 'We should put all this the right way up, Piss-Paul. Not leave it like this for all the nice nurses to straighten out. That wouldn't be fair to them, Pauly.'

'I don't know up from down. I think I must have taken more than I can think with this time.'

'Think with? You need to stop thinking. Go and lie down; you've got a bed here.'

'I'm wired. I think I've been plugged into the grid.'

'Lie down, you pillock!'

'Is Gloucester here?' says the younger man, voice now drained of his earlier anger. Paul Norton: Piss-Paul if Rice's nominated name has any purchase.

Rice laughs his head off at the confused young man. 'We're in the nut house, Paul. Mental patients as far as the eye can see. Don't expect friends and family unless they've reason to be in here too.' The younger man starts to hyper-ventilate. It is as if he has not previously understood his surroundings. The signage— saying The Princess Margaret Hospital, Psychiatric Department—is all on the outside, not a mention of it in its own lounge. 'What's his room number?' Rice asks the watching Cindy Walsh.

The nurse has stepped into the lounge, kept a few yards from the fray, felt a need to be on hand for this brave patient tackling the unruly Norton. 'Number nine,' she tells him.

'Come on Pauly-wally,' says Rice, an arm thrown around the boy's broad back. Walking him to the bedrooms at the rear of the ward. Giving the younger man no choice in the matter.

'I've done it, haven't I,' says the tall young man, his face crumpling, tears suddenly trailing from eyes to chin. 'I have, haven't I.'

'You and me both, Pauly-wally. Back in the fucking nuthouse.'

He walks him around the corridors, Paul grunting, his own name interspersed with 'Sorry' and 'I'm so sorry' as he passes patients on the corridor. Rice finds number nine. The door is open and they go in.

Rice pushes Paul Norton gently down into a seated posture on the lip of the bed. The nurse, hovering behind, plays no active role. Casey watches from the corridor. 'Feet on the bed, Paul. Sleep it off before the crack team shoot your bottom up with whatever magic potions they've got in here.' Rice looks at Cindy, to Casey behind her, still in the corridor outside. 'It might be his thing, eh? He might love that. His idea of a treat.' Turning back to Paul, he says, 'Sleep, young 'un. Just shut your eyes and do it.' The tall man's eyes duly close and Rice leaves the small bedroom.

Cindy and Casey are still on the corridor as Ken Tinsmith, another tall young male nurse and Dr Okafor pace quickly towards them. The nurse, Cindy Walsh, mouths a quick 'Thank you' to Rice. To his receding back. She has a look of astonishment on her face, cannot have anticipated the bald man's healing powers. She turns quickly to the junior doctor. 'Can we hold off doing anything more for now. I think he's settled after all.'

'Settled?' says the younger nurse, a look of disappointment on his face. He is built like a rugby player. No fun to be had on the bench.

'I need to assess the patient,' says Ahmed Okafor.

'Doctor,' says Casey, 'I think he's gone to sleep. I really do.'

Ahmed prevaricates over what course of action to take. In the attaché case which he carries lies a drawn-up syringe, a little draught of shut-you-up prepared especially for this eventuality.

'Listen,' adds Casey, 'he's snoring.'

Her nurse-in-charge nods along with the student's assertion. They form a united front against the injection which Cindy summoned just ten minutes earlier.

* * *

Paul Norton is not dead. However, his sleep mimics death sufficiently for Cindy, the ward sister, to look in every ten minutes. Those audible snores were short lived. He lies sideways in his bed, a foetal position, and Norton the most gargantuan of foeti. The bunched and ruffled blanket across him stays stock-still. Like a wild and frozen sea. The man's breathing makes no sound. She places the back of her hand near his blistered lips, feels the very faintest stirring of air against it. It is enough: Paul Norton lives.

In the office, amid files of medical histories, care plans of sketched futures with varying probabilities of success, Casey Taylor is telling Varina Pope about the happening of the morning. Rice's miraculous taming of the sofa-hurling Paul Norton. The most incredible thing to happen in Casey's short time on Mendip Ward. Varina has a longer track record, doesn't try to trump the tale.

'He's in a pretty manic phase,' Varina explains to Casey. One is qualified, one is a student, so patronise her she must. 'He will feel omnipotent, fearless. Ordering folks around who are in the state your Paul sounded to be in really is a mug's game. A dangerous pursuit. That doesn't preclude it from working once in a while. I think our Rice just got lucky.'

'It was stranger than that, Miss Pope. He called him a nasty name but Mr Norton didn't mind.'

'Please, Casey, I'm Mrs Pope, and you should better call me Varina. How is Rice now? Still high?'

'He calls himself the new Christ. Keeps asking Cindy and me for lepers to heal. I wish he didn't joke about mental hospitals so much.'

'Oh dear, oh dear. Let's you and I go see him. Will that be all right, Casey?'

They go into the day room, the lounge. Rice is sitting in a meditative pose, a glum and deflated look on his face. It brightens when he sees the two ladies approaching. 'Hello Briefcase, have you got any more fruitcakes I can suck the sultanas out of?'

Casey looks to the social worker, moving her mouth as if to answer while no words come forth.

'Can we pick up where we left off yesterday?' asks Varina.

* * *

The three of them are occupying the room in which yesterday's ward round took place. Varina laughing heartily, Casey looking perplexed. She repeatedly takes her ponytail in her clenched right hand and gives it a little pull. 'I should have asked how they knew each other.'

'Don't beat yourself up about it. I think Cindy believes in the same miracle and she might even have it black on white if she assisted Dr Okafor when he was booking in our new boy.'

Rice is laughing like Varina, it could just be a feature of his elevated mood. Their appraisal of his unearthly powers—the lion-taming act he performed with Paul Norton—might go straight over his head.

'Do you know if Paul has a social worker?' Varina asks him.

'Might do. Might do. I remember now. He's talked about one but it might be from when he was a kiddie. Or a teenager. He was a children's-home boy, our Pauly.'

'You don't think he has one now? A social worker.'

'Could do but probably not.'

'Not to worry, Rice. I'll look it up. Do you mind if I ask to be assigned; it makes sense because you both live in the same household.'

Rice shrugs. 'You'll have to stop him taking all the awful drugs if you want to get him well. And he won't stop at all is what Gloucester and me have learnt.'

'And Gloucester is another tenant in the house on Card Road?'

'No-o-o,' says Rice, his long stress on the word completely contradicting the suggestion. 'It's Gloucester's house. We pay him rent, me and Paul do. He might throw us out if he doesn't want a houseful of lunatics, mightn't he?'

'Well, that would be wrong, Rice. He shouldn't do that. How many others live in the house?'

'Others? No, we're pretty cramped as it is. Three big blokes.'

'And Mr Gloucester is the landlord?'

'That's not his name, it's just what we call him. He's called Stone. Roderick Stone, Rod, Baldy—his hair and mine are about the same—we only call him Gloucester because it's where he's from. Always banging on about how blooming marvellous life is up there. And Paul and I have one or two other names for him which I shan't let trouble your delicate ears.'

'I know the name,' says the social worker. 'You have him—Roderick Stone—written on your admission form. Next of kin. Are you related?'

'Gloucester? He's not next of kin at all, he just says I should put it on the form. That he'll look out for me. I've no family who bother with me anymore....'

Varina Pope lets out a sympathetic, 'Aw.'

'...or me with them. The thing with Piss-Paul...' Rice checks himself, looks directly at the younger girl; Casey is blushing at his attention, his inappropriate swearing that she doesn't dare to challenge. '...Paul, sorry miss...the thing is, he's a big softy. Daft. Can't help banging himself full of drugs which makes me and Gloucester get cross with him. He's messing up his own head really. We're always sending him to bed. Gloucester—Mr Stone—he can't handle it well, really can't. Says he wants to hit him when he's like that. It doesn't bother me. When you've been in and out of bins like I have, seeing a lad go bonkers on drugs can seem pretty normal really. Unexceptional, I should say.'

'In and out of bins?' asks Varina, interrupting his flow.

'Loony bins. They keep putting me back in and I'm pretty much like you really. Apart from taking my clothes off.' He looks at Casey as he says it; today she doesn't giggle. It's a heartfelt conversation and perhaps she feels sympathy, perhaps she worries he'll do it again with only her and Varina to intervene. 'And you wouldn't want to see that, would you?' he asks the gawping student nurse.

Casey Taylor shakes her head, pony tail swishing behind it.

Varina has a notebook open on her lap. She and Casey sit side by side on a single sofa, Rice at ninety degrees to them, upon an upright chair. 'Can I ask you about those previous hospital admissions, Rice?'

'Yes, Miss Pope. Ask away.' He places his hands on his knees, mirroring the posture Casey has adopted. Looks like a schoolboy, copying teacher.

Casey laughs. 'It's Mrs,' she tells him.

Now Rice looks a little puzzled. 'You're married, miss?'

'Not me. Varina. Mrs Pope.'

'Miss Pope cannot be a Mrs. It's not right. Popes aren't allowed to marry,' says Rice.

'I'm not worried what you call me,' says Varina. 'We know you were in this hospital two years ago. Do you recall when you were last in before that.'

'I bet you don't know I was in the bin in Brum. That was just before Christmas. They let me out in time for it. The turkey and what have you.'

'Last Christmas?' she asks.

Rice nods.

'In Birmingham?'

Rice nods again.

'What were you doing in Birmingham?'

'Walking around with no clothes on, I expect. That's my usual caper.'

'But why Birmingham, Rice? Why had you gone there?' asks the social worker.

'It was Gloucester, Mr Stone, he wanted help at the exhibition centre, so I went. Trouble is, we didn't have the right permit to be selling burgers there. At the conference-thingy that he was attending. Instead, I just went for a walk. Forgot to put my clothes on. My old trick. Something a bit out of kilter in my noggin, you see.' Rice taps a knowing finger on the side of his head. 'Couldn't help myself. It seems a nifty way to get a few nights in a loony bin. I doubt you'll want to try it, Miss Pope, but it works every time.'

3.

Nothing truer. Several months ago—before Rice ever cast his vote for Mr Blair—he was proximate to a political conference of a very different shade to the party he voted for. Up there in Birmingham. This was at the fag-end of the Major government. Rod Stone, the landlord who lets rooms in his small terraced house to Rice and Paul Norton, determined that he would attend the conference, the Referendum Party's end-of-year hullabaloo. The event with which its megalomaniacal leader hoped to launch himself towards great success in the forthcoming general election.

Rod was the driving force in the household's excursion to the NEC, Birmingham International. And he hoped to shift a few burgers—sell them out of the back of his van—while he was up there. Party conferences, like any gatherings of the masses, must infiltrate the dreams of hot food vendors the world over. Rod insisted Paul and Rice went with him. They were never party members, never "on-message" as the politicos say. And it was an odd message too, a vanity project more than a proper political movement. Even Rod had torn up his card by the end of the event, but on the morning that they drove up he was keen as mustard. Went there as a delegate, still to recognise that this was not a party which cared significantly what its members thought. Especially one who lived on a cramped street in Brislington, a dirty old burger van parked outside the house.

They arrived in Birmingham at six-thirty in the morning, a fairly pointless early start although it fulfilled Rod's master plan. By getting into the car park so soon, drapery covering the advertising on his van, hiding his intent to sell burgers to the Europhobic masses, he achieved his first goal: secured himself a prime spot. His parking space, close to one of the buildings side entrances, would attract the smokers as they came out, started to light up. Rod Stone knows his demographic.

'Are you a delegate or selling burgers?' Rice asked his landlord.

'Delegate. And I'm delegating burger sales to you and Piss-Paul.'

'What the...!'

'It's not my van Gloucester!'

Rod overruled their objections. The landlord using his position of rent collector—being of sounder mind, and not periodically disappearing into mental hospital—to demand the assistance of Rice and Paul for a few hours. Promised a few pounds their way in the bargain.

'British beef, that's what I've put on the sign, and that'll be good enough for this crowd. You'll see.'

'I'm not changing a gas cannister,' Rice told Roderick. 'Change it now, before you go off delegating. If you don't, we'll stop cooking when it runs out. I nearly set the van on fire last time you had me swapping. Can't be doing with all that palaver. How the blooming taps open or close, or whatever they're supposed to do.'

'All right, blockhead,' said Rod, who is also known as Gloucester. 'I'll do it before I go.'

And it was the strangest day. Just before Roderick went into the hall, he removed the fabric revealing the name upon his van. "Double Gloucester Burgers." A commercial name which misrepresents the generic cheese slices used in his operation. He stored them in the bottom cupboard, unrefrigerated, that device being full of burgers, bacon, margarine and milk for teas and coffees. Then he was away, off to listen to Jimmy Goldsmith, Rod Stone's hero for close on two months. An attachment which would not last the day.

Paul Norton had sold burgers many times before, Rod present on all previous occasions. He thrust his big ugly face out of the sliding window. 'We've forgot the onions,' he shouted at parking motorists, as if declaring it might entice them to the serving hatch.

The December day of the Referendum Party's conference was a cold one. Rice had brought only a light jacket. In his head the sound of jazz music perturbed him again. He likes it and he hates it. He imagined the other man, Stickerhand—who performed such music, lips and fingers, in that other life—drew the sound into the interior of his head. How or why, or where exactly Stickerhand stood or sat as he performed this sorcery upon Rice, was unknown to him. And it was not a trumpet he heard that morning, it was the sound of a cymbal, a drummer tap-tapping upon it. An insistent little rhythm that promised a wandering baseline. It wasn't Rice who was bringing this repetitive accompaniment into his mind. The other fella was up to his tricks. Rice greatly disliked the annoying sound living inside his head like a cuckoo. He has no feel for music. Stickerhand was back, was taking over. If this mysterious presence had first to suck out Rice's brains, he knew it would be no great loss. He, the jazz musician of old, could cook a burger, could fulfil Rice's role although the reverse was not true. Stickerhand is clever where Rice is a dullard: that's the truth of the matter. Probably knows when to keep his clothes on too. Rice manages that most of the time, most not all. Misses the mark now and then.

The paucity of custom that morning, in the frosty chill of the NEC car park, was a problem affecting burger sales, not that sales figures or takings were any kind of worry to the two purported to be cooking, serving. Paul Norton ate the majority of the nine burgers cooked that morning. The pair sold only four for cold money. It was mid-lunchtime, no queue, no punters, very few smokers—not that the Party didn't have its share, a different designated area was accommodating them—when the first brush with authority occurred.

'You don't have a licence, do you? It is all done through the management here.' The man accusing Rice and Paul—if Rice was still present which, physically, he appeared to be, whilst mentally it was a much closer call—was only a car park attendant. No warrant. No power to fine, summons or clamp.

'We've a ticket,' Paul told him, pointing to the pay-and-display slip which Roderick had left on the dashboard of the van.

'That's for parking not for carrying on a commercial enterprise.'

'But we're members,' Paul tried to argue in the manner Rod would have if only he were here to do it. 'We're only selling to other members of the party.'

'It's illegal,' the car park attendant told Paul.

'You tell him.' Rice was egging on the official. Sporadic nude pageantry aside, he is not a flaunter of authority. Nor does he have more than an associate interest in Rod Stone's comestible enterprise. None at all since the tap-tapping of the cymbal and a little background organ music had started rummaging around in his brain.

'I can get the site manager or you can just shut up shop now. Your call,' said the officious man in fluorescent yellow.

'Oh, I'm stuffed,' said Paul. 'We can call it a day. Will you tell Gloucester, please?'

Rice started to laugh at this; the car-park attendant looked at him through narrowed eyes. 'Who's this Gloucester?'

'The Mr Big who owns the van,' said Rice. 'He'll not be happy you've shut down his operation. I don't give a fig. Gloucester's the money man.'

'So where is he?'

'At the conference...' Rice pointed to the doors of the exhibition centre. '...getting himself a referendum.'

The car-park attendant looked blankly back, may not have known quite what meetings and conferences were taking place at the NEC on that day. The numbers participating were paltry, the Referendum Party's presence in Birmingham more discreet than is good form for an aspiring political movement. 'You're shutting up?' he said.

'Yep,' said Rice. 'Do you want a coffee for your trouble?'

'Don't try to bribe me, sir, I'm a professional.'

'I'm only being civil, and I'll take that for a no.'

They closed the burger van, pulled up the board. Paul Norton had never been to Birmingham before. He told Rice he was going to find out where the Brummy girls were. Rice advised him that they had parked the van miles away from the city centre. The NEC is near Birmingham rather than actually in it. This did not deter Paul. He ventured out with a bit of burger van money in his pockets, going far enough to find a dealer of something to loosen his mind, spin the chains in his head a little more hazardously. Girls have never really been in the equation where Piss-Paul is concerned, except for the imagining of them. Conjured fantasies in his room on Card Road.

The owner of the Double Gloucester burger van sat in the Referendum Party's rally all morning. A succession of unknown people talked about the European Union. They complained that their country was unrecognisable, so French and so German had its mores become. 'Our children are being indoctrinated by centimetres!' complained a speaker. Roderick, hamburger seller on a break, heard a bit, and he caught up on some of the sleep his early start cost him. When Sir Jimmy Goldsmith took the podium, he fired up the audience with carefully chosen words. Declared everything done in Brussels undemocratic. Hence his wish for a referendum. Give the people a say. Right the wrong. Then he took questions. Questions from the audience. Rod Stone stuck up a hand. He has a hatful of political views worth sharing. That's his assessment, Paul and Rice always seeming to nod along when he has a rant. In a barely alert state, he listened as half a dozen other questioners grumbled about this and that, and then the knight-in-charge of the Referendum Party pointed at Rod. Asked him to state his question.

'Can we have a referendum of tax, too? As well as the one about the French.'

Goldsmith looked intrigued. What do you wish to put to the public about taxation, sir?' he asked of the burger van owner.

'Lower for the likes of us, higher for all those toffs with hundreds and thousands in the bank, millions some of them. They can pay more and us less; it's only fair.'

Sir James Goldsmith may have thought the question an impertinent dig at him, the truth was Roderick Stone knew precious little about his temporary hero, had never read about the man's vast fortune. A single political broadcast going out at eleven-fifteen of an October evening had been enough to proselytise Gloucester into the movement. Send in his sub.

'Balls,' was the patrician's monosyllabic response before moving on to another questioner. Roderick was livid, felt slighted, ridiculed. He had made a better point than all the drivel that had taken up the morning. He pays tax once in a while and it is very annoying.

Shortly after not having his question answered, Rod Stone trudged out of the hall, already wavering on whether he would cast his vote for this fledgling party and its arrogant leader. He found a prickly dislike for Sir James Goldsmith replacing the previous certainty that he might be the ticket the country needed. When he was younger, he might have turned a wastebin over or vandalised a bus shelter, such was the mood Rod found himself in. These days he simply mutters expletives to himself, probably the better choice, and the way Jimmy Goldsmith dismissed his idea had him chunnering a babble of them. Shit, piss, fuck. Round and round in mouth and brain. In this mood, he strolled out to his van, surprised to find it shuttered, no sign of his co-opted employees anywhere.

He tried the doorhandle. Locked. He had entrusted the keys to Rice. The more reliable of a poor choice. He banged on the door on the off chance that someone was in but it drew no response from the interior. He looked around. The car park was only a quarter full, the hall used was a small area of the massive arena, no more than three hundred people in it. Mostly male, none of them young, moaning like hell over one thing or another: the very set Roderick Stone pictured taking him to their heart. Shame it hadn't turned out.

He walked away from the car park, shoulders slumped, trying to guess where his tenants might have taken themselves. The airport was the best he could come up with. They might be watching the planes. He trudged despondently in that direction. He had hoped to win the ear of Sir Jimmy, suggest his own adoption as the candidate for Bristol East. And he thought he would clean up on the burger front in the car park, do so while his political career was being hoisted up a flagpole. He forgot that his life is a more pedestrian affair. The burger van's sporadic offerings and the housing benefit that Rice and Paul put his way its highlights. Goldsmith's dismissal of his insightful question put it all in perspective.

He walked and walked until a familiar figure was in his sights. The six feet and four inches of Paul Norton, waving his arms as if he might be one of the aeroplanes that Roderick had imagined the boy gone to see. He was off his head. Not a new scenario, nor one which featured in the original plan for the day.

'Piss-Paul!' shouted Rod.

'Don't hit me!' the younger man shouted back, covering his face with his arms as if this were about to happen. 'Don't hit me!'

'Where's Rice, my son?' asked Rod.

Paul looked shocked by the question. If he still knew who Rice was, the expression on his face wasn't giving it away. He looked terrified of his friendly landlord.

'Have you got the keys to my van?' he tried. Paul's expression changed not at all. Narrowed eyes of fear, mouth taking in gulps of dank midlands air.

Back in the said burger van, Rice had transformed himself through sleep and the rising mania within his dormant self. He was dreaming of Stickerhand, dreaming that he had adopted that man's guise. Held aloft a triumphant, if imaginary, trumpet. These were predictable visitations. The elevation was rising within him and he could no longer be restrained by the middle-aged shell in which he is, most the time, cocooned. And in this heightened state he roused to full wakefulness, quicky irritated by the confines of the van, the limitations of trousers and underpants and polyester jackets. The clothes he discarded to the floor of the Double Gloucester van, unlocked the side door and left it open as he went out in search of a real trumpet. Birmingham is a large city, ergo, there will be one somewhere. Surely a true fact, although poor old Rice never seems to find what he's looking for.

After Roderick had coaxed Paul to sit in the airport lounge and watch the planes, then had a worrying skirmish with security staff who advised both should leave the building—the terror in Paul's eyes and his sporadic shrieking frightening others—the two returned to the burger van. Rod found the open door, keys still in the ignition, and the tell-tale clothes on the floor. He asked the unresponsive Paul if they should phone the police or the mental hospitals to try to locate their missing friend, housemate, tenant.

The boy nodded his head but its meaning was indeterminate.

'Fuck it,' said Gloucester. 'Let the doctors sort him out, it's what they're for.'

On the drive back to Bristol, Paul screamed periodically for no reason beyond whatever drug was coursing through his system. Misconnecting the neuropathways of a brain which has always been on the blink. The other crazy one was already in police custody, the good officers of the law busily sourcing a police surgeon to play his role in the detention of poor Rice into a Birmingham hospital. Unsurprising in the circumstances. A more handsome nude might be taken advantage of, this one is always binned for it. And Roderick, driving his burger van back to Bristol, talked to himself about the stupidity of Jimmy Goldsmith. His arrogance, his aloofness. He told Paul that the current shower will have to go. Major's lot. 'Young Blair's probably the pick of them,' he said. Paul Norton cowered in the passenger seat. Even thoughts of smiling Tony Blair scaring the drugged-up boy.

4.

'Have you been in other hospitals, Rice, other psychiatric hospitals?' asks Varina.

'Not me, really. The other fella. Manchester, that was.'

'The other fella?'

'Trumpeter.'

'Did you used to play the trumpet, Rice?' she asks.

'Never ever, Miss Pope.' A small smile wrestles a hold over the man's lips. 'I didn't used to be me. That's the nub of it. That's as why you've hauled me back into the bin, isn't it? I didn't even used to be me.'

* * *

After that confusing exchange, Varina and Casey make their way to the ward office. Cindy Walsh is sitting at the desk, a work roster in front of her. Planning the shifts for the next three weeks.

'Cindy…' The high pitch of Casey's voice relays an excitement not often seen by ward staff, inadvertently mimicking Rice's elevated mood. '…they live together, share a house. That's how come Rice was so good with the new one. With Paul Norton. He's talked him down loads of times before.'

'I thought so,' says Cindy.

'Are we all right to debrief in here?' asks Varina. She and Casey have agreed to talk over the interview. The social worker will help the student nurse to understand the strange presentation of Rice Bradford.

'Sure. Can I sit in? It'll help me because I'm Casey's supervisor.'

Varina agrees; the three sit down and she asks the student, 'Well, what did you think?'

Casey hesitates. 'It was weird,' is all she manages. Then as Varina waits for her to think it through, apply the learning of her days in college, she adds, 'He really shouldn't call hospitals bins. Not the psychiatric hospital. It's not right.'

Varina looks at Cindy. 'We've had a charge nurse or two who used the very same term. Mostly the older male nurses, eh Cindy?'

'True,' she confirms. 'Do Rice and the new one both live in a half-way house? Is that it?'

'Not by the sound of it,' says the social worker. 'Private landlord. I need to visit, get the lay of the land.' She looks directly at Casey. 'Meet the mysterious Gloucester.'

'Double Gloucester,' she replies.

This is going over Cindy's head. She asks questions, hears the backstory. 'What do you think it means?' she asks when Casey and Varina have unravelled the mystery of the trumpet. Told as much as they have learnt. It is not a precise tale.

'He's proper schizophrenic,' says Casey. 'A split personality.'

'Well,' says Varina, 'that's not really how we see it these days. There is a condition called multiple-personality syndrome but I don't think that describes Rice. It seems to me that he's disassociated himself from his past. He can recall it while imagining it all happened to someone else.'

'Wow,' says Cindy. 'We really get them on Mendip Ward.'

* * *

Rice is back in the day room, back on the not-so-comfortable sofa with the same two ladies with whom he sat the day before. Rose tells him she has a son, says that he might be visiting today, 'If he can get time off work.' He has an important job; she repeats this point in different formulations. 'The electricity. He's a very important engineer. Keeps it all ship-shape. Makes sure the electric can get down the wires and into our homes properly. It's an amazing job when you think about it.'

Rice knows this is a sure-fire lie. Electricity is not amazing, it's terrifying. And the more you think about it, the more frightening the alakazam. The current of a million epileptic fits trapped in the walls of our houses. Pick a socket, any socket. It could blow, spark the end for you and all who reside in your home. Rice hopes her son is a bloody good engineer, not spaced out on gallon after gallon of kaolin and morph like his mum. Hopes he works in a city far away, quite frankly.

'A son,' says Cheryl. 'Why do you have to say that!' She has tears in her eyes, many tears, her nose is congested by them. She uses her sleeve to dry the flood, frantically nuzzling the crook of her elbow. 'I've a son, a proper one. Not even in school yet and they won't let me see him until I stop self-harming. Don't go on about your son, Rose. He can fend for himself and you're about a hundred anyway. You don't need him like I need mine.' Rice puts an arm across the shoulders of the crying girl. She throws it off, looks a couple of daggers at him. 'I wouldn't self-harm if I had my son. I can't help doing it if I don't have him with me. Then they won't give him back until I do. That's how they all torment me here. If I kill myself, you can bet they won't let him come to my funeral. They all think I'm a piece of shit; you all think that about me in here.'

'You don't know any of that.' Although she rejected Rice's comfort, he's game to keep trying. 'It might look that way while you're stuck in the Princess Margaret, it will seem a lot better when you're out of here. If you just keep away from the razor blades, you might get your son back.'

'You don't know me, don't know a thing about me. I don't touch razor blades. Hate blood, hate blood, hate blood! It's tablets what I take. Do it whenever I get very, very down. When they won't let me see my son.'

'Oh, bloody hell, tablets. Your like Piss-Paul then. Tablets are a nightmare.' Rice makes a cross with his two forefingers, holds them up to Cheryl to keep her at bay.

Rose laughs at the sign, does the same, repeating the single word, 'Unclean,' at Cheryl.

The girl stands with tears tracking down her cheeks, leaves

hurriedly, her head bowed. A flailing arm knocks a small vase of flowers off the side-table onto the floor as she does so. Vase and Cheryl equally upset.

5.

Six days pass before the next ward round. Rice is both restless and exhausted, frequently asks nurses about going home. 'I mustn't lose my job,' he tells them; however, he also sleeps for hours and hours each day and then through most of the night too. Cindy tells Casey that his overactive brain is finally slowing down. She might be right but they can neither see inside it. At what speed anything in there truly moves is beyond their ken. Externally, the head does not rotate, whatever is going on, the external appearance is static first to last. The pair of them are on shift for this ward round, Varina also in the room. She works closely with Dr Kavanagh, social worker to most of her patients. Any who need one. It's as decent a working relationship as these contrasting professions generally muster for each other.

Today Caitlin Kavanagh wears a different summer dress. Navy blue, with the outlines of small white yachts upon it. Her legs are white as paper despite the August sun, the June and July sun that proceeded it. The junior doctor is not in today. He is at a seminar, representing the Princess Margaret psychiatric wing. It's all sponsored by a pharmaceutical outfit. A bit of learning and a bit of propaganda.

'How's he been?' asks the consultant.

Cindy Walsh, ward sister, confirms that Rice Bradford is the most compliant of patients, give or take the odd upset that his excitability has caused. He has troubled Cheryl Harrison once or twice, always makes up with her. The ward staff like his temperament; the other patients seem to share that appraisal. No one minds him. Charming, northern and a tiny bit unpredictable.

'He still calls the hospital a bin,' adds Casey.

Dr Kavanagh lets out sympathetic 'oohs' and 'aahs' as she hears the nurses tell of Rice's week, the ups and downs of ward life. Then Cindy turns to her student and asks, 'Do you want to say about, you know...?'

The girl dips her head, glances at Varina who's story it is too. 'We think he used to play the trumpet in Manchester but he pretends not to be that person. Talks about that time as "the other man." It's like he's got a split personality but Cindy says he hasn't. Or Varina does. Or they both do.'

Dr Kavanagh nods along to this. 'Classic disassociation,' she says. 'Do you think there is any chance we can pull the hospital records from any stays he had in Manchester? The longer ago the better.'

'Social work records are mostly useless,' says Varina.

'I'm not sure. I can ask,' replies Cindy.

Casey looks pleased to have contributed so much to the meeting, to have piqued the consultant's interest.

'Bring him in then,' says Caitlin.

Today they trust Rice to come into the room without an escort. Varina has already advised Dr Kavanagh, that he is a pussycat. A balding pussycat with a stomach paunch and limited interest in personal hygiene.

'You look like a pop group,' Rice tells the assembled room, the four seated women. Says it before his bottom has touched its seat. 'A good pop group, I'd buy the record, I would.' Then he points at Casey. 'Put the pretty one on the album cover, eh?'

Dr Kavanagh laughs while Varina puts her face in her hands. The man is inappropriate to the last. Cindy looks at Casey, a protective smile for her young protégé.

'Mr Bradford, I've been hearing that you know a little bit about music,' says the doctor.

The man in tracksuit bottoms, a grey sweat shirt with a hole at the elbow, shakes his head. Indicates some form of rebuttal of the assertion. Nothing specific.

'Did you not play the trumpet in Manchester?'

'Who says I've ever been to Manchester,' he states. His tone of voice changes—becomes adversarial—a lower register than that with which he enthused about the imaginary pop group.

'We understood that was so when you were in here a week ago, Rice. I recall you gave Dr Okafor a Manchester address when you were first admitted.'

'Maybe I was mad then. I'm better now, I know I live in Bristol, don't I? That's me cured.'

'But where did you live twenty years ago, Rice?'

'Now, none of us can really remember that, can we doctor? We might wish we did. We remember our mummies and our daddies, perhaps, but we can't remember-remember. We can't ever again be the person we used to be, can we doctor?'

'Mr Bradford, you seem a little agitated by this question. And you are really just going around the houses, not answering the one I have initially asked. Did you once live in Manchester?'

'Yes and no.'

'Yes and no. How can it possibly be both?'

'No then. Never lived there. Never been there in my life. If someone else has, it's not somebody as shows their face around my place very often.' As he says this last phrase, Rice slumps forward in the chair, hangs his head as if it weighs more than the largest sack of potatoes he could possibly lift. The big man lets out a groan. 'Grrrrhaah.'

'Rice,' tries Varina in a kindly voice, 'I've noticed you have a bit of a northern accent.'

'Sherlock bloody Holmes,' he mutters.

This ward round offers the professionals as much intrigue as it did last week and, like his last foray in front of them, it is no more conclusive in pinning down the condition of the poor man. Varina Pope agrees to find out more about Rice Bradford's home life. Meet the landlord known to his tenants as Gloucester. Figure out if it is a supportive relationship or part of the problem; try to learn if Paul Norton—discharged once his reaction to whatever drugs he ill-advisedly consumed had worn off—is coping, keeping clean. Always plenty to occupy a mental health social worker in Bristol.

6.

Overnight, Fiona Cook is on shift, the same Fiona who Rice has seen on the ward on many day shifts. The one whose classical features mesmerise him. She is covering a colleague's absence, not a regular on the nightshift. The ill man cannot sleep for thinking over the trick the psychiatrist played upon him. The contrivance of the nice woman too, Miss Pope, fancying she can link his place of origin to the lilt of his voice. It cannot be so, not really. We all walked out of Africa those finite number of generations back. And before that there was bugger all. We didn't make any sense at all, chattered like chimpanzees. He needs to talk to the nurse, the beautiful one. A girl with a face like hers really should know what's going on.

'It's Fiona, isn't it?' he shouts up the empty corridor.

She starts walking towards him, then instantly stops. 'Mr Bradford,' she hisses through the still of the night-time ward, the bedroom corridor, 'go to your room and put on your pyjamas.'

Rice glances down, immediately self-conscious. He has offended this nurse whose help he requires. He was unstirred before she reprimanded him, and now this sudden awareness of his unseemly state has aroused something in his cock. The rarest thing on the cocktail of medicines he has to consume, and he has something or other injected up his rear on a three-weekly basis too. He turns quickly aside, barking, 'Sorry,' louder than is needed. Once back in his own room he studies the mess upon the floor. All the clothing and possessions fetched to the hospital for him are strewn across it, a few on his unmade bed. He cannot see the pyjamas she has instructed him to wear. He pulls the underpants from yesterday over himself, covers his privates, takes the unflattering grey sweatshirt off the floor, pulls it over his head, hides his swollen stomach. The man-boobs which he feels inherently embarrassed by. Hopes Fiona was far enough up the corridor not to have noticed. He finds a pair of track suit bottoms, sniffs them. Not bad at all. Once through the hospital laundry and back to the right patient: this is a better hospital than most.

When he returns to the corridor, Fiona is there, close to his door, listening or waiting for him.

'I'm sorry, I forgot. It's hot and I don't wear...' The nurse is waving a dismissive hand, she has doubtless seen cocks from closer than ten metres in the course of her taxing job. Her social life too if she cares for that sort of thing. '...they can make you sweaty. I didn't mean anything by it.'

'I understand,' she tells him. It's a nurse's phrase, sounds helpful but may just be encouraging him to move the conversation on.

'Your voice,' he tells her, 'it's a lovely voice. Is it a Manchester accent?'

'Rice!' her face lights up at the funny personal question which she cannot take offence to. 'You can hear my burr, I'm a Bristolian. You must hear that. You've got the Manchester accent, I'd have guessed, Rice.'

Rice takes a hold of Fiona's hand. She tugs it back fractionally; the man was naked on the corridor just a couple of minutes previously.

'Talk to me,' he says. 'Help me sort myself out. It's what hospitals are for.'

'Go through and make two teas,' says Fiona. 'I'll tell Barry what we're doing.'

Rice smiles; he thought—gleaned it from the serenity forever in her face—that she would understand, would make the effort. 'But we don't need that Barry talking with us, do we? Three's a crowd, you know? I'm not a fan of crowds. Not tonight. Not ever, really.'

Fiona smiles assent, takes herself to the nurses' station where she tells the other member of the night staff that Rice is awake, wants a chat.

'Is he trouble?' asks Barry.

'Not as far as I can tell.' That is a kindly assessment in the circumstances. The nurse does not tell her colleague of Rice's recent nudity. It's a hot summer, maybe she walks around her own home that way. It's tougher for patients on Mendip, their privacy long vanquished.

In the ward's small kitchen, Rice has found two mugs and boiled a kettle of water. The teabags are odd little things stuffed into plastic Tupperware boxes by the central kitchen. Some patients say the taste is terrible, that the bags contain the ashes of the cremated. Rice is not a fussy a tea-drinker: if that's how they make them, the outcome is still drinkable. He pours the scolding water onto the two bags, pours in a dash of milk, walks back to the day room, mugs in hand. Teabags drowning without hope of rescue in the murky grey-brown brew.

'What's troubling you, Rice?' says Fiona.

'I'm back in this place again, aren't I? Getting in's a doddle, you know. Pretty twisty to get back out again, back to normal. I might have lost my job, really might have.'

'What job, Rice?'

'Oh, it's not a good job. I can't pay my way without it, that's the problem. It's like a factory where I work but not much machines. I just put things in boxes. Wrap 'em and pack 'em, that's what I say. Wrap 'em and pack 'em. Stack 'em if the goings good.'

'Who's your employer, Rice? We've no record of you having a job. I'd have remembered if there were.'

Rice taps the side of his nose with his right index finger. 'A bit hush-hush. Not MI5, just the next best thing, if you know what I mean?'

'Is it a bit of on-the-side work, Rice? You know. Not quite on the books.'

'Oh, you're good, you are. Not just a pretty face, eh? And my life isn't likely to get in a book, is it? People like me are generally off the record. I'm too peculiar for writing anything about, aren't I, nurse? Nurse Fiona, I can call you that? It's not wrong. Your boyfriend won't punch me for saying Nurse Fiona, will he?'

'No, that's all right. What do you pack into boxes?'

'Oh, just the sorts of things that need packing. I'm not one of Santa's elves if that's what you're thinking.'

'No, seriously,' says the nurse, 'do you think you might lose the job because you're staying in here? We can talk to your employer, provide evidence of sickness.'

'They won't want me back at all if they think I've gone crackers, Nurse Fiona. I used to think places like this should supply patients with a double, a lookalike who can get on with their life so no one knows they're in the nuthouse. It's shaming, you see?'

Fiona finds herself laughing at this. 'Sorry, Rice...' she puts a hand over her mouth to hide the grin. '...how would it work? You know we call it a hospital; it's a psychiatric hospital and lots of ordinary people—even famous people—have needed them. You know that. But you can't have a double being you. What if you were married?'

'Ha! You're a cheeky one, Nurse Fiona. If you're husband looks a tiny bit like me, I'm volunteering to work as his double. Bring him into the bin and I'll be straight round your house, doing my best.'

Still Fiona is laughing, trying harder to stop. 'Rice! That's not really talk I want to hear. And I'm not married. I've a boyfriend.

He doesn't look like you. Sorry.'

'I didn't expect he would. That'd be a sorry state if he did. You looking like a glamour model and...'

'Rice! I do not, and I'd like us to talk only about what's troubling you, please?'

The man leans forward on his seat, holding his balding forehead in both hands before sitting back up. 'I'm free to leave but will I be sectioned if I do? Will they stop me, detain me? The Princess Margaret, eh. Detained in Her Majesty's loony bin.'

'Rice, I understand your problem. I can't say if Dr Kavanagh would or would not wish you to be detained. We all think you should stay a little longer. You were not at all well when you came in...'

'I forgot to put my clothes on. It's not a crime. People would applaud if you did it.'

'Rice! It's a symptom that you were high, manic. You know about it, don't you? The doctor must have explained. You did it earlier but I know you'd just come off your bed. Being disinhibited, it's called. Not bothering that you're living with strangers in a hospital, treating it like it's your own home.'

'I live with two ugly brutes, Nurse Fiona. No one to get my clothes off for where I live.'

Fiona looks closely into his face. 'Did you want a little spell in the hospital?' she asks.

'No-o,' says Rice resolutely. 'No one in their right mind wants to be stuck in here, and not many of the crazy ones either. Looking into your lovely face is a bonus but generally...' Fiona is shaking her head, wagging a forefinger. Reminding him to stop flattering her. '...it's a bonus. These places are depressing, Fiona. They can't cure anyone. Doing the hokey cokey with a bunch of lunatics is not a good way to prepare your rehabilitation back into society. They cry and scream and break flower vases for no reason. I can get all that at home with Piss-Paul, can't I?'

'I see that you'd like to leave, Rice, but you still sound excitable. And why do you call Paul by that nasty nickname?'

'You haven't smelt his bedroom, love. You haven't, have you?'

A shake of the head. 'It's not a nice name. It won't help him.'

'What if I go to work first thing in the morning and come back for tea time, supper time? Would that be all right?'

'Rice, I'd rather you wait one day, so that I can clear it. What's the name and address of your employer? We should go to the office. I need to write it down.'

'It's just a packing place, Nurse Fiona. It's not the actual MI5. I think I could get in trouble if I tell you where I work.'

'Because it's the black economy?'

'Any reason you care to believe. I can't tell you because I'll get in trouble. End of.'

'Stay one more day. I'll speak to Varina before I leave shift in the morning. She's usually here early. She'll help you. Varina's very conscientious.'

'That's Miss Pope, isn't it? Varina?'

'Mrs Pope.'

'There is no Mrs Pope. Old John Paulio never got married, not allowed to. He might have got himself a couple of little Miss Popes though, eh? You don't have to be married to have fun. Ha-hey!'

Fiona stifles a laugh. 'Tomorrow. I'll talk to her. To Varina. Okay?'

'You're in charge. I always do as I'm told, you know.'

As she rises, Fiona Palmer gently taps his upper arm. 'Then keep your clothes on, Rice. That way there will be no need to keep coming back in here, will there?'

7.

In the early afternoon, conversations and phone calls paving the way, Roderick Stone is in the social work offices, occupying a small meeting room, speaking with Varina. He wears a white shirt and a stained paisley-patterned tie above navy blue trousers. A heavy double-breasted jacket was upon him on arrival but that is now over the back of his chair. Cumbersome in the summer heat.

'You know nothing about this job, Mr Stone?'

'First I've heard of it,' replies the visitor.

'You see, Mr Stone, Rice wants to go back home—your house—and I don't feel we should stop him, while not really thinking he's entirely well either. Do you understand me?'

'Go on. I'm not sure.'

'We only detain people in hospital who are seriously unwell. Rice seems a gentle sort really. He means no harm. We think he'll take his medicine but if he forgets he could get quite poorly, quite quickly...' As she is saying this, trying to describe the dilemma in layman's terms, Varina struggles to get a sense of Rod Stone. Doesn't know if he understands her or not. Rice put him down as next of kin on the admission form but the man is only his landlord. The rental income may be his principal interest in Rice, in Paul Norton too. She tries changing tack. '...I hear Rice helps out with your burger van sometimes?'

'Help! Day care, I call it. Those two, Rice and Tall-Paul too, they wouldn't see sunlight if I didn't push them a bit, this way and that. I'm a business man, Miss Pope. I'm not sure that taking them with me for the day increases sales, at least they wash up all right.'

'I see. Do you not think Rice has the concentration to hold down a proper job?'

Roderick laughs, shows a couple of missing teeth as he does it. 'He couldn't do your job, could he? A right mess he'd make of that. You're doing all right. Together, me and you can sort him out. Get Ricey-boy back on his feet, eh?'

'And you've seen him on the ward earlier, Mr Stone?'

'Yep.'

'And does he present as he usually does to you? Is he his old self?'

'I'll have him back in the house if that's what you're asking. What he's like doesn't bother me. Paul on a bender is much worse than anything Rice gets up to.'

'I was going to ask about him. Is Paul behaving since he left hospital?'

'I can't say about the drugs, can I? You could arrest me for not reporting it before or something.'

'Mr Stone, I'm a psychiatric social worker, I'm interested in Paul and Rice keeping well. I'm not the police. The taking of a particular drug doesn't bother me legally, I think we can all see that Paul Norton cannot cope with them. That's his problem, he takes too many of whatever they are, and none is enough for Paul. For his own good he needs to keep off them. Do you know who supplies him with drugs?'

Roderick leans back in his chair and narrows his eyes. He knows and he's keeping it to himself, says his body language.

'We really need to keep Paul away from them, Mr Stone. Easier said than done, I know.'

'He's a sight bigger than me, Miss Pope. I can't grapple with him.' There is truth in this, Rod Stone is some eight or ten inches shy of the humungous Paul Norton. Two or three shorter than Rice. 'If I find any in his room, I take them out, if he has any tablets that aren't the whatsits.'

'Whatsits?'

'Hay fever or whatever it is Doc prescribes for him.'

Varina Pope feels slightly perturbed that this landlord has assumed the authority to enter rooms and the discretionary right to remove items he thinks unsuitable. He might be an entirely benign force, a landlord-come-ward-sister within his own ad hoc halfway house. It is odd though. At best it is well-intentioned oppression. And that only if he is getting the calls right, intervening when necessary and leaving alone when not.

'Mr Stone, can I make an appointment to visit your home, see Paul and Rice, next Tuesday. I can go through their medication, benefits, other issues with them. With you if you chance to be present.'

'Tuesday. It's a bit soon, I'll try and clean the place up. You'll have to take us as we are, Miss Pope. So that means he's coming home?'

Varina nods absentmindedly. Thoughts of the hay fever tablets. She and the doctor spoke at length before Paul Norton's discharge. He was taking no medication whatsoever. He said it, his records said it, Dr Kavanagh said it. She must see his room, get to the bottom of it.

'I'll look after the pair of them for you,' says Rod Stone dutifully.

Chapter Two

Yes, My Son

1.

'Can I take your details please? This is all new to me.'

Varina Pope speaks quietly into the telephone, an unexpected call from a woman in Droylsden. No prior knowledge of place or lady. She gathers that it is near Manchester, possibly the very part where Rice Bradford lived many years ago. The lady would like a divorce and says that her ex is not helping. Won't agree, won't so much as engage a solicitor about the matter.

'I've always felt sorry for him,' says Pamela Bradford. 'Never wanted to put him through more upset. It's just that I've met someone and it's serious this time.'

'I see, Pamela. Can I ask—because I don't understand it—how did you learn Rice had been in this hospital?'

'Oh, his nutty friend, Gloucester, phoned me. Told me.

'Roderick Stone.'

'Yes. His nutty friend, Gloucester.'

* * *

Next up, young Casey Taylor is knocking at her office door. Stands in the entryway, door wide open. They always are on the social work corridor. All doors open except for Dave's when he's giving supervision. Dave Thompson, manager of the team. Maybe when he's having a nap, too, not that it's any more than hearsay.

'Come in Casey,' she says. Varina likes this girl. Not the brightest but she's always keen to help. That's the cornerstone of a decent healthcare professional. And she brightens the place up, smiling face, a nice one to look at.

'Yesterday I had my one-to-one with Cindy, right. And she thought it would be good—a good thing for learning to be a better nurse—if I went out with a professional into the community. See where patients live when they're not in the hospital. Find out about the other side. I was hoping you might take me. She said you get out of the hospital quite a bit.'

'Aye, I've done that for students before. Happy to help if I can find a visit that won't be disruptive to the client.' Then she looks at the telephone she has so recently put on its cradle. 'You remember Rice, don't you?'

'No forgetting him; he's one on his own.'

'I've just taken a telephone call from a lady who used to be his wife.' Casey Taylor's mouth opens, not to speak words, probably just imagining a such marriage, a partner for a balding strippergram. 'She's still his wife, actually. Never divorced. The thing is Casey, I need to speak to him about it, and I expect his marriage goes back to the time he doesn't remember. Or doesn't acknowledge. She wants a divorce, time's up and all that. Poor old Rice thinks it's somebody else, a painful memory which he won't allow himself ordinary access to. I think it will be easiest for him if he simply consents. The trouble is, I don't know what he'll say. If he will indulge me with the belief that he might be married. He doesn't say he's forgotten the past, he says it didn't happen.'

'The other fella,' says Casey, quoting Rice from the interview she sat in on. 'Thinks it was someone else it all happened to.'

'Well remembered.'

'It's dead sad,' says the student nurse. 'I don't blame the wife, it's just that Rice will never get another chance, will he? Not likely to marry again.'

'Hard to imagine it. Now, if you're free later, I'll be going round the house this afternoon, talk about it best I can with the man himself. Check in on Paul Norton too.'

Casey is still standing in the office doorway, she wears white jogging bottoms, a double line of navy running up the outside of each leg, a pleasing T-shirt, yellow, tight fit but not ridiculous. Half of the nurses in the psychiatric wing dress this casually throughout the summer; at least Casey has the good sense to cover herself up properly, nothing low cut that would magnetise the hungry eyes of all the male patients on Mendip Ward. Snag the gaze of a male doctor or two, most likely; they don't have immunity, not from the attractions of the likes of Casey. 'I'd like to go but I was thinking more of later in the week. Can I really visit in the community if I'm dressed like this?'

'It'll be my first stop at forty-one Card Road; however, I'm not anticipating any semblance to Buckingham Palace. Your clothing is fine. Can you come back at two? We'll go then.' The girl nods. 'And Casey, you're not scared of Paul Norton, are you? He's a big lad.'

'No. I'll be fine just so long as you're there.'

* * *

Varina and Dave Thompson are having an ad hoc supervision session. Thompson is an unorthodox team manager, a standoffish man. Only ever informal when it's a poor fit. Varina only popped into his office to pass on the information about Rice's wife, tell him that she was in the mix. She said it could discombobulate the patient, land him back on square one. 'Let's do a supervision around it,' Dave said, waving her in. Varina hates this. It really isn't a proper supervision, neither party has prepared a thing. A quick chat and then the rum bugger will make a few notes, meet a target that the City Council sets him. Tick off monthly supervision on the hoof. For the most part, the wider social work department leaves psychiatry to itself. This team doesn't work with children, doesn't spend a lot of money. The Director mirrors the world around him: won't worry about mental illness unless it hits him over the head. And that's virtually Dave Thompson's catch phrase: 'Don't upset the big cheese.' Now she and her manager are talking, doing as he has bid. Varina hasn't the will to call him out, tell him that his style of management adds up to nothing. Keeping your head down isn't the point of social work.

'So let me get this right,' says Dave. 'Your Rice is married in Manchester and you think it's years and years since he and she have had anything to do with one another?'

'In a nutshell. A decade is what she told me. Rice moved away ten years ago. They separated several years before that. Probably when he first became ill.'

'And did you ask her about that, Varina? Was he always taking his clothes off, even as a young man?'

'Dave! I can't ask that of a woman who phoned me out of the blue—no contact for yonks, even in her version—can't tell her all about the different symptoms he's been having. I don't disbelieve her but nor do I have proof she even is his wife. I'll see what Rice says about that. The trouble is, the past is clearly difficult for him.'

'And what does Caitlin say?'

This is another thing that bugs Varina about Dave Thompson: he treats the psychiatrists as if their word is gospel. Caitlin Kavanagh isn't the worst of them, a bit wishy-washy much of the time where normal psychiatrists are arrogant. And slightly unhinged. Dave's reliance on the doctors knocking around the place just goes to show he's as institutionalised as the patients. 'I've not talked to her about the wife yet. Only just heard it myself.'

'Steady on,' says Dave. 'Don't you think you should clear it with Caitlin before waltzing into the house and asking questions that might set him off again?'

'Dave, this landlord fella, Rod Stone, he phoned her to say he was in hospital. Why he never mentioned Pamela—the wife—to me is a complete mystery. I asked if there was anything else that he thought I should know about Rice. He doesn't know anything about the packing job which Rice says he has, knows about the wife then doesn't tell me. Pamela thinks Rod is as barmy as his tenants. The two who live between his house and our ward.'

'Does she visit him.'

'It doesn't sound like it.'

'Okay. That's an interesting supervision, Varina. See if you can get a word with Caitlin before you go out. Clear it with her just to be on the safe side.'

Varina rises, says, 'Good weather for golf.' It's a pursuit of Dave Thompson's in which she has no interest. She does not confirm or contradict the request to run her mission past Caitlin. It's a fool's errand. She wouldn't get hold of her if she tried, not today. If he was smarter, Dave Thompson would know that Dr Kavanagh spends Tuesdays out at Bath. Doing a day's work at the private hospital there, earning a small fortune alongside her NHS salary. And that's another reason why it's not worth running so minor a matter past the consultant: she's only half interested in her patients anyway. Not in it for the cause like the social workers. Dave Thompson is saying something about the greens being too dry. The hardness of the ground exaggerating the effects of bumps and divots. His thoughts flit away from work at the first opportunity. Her comment on the weather opening the door of the birdcage. It wasn't a proper supervision and Casey Taylor agrees with the plan, she and Varina outvote Caitlin whatever her hypothetical point of view. Democracy! Varina is happy to work with doctors but she doesn't look up to them. We are all equal. She doesn't look down on Rice or Paul, either. All equal. Tries not to look down but those two are bumping against her outer limits. One going out without his clothes on, one stuffing himself full of ecstasy or amphetamine or quaaludes. Whatever it is that he can't stop taking.

2.

When Casey comes to the office door at ten-to-two, Varina is pleased to see how very eager she is. Arrived early and the girl has really gone to some effort. No jogging bottoms upon her now, Casey wears a summer dress that could have come from the psychiatrist's wardrobe. Slimmer fit than Caitlin wears, equally tasteful design. Cream in colour with a smattering of red-roses stencilled upon it. Higher hemline, something Casey carries off better than the doctor ever could.

'Lovely outfit, by the way,' says the social worker.

Casey blushes ever so slightly. The Mendip Ward—the world of psychiatry, consultant psychiatrists aside—is a dress-down workplace.

'Do a twirl for me,' says Varina.

The young girl spins as asked, does so on the toes of her high-heeled shoes, fast enough that the dress begins to rise. She holds it down with flattened palms so nothing within shows above her knees.

'Beautiful.' Odd commentary from a social worker who wears charcoal-coloured slacks and a blouse from the decade before. Flat training shoes are all that have adorned Varina's feet in fifteen years. 'Let's go to the car,' she says. The two go together down the corridor of the Princess Margaret Hospital. Walk in step, Casey's shoes clicking in time with the squeak of Varina's rubber soles.

* * *

Varina drives slowly through snarled-up city traffic. The smells of sun-parched tarmac and petrol fumes sit heavily in the still air. The car windows are open and it all blends with the residual fug of smoke which lives in the social worker's old Ford Capri. Smokes a ciggie or three on her way to work, the same every return journey; prefers her car to the hospital smoking room if she fancies one during the day. The Capri was an attractive car in a bygone era. It is ten years since production ceased and this vehicle far from the last off the line. It reflects its owner: best days in the past while remaining serviceable. Does the job. Never had air conditioning although it is hard to find a car without it these days; no functioning radio, there are dials and buttons but the device is moribund. The car runs noisily, would growl if the traffic cleared enough to let it exceed fifteen miles an hour. To Varina it is a haven from all the mental illness in Bristol. From Dave Thompson too. How Casey Taylor might perceive it—the utter mess of her vehicle, fag packets and sweetie wrappers on the floor, screwed-up notes to self—Varina cannot guess. 'Tell me about yourself,' says driver to passenger. 'What brought you into mental health nursing?'

Casey looks sideways at Varina. 'I just chose it,' she says. 'When I was doing sixth form it was obvious that I wasn't going to get great marks or anything and the entry requirements were not too bad. I needed a job and I think you should help people. Help all those who need it, not the others.'

Varina contemplates this reply for a moment. The car sits motionless at a set of traffic lights; she glances at the pretty girl, hair tied back, tanned forehead exposed. The darker grain of her dyed fair hair visible at the temples, pulled back tightly by the toggle behind her head. 'Did you have a connection? Had you come across mental illness before you decided to do the course? Get trained up.'

'No,' she answers. Then after a long pause, she says, 'Well...yes.'

The traffic moves and the girl offers no explanation for a moment, seems caught in a reverie. 'You did know someone?' says Varina, and then as she says it, she stretches a hand out, places it upon Casey's forearm. The girl is crying—silently falling apart—shoulders moving as tears flood her cheeks, stain the crumpled face Varina so recently enjoyed looking upon.

'I'm sorry,' gulps Casey. 'I shouldn't be like this. I'm sorry'

'Don't be,' says Varina. 'I shouldn't have raised it.'

'I've a brother, you see,' Casey starts to explain. It is as far as she gets before another squally mass of bitter tears erupt within her. Varina tries to listen and Casey tries to talk, impeded by her upset. Says something about her mother's remarriage. That her brother is a half-brother. Then the girl puts her head in her hands. Sobs without speaking.

Varina pulls the car into a side street, they are close to the city centre, must drive across it to reach Brislington. It is unclear to Varina if she can or cannot park here. Sod it, she thinks to herself, the girl needs a shoulder to cry on. She turns off the engine.

'I'm making you late,' says Casey. She is unable to compose herself. 'Oh God, I'm sorry.'

'I think Mr Bradford will wait for us. Sometimes you need to get things off your chest, young Casey. I'm sorry my question did what it did. Now tell me, sweetie.'

'I was ten but Fergus didn't live in our house. He's a lot older; my mother was old when she had me. Fergus killed himself when I was ten. I don't think about it, never think about it; I used to have nightmares and then they all stopped—I just stopped having them—put it all out of my mind. I only knew him from Christmases, weddings, that stuff. He lived with his dad, who my mum hated by that time. But she was depressed after...' The girl pauses her torrent unearthed memories, shakes her head, her pony tail making a sympathetic wave. '...after all that. When I started working here, when I applied for it, all that, Mum never mentioned Fergus once. We don't, you see. I don't think I even made the connection.' Casey turns into Varina, leans across the handbrake and hugs her. She is sobbing and sobbing and sobbing.

* * *

'No, it's fine. I hardly knew him.' Casey is trying to excuse her behaviour, her emotional tumult, to Varina. Or not trying. The explanation—that she cannot explain it—doesn't amount to very much. 'I think I felt for my mum back then. It wasn't something to talk about because it just wasn't.'

Varina nods as she drives, repeatedly asks the young girl—face looking surprisingly composed, beautiful even, after a couple of careful wipes with a tissue—if she is sure about continuing this visit.

'Rice is funny,' says Casey. 'He won't make me cry!'

'And Casey,' says Varina more quietly, wanting to have a considered answer, 'he might have a little thing for you, you know. The old-man-crush rubbish, you being so pretty and everything. That won't bother you?'

'No.' Her monosyllable is a reflex. Varina lets the matter sit in the moving car. 'I've a boyfriend,' Casey adds.

The social worker is not surprised that pretty Casey Taylor has acquired one, nor was she suggesting the mental patient as a stand-in were she not already spoken for.

* * *

Varina parks her car on Card Road. There is a space next to the Double Gloucester burger van, a commercial vehicle not currently in use. Red-brick terrace houses line the street, plenty of them. Small front gardens, four paces from gate to door; two-foot-high garden walls, built of the same red brick as the houses; a few have roof tiles tented across their top forming a pleasing finish. It was once the way of all these garden walls, back in the Victorian age. An era of elegance the road has forgotten. There has been attrition, removals, damage. Flower pots are prevalent in many front gardens, large and small, terracotta mostly. Some broken, all untended. Varina doesn't see a decent display on the whole row. Weeds gone to seed. Pages of newspaper, chocolate bar wrappers and cigarette packets accompany the uninspiring plant pots. It looks as messy as the inside of her car. Number forty-one has a wrought-iron gate, terribly old fashioned. The ladies must walk around it—the gate lies across the garden path, far from its hinges—in order to reach the front door.

'Welcome to the high life,' whispers Varina to Casey.

The younger girl looks behind her where children play on bikes, shouting and swearing. 'It's not, is it?'

* * *

'Ha-ha, you again, Miss Pope. Come into the madhouse.' Rod Stone flashes the two ladies a smile of welcome that could swallow a banana sideways. Shows them the gaps in his teeth.

'You don't mind that I have a student with me, do you?' asks Varina.

'No, no. Come inside, love. The both of you.'

They enter the narrow hallway, stand upon an old and rucked carpet, red and black patterned, with about twenty shoes strewn upon it. Not a single one sits beside its match. A blown-up bicycle inner tube lies across the bottom two stairs. As Varina glances up, she sees that the wallpaper in the hallway and up the staircase has been poorly stripped, never replaced. Small snippets of white, flecks of long-gone lining-paper, remain adhered to the wall. As if confetti from a long-forgotten wedding is still to be cleaned away. The wall is mostly pale green, not recent paintwork. The wear and tear of thirty years displayed in this tiny space. There is a little graffiti partway up the stairs. Varina can't read what it says from where she stands.

'We're in the back,' says Roderick.

There are two doors with frosted glass panels leading off this ground-floor hallway. Varina and Casey follow Rod through the second of these. They enter what must be the dining room. A table large enough for that function fills it, piled high with newspapers at one side, nuts and bolts, pieces of a small engine on the other. 'Who's the engineer? asks Varina, pointing at the assemblage.

'No engineers here,' says Rice who stands beside the wall. Stands to attention as if these lady visitors are inspecting the troops.

'Tea. You'll have tea won't you, doctor? I'm good at making it, aren't I, Rod?' This shout is from Paul, it comes from the open door into the kitchen. A narrow galley affair. Unwashed pots in the sink and upon the Formica top; empty cans of tinned fruit on there too, plus jam jars, their contents absent. Empty packaging, the slick wrapping paper from long-eaten loaves of supermarket bread, nestle together on the floor.

'Oh, yes please,' Casey replies before Varina can forewarn her.

'Sit yourselves down,' Rod Stone instructs the girls. Casey steals a glance—eyebrows raised—from Varina. The dining chairs are as laden with paper and junk as the table, no seating available. 'Through here,' he adds, pulling apart the handles of a concertina-style division, opening the way from dining room to lounge, turning the ground-floor of the small house into a single whole.

As they step into the lounge, Varina sees an old sofa, floral yellow cushioning, wooden armrests painted black, scratched by a sharp knife or similar. Mild vandalism. Everything in this house is dilapidated. Worn out. They sit on it for lack of an alternative, Casey immediately pulling down the hem of her dress which has ridden up when sinking into the seat. Her knees have attracted the gaze of the old landlord.

'I've a nice place for them, you see,' Rod boasts. Varina lowers her eyes, suspects this is his sincere judgement. Rice has followed them into the lounge, hovers above them at a respectful distance. There is one other armchair in here, a recent copy of News Explained—crummy tabloid, pernicious peddler of half-truths and lies—rest where a person might sit. 'How are you keeping, Rice?' asks the social worker.

'Good. Good Miss Pope. I'm taking all my tablets...' He gestures to his landlord, a flat palm offered up in his direction. '...aren't I, Gloucester?'

'Aye,' says Roderick, standing to Rice's left. 'I watch out for him. Keep an eye on both of them. For my sins.'

'And did you go back to work?' enquires Varina.

'Laid off,' Rice replies.

'Oh dear. Would you like us to write to them, intervene on your behalf?'

'There's no work, Miss Pope. Nothing can be done. Contracts have dried up. It's what they said.'

While Rice explains his hopeless work situation in a monotone which contrasts greatly from his hospital high, Rod stands beside and slightly behind him, tapping the side of his head with a forefinger. Rice's commentary is to be disbelieved: this appears to be the landlord's analysis.

'Would you like to say something, Mr Stone?' Varina asks of the gesticulating man.

He desists from pointing demonstratively at his own temple just as Rice turns to him. 'No. Nothing to add.'

Paul Norton stoops his tall frame to come through the dividing partition between dining room and lounge. He carries two mugs of hot tea. 'For the lady doctors,' he says. When he is standing in front of them, holding the mugs forward and both girls stretching to relieve him without spilling anything, the man looks awestruck. 'I remember you,' he tells Casey. 'I thought you were only a dream because I was a bit off my head when I was in the hospickle. I remember you, now. And you still look like a dream.'

'Thank you,' says Casey, dipping her head, lips on the rim of the beaker, embarrassed by the attention she is getting in this household. She might be the easiest thing on the eye for streets and streets. The three men look nowhere else.

'Thank you, Paul,' adds Varina. 'And I'm a social worker, not a doctor. Casey here is a student. Here to learn. How are you keeping?'

'Eh, eh,' interjects Roderick. 'What about our tea, Piss-Paul?'

Paul turns around to fetch their drinks. Varina says quietly to the landlord, 'Could you not call him that, please. It isn't nice for him.'

'Aye, ladies present,' says Rice.

Paul turns back around, must have heard the whispered comment. 'Don't worry, Miss. It's only a joke. We're all pals in this house. Aren't we, Gloucester?'

'I treat him like my own son,' says Roderick as Paul goes back to the kitchen. 'I'm keeping him off the rubbish best I can. What do you think, Rice? He's not taken anything, has he?'

'Robson's not been round,' says Rice.

Varina gives him a questioning look.

'His dealer, Robson.'

'Shut up!' Paul is back, two further steaming mugs of tea to distribute. 'I said, I'm having nothing to do with him anymore. Nothing.'

Rod and Rice take their teas from him. 'Have the chair Tall-Paul,' says the landlord. Paul sits on top of the newspaper, sinking deep into the comfiest-looking chair in the room. 'He's no bigger than the rest of us now,' Rod announces. Then he steps forward and places a hand on the top of Paul's head, ruffling his hair, roughly but not an unfriendly action, a vigorous motion, not one to cause pain. 'Yes, my son!' he says in a loud voice. The word yes is trilled—yesssssss—a long and happy hiss, the landlord bobbing his own head from side to side as he wobbles Paul's. 'Yes, my son.' The same meaningless formulation is restated, the same glee expressed in the doing of it. Head wobbled by Roderick's spreadeagled palm on top of the boy's head.

'Give over,' says Paul, wearing the most enormous grin on his face. Then he stands up from the chair. Rod steps behind Rice. 'Gloucester, Gloucester, where are you?' says Paul. The girls might be watching the world's worst game of hide and seek. The tall young man places his large flattened palm on Rice's balding head, ruffles it around saying, 'Yes, my son,' repeatedly. Hissing on the es sound as Roderick did before. The three men are laughing and laughing.

'Calm down, please,' says Varina.

Spoken to no avail. Rice has a hand on the landlords thinning hair, his greasy head. 'Dr Foster died in Gloucester,' he says.

'He didn't die,' says Roderick.

'Yes, my son,' adds Rice, moving the head back and forth, hissing the longest of es sounds. Repeating the phrase twice over. 'Yesssssss.'

All three men are standing, a hand on another's head.

'Can we have a serious conversation, please?' pleads Varina from her seated position.

The three bow their heads like schoolboys. Rod Stone exhales, 'Aye.'

'What was all that about?' asks the social worker.

'Fun,' says Paul. 'A bit of fun.'

'It's only fun,' Roderick confirms.

'It's therapy,' adds Rice. 'A lot better for young Paul than a fistful of those uppers and downers and every-which-wayers.'

Now it is Varina's turn to laugh. 'You can't be wrong there,' she grants him.

'There you go, Paul,' says Rod. 'We don't tease you, it's therapy.'

'I wouldn't go so far as to say that,' says Varina.

Casey shuffles in her seat, again pulling her ridden-up dress back down over her knees. 'You don't mind at all, Paul?' she asks.

Paul Norton shakes his head. 'It doesn't hurt,' he says. Then he dips forward, places his large right hand on her hair, lightly, almost delicately, he wobbles the head of the realistically bleached blond. He is careful not to disturb the tight pony tail in which her hair is corralled. 'Yes, my son,' he says, the es is just as long but his voice much softer than before. 'Yes, my son,' he repeats, laughter in his throat.

Casey brushes his hand off with her own.

Varina says, 'Stop it.'

'Give over, Piss-Paul,' says Rod. 'It doesn't work with girls.' Then he glances at Varina. 'Sorry.' He puffs out an exaggerated sigh. 'Tall-Paul, did you notice that this one's a girl? Or has that passed you by? Big Mr Gormless?'

'Sorry,' says Paul looking at the girl whose hairline he has assaulted. 'I didn't hurt you, did I?'

'No. I'm all right.'

'Are you sure?' asks Varina, feeling responsible for the student she has brought from mental hospital to madhouse.

'I'm fine,' she replies. The kindly tone from the social worker is as it was in the car. She has declared herself fine but there are tears welling up in Casey's eyes, the cause of them remote. There was a moment of excitement that included fear when the man put his hand upon her scalp, not that Paul did her any obvious harm. Every hair on her head remains flawless.

'Look what you've done, Piss-Paul!' says Rod scornfully.

'It's all right,' says Varina, keen that the men should not fall out. Casey brushes the tears away with the back of her hand; communicates that she is okay with a smile directed at Varina. She doesn't speak and the social worker guesses she is struggling. Varina squeezes Casey's hand and looks intently into her eyes, wills her not to tell these men about her half-brother's suicide. One can never guess how clients in their situation will react to such an explanation. 'A little misunderstanding,' states Varina. 'Rice, are you able to take us to your room to talk, or would you rather we don't go in it? It's just I'd like to speak to you alone.'

Rice doesn't answer; his face wrinkles up in thought. Her request might be a mathematical equation, the answer beyond his grasp.

'You and I, with Casey just listening,' she adds.

'Upstairs then,' he says finally.

As the three go up, Rice leading, followed by Varina then

young Casey, the other two go into the hallway to watch them climb the stairs. Casey keeps a hand on the back of her dress, preventing it from fanning outwards.

* * *

The stench in Rice's room is overpowering. Varina looks into Casey's face and decides she is still upset. The bad smell is not the cause, it simply doesn't help.

'Will you give us a moment, Rice? We'll be back.'

She draws Casey out by the upper arm; on the landing she sees a half-open door, tiled walling inside. She takes Casey into the bathroom, pushes the door closed.

'Are you okay, Casey? Did that business with Paul frighten you?'

'No, I'm okay. What was the smell in his room?'

She leans into the girl, whispers it quietly in her ear for fear of being overheard: 'Spunk, most probably.'

Casey starts to laugh. 'No! Oh, God.'

'Just the educated guess of a social worker with too many single male clients. Are you all right to go back in there? You won't gag?'

'I might now you've said that.'

Varina sees that she is smiling, not objecting. Casey volunteered herself for this visit, seems to be game for most that happens in the psychiatric trade. Even having her scalp wobbled as a large man trills the word 'yes,' like a sitcom catchphrase. Not that this one will ever catch on. The particular sequence—hands on heads and the screech of 'Yes, my son'—is a first on Varina's community rounds. Thoughts of Fergus, thoughts prompted by her own needless questioning before they had so much as arrived, are the cause of the upset. That is Varina's analysis. 'I need to see the room again,' she continues. 'Adjudge if it is fit for human habitation.' She says it very quietly, it is a serious put down of all who reside here.

When they return to Rice's room, he starts to apologise for the mess, says he did not know they were coming upstairs. Varina looks at the bed, carefully places a hand on the mattress, feels a metal spring within. Can imagine little comfort being gleaned from so worn a bit of old tat. 'Rice,' she says levelly, 'I don't know how you are doing financially. We have a welfare rights lady who

I can put you in touch with.'

The man pushes out his lower lip, it could be a gesture that he is considering the matter. He does not look pleased at the prospect. 'When I get my job back, I'll be in the money.'

'But you said that was off the books, Rice. Do you have any old pay packets, or can you remember how much you used to earn?'

'Yes, but I doubt they'd want me blagging about it.' He touches the side of his nose with his forefinger.

'And there's no work now, Rice. Is that correct?'

'None until the new orders start coming in. More packing jobs.'

'Do you need to sign on?'

Rice looks at her blankly, Varina stares back, each waiting for the other to add to this stalled conversation.

'Are you signed on already?' asks Casey.

'Like a knife through butter, isn't she?' says Rice.

'Is that right, Rice? Have you got money coming in each week?'

The bald man nods his head, looks a little sheepish as he does so.

'Can you show me your benefit book? I want to see if it is all you should be getting?'

'A giro, Miss Pope. I get a giro.'

'You don't have a book for it?'

'Nope. I get my giros through the post. It's how they do it.'

'Then I don't think you're on the right disability benefits.'

'Don't you start interfering with my money along with everything else. I'm embarrassed to be fiddling at all, it's just that you can never tell when the packing job might dry up. Can't do with being skint.'

'I'm sorry, Rice. I'm only wanting what's best for you. How do you pay for this room? When you pay Mr Stone?'

'Out of the giro. Or my pay packet if I'm getting one.'

'And how much does Mr Stone charge?'

'Gloucester-the-fleecer wants twenty-seven pounds a week for this little room. What do you think about that?'

Quite reasonable, in Varina's view, were it not such an abject dosshouse, and if a bit of the collected rent had been spent on the place in the last five years. 'What do you think, Rice?' She needs to know his opinion, encourage him to demand better from Roderick if possible. He has been living here years before she came along and may stay here for years after.

'He can want. I pay sometimes, not others.'

'Does he get on at you about that?'

'Not really. I pay him now and then, and Paul and I work for him. Helping out on his van, we're professional burger sellers. He's got nothing to complain about. We're no trouble.'

'Do you have a contract for the room, Rice? Security?'

'I don't have any security at all, Miss Pope. That was what the other fella took. Maybe filched a few of my clothes along the way.' Then he rubs the top of his own head, hisses a quiet, 'Yesssssss,' to himself. 'Hair too,' adds Rice as an afterthought.

Varina turns her face to Casey, they exchange knowing looks. Earnestness upon both faces. 'The other fella,' says the young girl. 'Does that mean you before you were ill?'

'Butter's gone a bit rancid now, Miss. That's a nasty thing to say. I have never been ill. Forgotten my clothes once or twice and I'm sure everyone does that now and then. Calling the police is the biggest part of my problem, people call the police because I'm not handsome enough for them. They don't like watching me that way, might not mind so much if I was in shape.'

'Rice, Rice,' says Varina. She glances quickly at Casey, gives her a sympathetic look. The girl hasn't a nasty bone in her body. 'You were in the psychiatric hospital for nearly three weeks. Dr Kavanagh was not too sure about letting you go as soon as she did; in the end we agreed you weren't ill enough to section. To keep in there against your will. You are not a well-well man. Your thoughts can get very muddled, things trouble you.'

'Says clever clogs.'

'Rice?' Varina waits for the man to nod at her intonation. 'I took a phone call this morning from a lady named Pamela. Pamela Bradford. Do you want to tell me about her?'

'You took the phone call, you tell me.'

'She told me that she is your wife, Rice. Said you were married to her many years ago. Up in Manchester. Still married to this day but not living together in a long while.'

'I think you might need to section her then. Whoever she is she's clearly crackers.'

'Do you not have a wife, Rice?'

'No.'

'Have you ever had a wife?'

'No. I'm thinking of asking this young-un,' he points at Casey, 'but I might be a bit long in the tooth for her.'

'Rice, I don't like to hear you embarrassing Casey.'

'Sorry, love,' he directs at the student.

Casey shakes her head lightly, indicates acceptance of the apology. The briefest smile.

'Pamela said she's not seen you in fifteen years, ten or fifteen. What do you think about that?'

'Well, Miss Pope, I don't expect you remember every face you saw fifteen years since, so maybe she did. Married? Not a chance. That wouldn't slip from my mind or your mind, would it? It's not like remembering to put your clothes on...' He makes a point of grinning directly into Casey Taylor's face. '...that's just a little tiny blunder which I make once in a while. I'll be the first to admit to that one.'

'But, Rice, I think you might be getting a letter from her, or from her solicitors—Pamela Bradford's solicitor—about divorcing after all these years.' Varina looks closely into his face as she says this. Rice holds her eye, swallows suddenly, and she wonders if it means recognition but that is not the only plausible conclusion. Attributing meaning to every gulp, grunt or slip of the tongue is a fool's game. She's known a few social workers who swear they can read body language but it's all kidology. Hit and miss: for every one they get right, there'll be two which they've convinced themselves they did when they didn't.

'I need to talk to Paul and possibly Mr Stone,' she tells him.

They move onto the landing, Rice following. 'Here,' he says. Varina has reached the top stair, turns around as he says it. Casey is between them. He pats the door next to his own. 'This is Paul's room.'

Casey and then Varina step past him to go through the door that Rice has opened, into the bedroom next to his own. Casey finds herself in the messiest room of the house so far.

'Bloody hell!' shouts Paul from the bed.

Casey backs out quickly, stepping on Varina's foot with her narrow heel, clattering the back of her head into the social worker's chin. 'Sorry,' squeals the younger.

Varina narrowly avoids cursing, puts her left hand on Casey's shoulder as she feels her bruised chin with the right, then lifts and shakes the ever-so-slightly damaged foot. Casey has already pulled the door to. 'What was in there,' asks Varina.

'No clothes on,' says Casey, her face turned a bright shade of red.

'He was doing like I do,' says Rice. Greater animation in his voice than for any earlier pronouncement.

Varina knocks on the door, lets it remain closed this time. 'Paul, can you come down stairs when you've dressed? Come down to speak to us, please?'

'Yes, my son,' he shouts in reply.

As they go down the stairs, Casey again leading, Varina whispers, 'What was he doing in there?'

'Making that smell,' says Casey.

'Oh God, I'm sorry. Not all community visits pan out like this, honestly.'

* * *

They find Roderick still in the lounge where they left him. He is sitting on top of the newspaper on the only chair which looks comfortable, sipping on his now-cold tea. Varina takes again to the cramped sofa. She pats the seat beside her where Casey might sit. 'I'll stand,' says the younger girl, adding after a pause, 'to stretch my legs.'

'See. They're all right here,' says the landlord.

'Mr Stone,' says Varina, 'does Rice go out to work, stay out, many days or is he always here?'

'Walks about a bit, can be gone for hours, he hasn't a job if that's why you're asking. I put them both to work in the burger van but...' He glances at the ceiling; it creaks to the sounds of Rice and Paul walking around above them. '...that's therapy, isn't it?'

'I think you're using the term very loosely.'

As Varina gently probes the man—seeking to learn how much he does or fails to do for his poorly functioning tenants—Casey is examining the bookcase.

'They're not for you, love,' says Roderick.

There are thick magazines tightly packed, standing upright, so that only their spines show. The girl's own mother similarly arranges Good Housekeeping on her shelves; these periodicals are not those. Casey has started to remove a single magazine, unaware from its title as to the type of journalism it contains. Now dislodged, the front cover reveals a naked woman, the promise of oral and anal titillation within; straight-away she tries to push the magazine back where it came from. It will not slide in, all are too-tightly packed. 'Sorry,' says Casey. Meaning it most truly, one way or another.

'Don't tear it, love,' says Roderick.

'Just leave it,' suggests Varina, as she sees the girl's face reddening up once more.

'You can borrow it if you like that sort of thing.'

She dips her head down, magazine left across the tops of the others, and slides on to the seat next to Varina.

'Now, Mr Stone, I understand that you've had conversations with Rice's wife.' The man says nothing and she adds, 'Or ex-wife. Whichever.'

Roderick laughs. 'Not biting,' he says. 'You're not catching me out with that one. There's a nutter out there says she's his wife; you see, he's met a lot of them, the places he's been in, hasn't he? He never married, didn't Rice. He told me that. I'm sure he'll tell you the same.'

'Are you certain, Mr Stone?'

'Look at him! Would you marry him, love?' Then he turns to Casey. 'You definitely wouldn't.'

Paul Norton enters the room, clothes thankfully upon him. He shouts, 'Gloucester the imposter,' and places a big hand on his landlord's head. Rubbing and rubbing.

'Give over,' says Roderick.

'Yesssssss, my son.' He screeches the es sound for longer than any previous yell.

Varina makes a hand gesture, patting the air in front of her, as if it might calm him down. When he has stopped, she says, 'Can we talk now?'

'I'll wait in the car,' says Casey, leaving the room.

'I don't know what's with her,' says Paul, as he sits himself down on the sofa next to Varina.

As soon as his bottom touches the cushion, Roderick crosses the room, hand on Paul's head, yelling out the 'Yes, my son' phrase. Some kind of retaliation.

'Can you just give over,' says the social worker. She feels that she has let Casey down. A keen student wanting to see community social work in action, Varina has found her only mayhem, let her become embarrassed beyond anything she will have experienced on the ward, ushered by Rice to watch this tall boy having a not-so-private wank. And Varina knows that it was all her own prying—the inadvertent speculation about her family, the link to mental health which none are truly without—which upset the girl. Put her on edge before the visit had even started. 'Paul, what are we going to do for you?'

'I don't need anything, not unless you can get me more benefits.'

'I'll book you in to see welfare rights. Before I do, you must promise me you'll keep the appointment.'

'And then I'll get more money.'

'I'm not saying that. They will determine if what you are receiving is correct, or if you are entitled to any additional allowances, and...' She turns her whole body along the sofa she shares with the large man. '...you've also got to promise me you'll not be spending any of it on drugs. That'll only land you back on Mendip Ward, won't it?'

'I know that, Miss Pope. I've stopped it now. It's just that I can't help myself if I get some. I'll try anything, me.'

'I'm not hearing the right answer. Stop means stop.'

'I'll keep an eye on him,' offers Roderick.

'Have you any in your room?' she asks the younger man.

'No. I don't think I have or I would have done 'em.'

'I've been in and taken stuff off him before now. Haven't I, Tall-Paul?'

'He has, Miss Pope. He looks after us, does Gloucester.'

* * *

On the drive back to the hospital the girls barely talk. Both might be contemplating the chaos of the Card Road household, the childishness of three grown men. It dominates Varina's thoughts throughout.

Only eight-hundred yards to go—the red H for hospital on all the signposts—Casey starts to speak. 'I'm sorry I messed up your visit.'

Varina lets out a sigh, then laughs self-consciously. 'I messed up my own visit, thank you. I thought I was going to see two clients but then old Double Gloucester was the worst of the lot.'

'Thank you for taking me. It was dead interesting. And odd, very odd.'

'Casey, I think I'm to blame for putting you in a funny mood to start with. I am sorry about that...' Casey shrugs. '...and with hindsight, taking you to that ugly fellas' lair, well, you must have felt a bit on show.'

'I was angry with Paul—doing what he was doing—but men do that, don't they? On the ward, we always knock on their doors and wait for a reply. Rice didn't but I'm meant to know better. I shouldn't even have gone in.'

'Don't criticise yourself, I was right behind you. We'd seen him in the lounge ten minutes earlier. Never guessed he'd be getting up to that while we were still in the house.'

'Will he report me for entering without knocking?'

Varina laughs. 'He might worry that you're going to report him for jacking off in broad daylight. There are no police for any of these matters. It happens and I'm sorry it happened to you. I'm the one that should have known better. It was a bit much, three of them in that shithole.'

Casey laughs. 'It was a shithole, wasn't it? Did you see what was written on the stairs?'

'Yes. No. I saw there was writing but it was small and I didn't have my reading glasses on.'

'It was small but dead rude. He should paint over it.'

'Do you remember what it said, Casey?'

'Yes, but I don't like to say it.'

Varina touches her shoulder, it is a secret she has no need to keep.

'It said...' She breathes in and allows her chest to expand, as if about to recite before her English class. 'Gloucester lost a stick of charcoal, halfway up his furry arsehole.'

Varina can only giggle. 'A house full of poets and then "Yes, my son" is as much as they can shout at each other.'

'The graffiti was disgusting really. Not poetry at all,' says the student, before joining Varina in laughter. 'I'd have painted over it if I was Mr Gloucester. It's a terrible thing to say.'

'Mr Stone, Casey. And he might have penned it himself, pleased as punch with rhyme and metre.'

3.

Becker's back inside his head. Shouldn't be there, by rights. Someone else's girl. She's got nothing to do with Rice. Pamela Becker: what's she wanting now? The picture in his mind is of black hair falling down in ringlets across her face, green eyes like a cat. Whoever this Pam Becker is, she has features which might entice a man to get closer; however, Rice doesn't know her. Somebody else has planted the memory, the thought. Quite a picture; how it got in his head, he doesn't wish to dwell on. She isn't on the pages of any of Gloucester's glossy magazines. This one tunnels into a man's head by a funnier route than that.

There was a man once who loved Pamela Becker and he wasn't a stupid man, so he can't have been this one. Not Rice of the bald pate and pot belly. Obvious really, a girl like her can do better than a daft looking codger who keeps forgetting to put his clothes on—she's a proper head-turner, one of the sultry ones—so there's no point dwelling on it at all. Rice can picture the face, the gorgeous green come-to-bed eyes, despite not actually knowing her. Someone is planting thoughts in his pudding-bowl brain. Up to those tricks again. Rice isn't smart, just smart enough to know he must keep thoughts of her at bay. Pam Becker and any woman like her. They laugh at fat bald men in the nude, that's what that sort do, it's happened once or twice when he's been out there in the buff. Bristol, Birmingham, that time in Taunton too. Then she claims she's his wife when she's a darned sight foxier than would usually stay in the same room as the likes of him; it's as if she's trying to drive him crazy and making a fool of herself at the same time. He can't stand it. Other people's thoughts lodging themselves in every crevice to be found, deep inside of his cavernous head.

If Pamela Becker comes to the house, Rice will need to make himself scarce. He's worried sick that she's already played a trick on him. He can't be sure if the face he keeps picturing is even her. How would he know, seeing as it's all in the other fella's memory.

The snag is that this state of not-knowing makes it easier for the wily siren to trick him. She can be tall or short, blond or redhead. The ringlets—black curly hair—she might have planted that image just to baffle him. She could outwit Rice Bradford easy as shelling peas. How can he possibly remember who the other fella was and wasn't married to? It's a taller order than juggling fish.

Then there's Miss Pope. She's like all the social workers who have gone before. Means well and cuts her own hair. That is as much as Rice thinks about her. This other girl, with a name like she's a cowboy, not a girl's name at all, but golly is she a girl— Piss-Paul's eyes came out on stalks for the looking at her—more girl than in all Gloucester's magazines put together, frankly, she might be Pamela. Might be, must be; that's how come Miss Pope knows so ruddy much about her. About Pam Becker, the woman who is not his wife, just chooses to humiliate him with some pretence about it. Typical little trick to use a funny name, dye her hair, straighten it out. All girls know how to do that stuff. Pamela never did it before—or if she did, the other fella didn't say—a crafty ruse to entrap him. It's got him muddled up every which way. And he almost proposed marriage to the little minx. Playing a blinder, that one, getting the better of him all ways up.

What might she do next? Seems like she's staked out his house, hornswoggled her way into his bedroom while she was at it. That's the sneakiness of the girl, taking what isn't hers and acting all the time like it is.

'What did they want in your room?' Gloucester asked him when they'd both gone.

Rice said the first thing that came into his head, didn't really figure it out first time. 'Coming up to my room was just an excuse, Rod. They're lesbians. They just wanted to get upstairs. Went into the bathroom to do whatever lesbians do, then came back into my room to pretend they hadn't.' That was his answer and already he thinks the bathroom was another trick. Miss Pope might be a lesbian, Pamela definitely isn't. Why would she bother with any of that? Men must follow her like they did the pied-piper.

'Lesbians!' said Piss-Paul. He sounded crosser than he ever gets without drugs. 'Lesbians!' He shouted it for the whole street to hear. 'I've wasted a wank.'

Gloucester laughed at the tall one, while Rice thinks Paul

Norton is onto something. The pair of them are playing with their heads. Even the dumbbell landlord fell into the ambush. Ogling the young one, smitten. He says he isn't mental but he's on the same tram ride as Paul and the bald bloke thinking these thoughts. Rice worked that out long ago. His tongue was halfway down his chest following the temptress. Eyes following Pamela-calls-herself-Casement. Playing with their heads more dangerously than a little wobble of a hand on top, a little shout of 'Yes, my son'. Playing with all the goo on the inside, that's Kiss-me-Casey's game. Pamela-pay-later. He never thought she would come rooting around Brislington; it might be getting too much to bear. Tough times to keep your clothes on.

4.

Roderick Stone is having a chin wag with one of the regulars, a guy who owns a couple of greyhounds. Paul Norton has gone into the stadium, a few pounds in his pocket. He will lose it quickly, at a speed that is almost a talent. That is Paul's way with gambling: enthusiasm and ineptitude compete greedily. It leaves only Rice in the burger van. He doesn't mind; flipping slabs of meaty cardboard around is easy enough, and Gloucester can cop it if the punters get food poisoning. Rice isn't the buyer, the supplier. Not responsible for quality control. And there isn't really any if about it. Food poisoning is Gloucester's plate-de-jour. Every fucking jour.

'Do you have brown sauce?' says a fat man who has not buttoned up the bottom three buttons of his shirt. A fuzz of stomach hair, three folds and a belly-button shared with the world.

'Red and brown, just there.' Rice gestures to the stained plastic squeezy bottles to the side of his serving hatch.

'Burger then, please. Do you do onions?'

'He's out.'

'What?'

'He's run out of onions. I'm just helping.'

'No worries. I'll just have the burger. Starving this evening, pal. I'm starving.'

Rice spreads margarine onto a bap and, with a plastic flap, he pulls one of the sweating disks from the griddle and slaps it on the bread. Pulls the brown sauce bottle across, and offers both to the fat man. 'One pound forty.'

The man dips a hand in his trouser pocket and then passes a clutch of change to Rice.

'Ta then,' says Rod's helper. Doesn't count the coinage. This business lives on trust, on goodwill. On indifference.

* * *

The greyhounds are shut in the starting gate, straining and salivating. The bell sounds. Brian Pope is wringing his hands together, thirty pounds riding on this one. Varina is in the stadium for the first time in more than a year. She notes how small the crowd is this evening, not a quarter of the numbers this venue used to get when she and Brian first spent an evening here. The late nineteen sixties. Varina had left school, started working in the old people's home, and Brian was the older boyfriend she was widely envied for having. Parents worried over it; teenage daughter hanging on the arm of a man a decade older. Even tried to put a stop to it. Hadn't the authority; they were changing times, those nineteen-sixties.

Now she watches on as the retired fireman, who has long been her husband, eggs on his nominated dog. Brian pants like he might be the one on the track while the skinny creature on which his flutter rests, scurries down its lane—one of four—to determine whether his thirty makes good or tilts down the pan like many a good bet he has laid before. Varina thinks over how she used to relish being in this place, even when her work colleagues raised their eyebrows. Not in her care-home days: care assistants love the dogs; there could be one or two here tonight, Varina never kept in touch. The shift in her perspective came when she qualified, left the big-hearted care assistants for the more circumspect professionals. Social workers and dog racing don't really mix. Dave Thompson says he goes to the opera but Varina can't picture it. And his golf isn't earthy, working class. It's a disgraceful activity for a man with a social conscience: bagging a vast quantity of the countryside for the exclusive use of a handful of men in chequered trousers. Dave hasn't got one, that's her conclusion. Conscience went walking on the links and failed to find the way back home. He's more golfer than social worker when you analyse his practice, weigh up the effort he puts into each. She used to think herself more proletarian, more at one with their clients, for following her husband's hobby. Still there is no denying that the dogs lead a dog's life. It's another kind of moral issue—not social work—but no less real for it. That's what's bugged her for four or five years now. Animal rights. She doesn't say it to Brian. And while she watches her husband watching the runners—angular dogs swirling around the stadium—she feels a hand placed upon her upper arm.

'You've not brought her with you, have you?' Varina looks around, blinks once. Rice Bradford is at the dog meet. 'Tell me, you've not brought her with you?'

'If you mean Casey, of course not. We work together, we don't live together.'

'Oh, I know what you are.'

Varina feels irrationally annoyed, wishes she'd not come. Meeting clients by accident has happened before; this one, Rice Bradford, is proving hard work. Her husband's choice of pastime gets her among the class of people she wants to identify herself with; however, a little social solidarity hardly makes them pals.

'Second, the bloody thing came second,' says Brian turning directly to Varina.

'Did red win?' asks Rice.

'Red, yes. Is this a work colleague, Varina?'

'No. Kind of.' She would not want to label him a mental patient in a public place, while sincerely hoping the fact doesn't make itself too obvious. She won't say it but Rice really must keep his clothes on.

'Whoo-ooh.' Rice puts the palm of his hand on his own head, wobbles it in a victory celebration. 'One pound forty turns into four quid. How about that Miss Pope!' He is drawing his stub out of his pocket. 'Four fucking quid. Excuse my French, won't you. Good money, and more of it than I started with.'

Varina nods to Brian that they should walk up the rail a little, no need to stay with this man. She thinks Brian has cottoned on, then a younger man is beside them.

'Is your lesbian friend with you?' asks Paul Norton.

Brian stares at the tall young man and then turns to Varina. To his wife. Lesbian? he appears to say, at least, his lips move, no sound accompanies the word that she lipreads. His mouth went round it, nose turned sideways with the questioning intonation. He didn't say it, couldn't. He must know what they are; everybody does. His face suggests Varina might explain why the tall young man said it. Asked such a thing.

'I don't have...I don't know what you mean, Paul. Enjoy the races.'

She tries to walk up the rail, get away from the strange pair, but before Varina has prompted movement in Brian, the third member of the Card Road household is beside them.

'Miss Pope, is this your father?' She shakes her head, insulted not flattered. Nine years is all there is between them, and neither are ageing especially well. 'There's a free burger for you at the front entrance, when I can get my lazy helpers back cooking. You'll have one too, won't you, mister?'

'A hamburger?' says Brian Pope. 'I am a bit peckish.' As Varina contemplates how to counsel her husband against it, he adds. 'And I like the sound of free.'

'Rice, cooking!' Roderick positively barks the words at the man. 'Piss-Paul, go and help him.'

Varina glares, shocked that Roderick speaks to his tenants that way.

'He can call me that here,' says Paul, a grin on his face as though the insult is his evening treat, 'seeing as no one's at work.'

'I am. I'm cooking.'

For his comment, Rice gets a big hand on his head. Paul Norton's frying pan of a hand, wobbling it this way and that. 'Yes, my son.' The es trilled in their unique fashion.

'Yesssssss.' Now Roderick has a second go at the same neck-stressing pastime. Rice doesn't seem to mind: he holds a winning stub.

* * *

'It's a bloody good offer,' says Brian. Varina thinks he is trying too hard to be one of the lads. Not the smartest strategy with this triumvirate of misfits.

'I'm cooking you one whether you want it or not,' Roderick says to her. He has come down to the van with his conscripted helpers.

The three from Card Road have managed not to swear for well over a minute. Rice asks a question or two about Casey Taylor in which Varina hears paranoid undertones. Does she know he is at the dogs? She's not waiting back at the house, is she? Understanding what old men are really thinking when they contemplate pretty girls like the young student nurse is only guesswork for Varina. A smile and a wink from pretty Casey Taylor might turn her Brian into a gibbering idiot worthy of a few nights on Mendip Ward, she knows that much.

The burger doesn't taste too bad. Shame there are no onions. Brian is ready for going home once he has thrown the modest fare down his throat. His betting money long left his pocket on the promise of an underperforming dog.

'Thanks, boys,' says Varina.

'Thank you, gentlemen,' says the husband.

He never asks about the funny men she happens to know, not a single question as Varina drives them the short journey to Two Mile Hill. Licks his lips once or twice, Varina copies him unintentionally. The taste of the burger was not so dire. Then, in the late evening, Varina spends an inordinate amount of time on the toilet, gets up to use it twice in the night as well. Not her usual practice. Brian is upon it when she is not. Neither mention the burger but there can be no other culprit.

* * *

Paul Norton belches out a house-shaking burp; it is what he does best. Rice holds his tin of lager stock still, he has not pulled the tab. A most particular thought has him in its grip. Not one he wishes to share with these two chance-companions.

'We hardly made any money tonight,' complains Roderick. 'They make me pay to park my van there, you know. I might stop going. That, or I'll ask them to lower the price. Fifteen quid profit and that's only because the buns cost nothing.'

'Out of date buns again?' asks Paul. 'You're a cowboy, Gloucester.'

'They were not out of date. Use by, sell by. Not the same thing. And it'd be a shame to waste them. Too much waste in the world. Butter mountains and I can't get it for under eighty pence a pop these days.'

'Yeah. I ate loads.' The tall man gives a smaller belch, does so as if it proves his point.

The other man had the woman called Pamela. Really had her, in the biblical sense of that word. All the shenanigans that get wrapped up in that type of having. That is what Rice Bradford is thinking. A woman claims she was married to him, does so because she doesn't understand how everybody is really someone else. He had always thought her marooned in Droylsden, people from there no longer able to get down here. There is no route from East Manchester to Brislington, not any longer. Not one known to women and the men have long been sworn to secrecy. Must keep the tunnel for their exclusive use. So how did she make it dressed in cream? Pamela calling herself Casebook. Rice should have told the social worker to drive her back up north. That's what he thinks now he's had time to figure out what's going on. Wouldn't want a wife who looked that way, although he knows every other man on Earth might be pleased with the prospect. Stickerhand is free to agree, disagree or blow on his trumpet. He could be doing just that, or might as easily be having no part in those activities. Might be resting in that shallow grave of forgetting. Rice has never wished anyone deader than he wishes Stickerhand.

'How many did you sell?' Rod directs at him.

He allows the faintest of motions, a slight shake of the head. 'Burgers? I sold a few burgers. We had no onions, Gloucester. That was your mistake tonight.'

'How many?'

'I don't count them.' Then Rice sharpens himself up, looks alert for the first time in twenty minutes, pinches on the ring-pull, finally opens the tin of lager that has lain static in his hands. 'Did you count how many you started with? Tot up however many you have left; we sold the difference. It's called stocktaking, Gloucester.'

'Ooooh, stocktaking,' parrots Roderick. 'What about the shitload you and Piss-Paul ate...'

'Not me,' says Rice.

'I ate a proper shitload,' says Paul. 'Gonna do a big one later.' A broad smile for his genial landlord.

'...and giving free ones to your two friends. That was daft, wasn't it?'

'They offered to pay, Gloucester,' Rice reminds him.

'Can't take money off friends, can we?'

Paul tries to cover up a small, uninteresting belch. 'It's his lesbian social worker, not a friend, Gloucester.'

'Your social worker too,' says Rod.

'No, I think I'll have the young one. Training to be a doctor, she is. You can keep the oldie, Rice.'

Rice is sitting on one of the dining chairs, the can of lager at his lips dribbles the tiniest amount of liquid down his throat. It is a trickle to sustain life, he thinks, not to fade away like nasty stupid Stickerhand. The old one and the young one might be the same, might both be Pam Becker. Pamela is young, flaunting herself around with her new blond hair. And Pamela always liked a ciggy, she could be old Varina too. It depends whether she's just come from Droylsden in the blink of an eye, or if she's been around the block to get here. How does she do it? Bloody conniving harlot. Rice feels a little sick at the thought of all he is up against.

'Did you watch, Rice?'

'Watch what, Paul?'

'Look through the key hole when they were doing the lesbian stuff?'

'No, Paul, I didn't. I might have it wrong, you know. Women sometimes go to the bathroom together to keep an eye on each other's handbags. That might have been it.'

'No. Mine was definitely a lezzer. It's growing on me. I didn't know I liked them that way, but I do now.'

Now Roderick starts coughing and spluttering on his tin of beer, so amused is he by Paul's assertion. 'Are you going to join in, have a sex-change and be a lesbian just so you can join in?'

'Oh, Gloucester! You've just made me remember.' Paul talks excitedly, voice up a pitch. Two pitches, an octave and then some. 'There was a bloke on the ward. Wasn't there Rice? You remember him.'

'Yes. No. What bloke?'

'The man with the eye make-up. Silver and gold, it was. Sparkling eye make-up on a bloke. Did you talk to him?'

'I avoid talking to the men in bins. Even the ones that aren't homosexual are happy to try it. Not my scene, Piss-Paul. You can give it a go if you wish.'

'If you took all the drugs I take, you'd try anything. But Rice, the bloke I'm talking about wasn't really ill.'

'He must have been, if they put him in the hospital...' Rice scratches his head, mouth turns up into a little smirk. '...or had he just forgotten to put his clothes on.'

'He told me you can't get a sex change unless they assess you in the hospickle. In the psychiatric.'

'And you're going back in to get yourself flipped?' says Roderick. 'Become a lesbian and join your friends in the bathroom. Is that your latest plan?'

'No, Gloucester, it's true. This funny man was in there so the doctor could assess him for a sex change. Hey, Rice, what would they do with your old dick, if you had that done to you?' asks Paul. 'What happens to all the dicks they chop off all the people going in for sex changing? What do you reckon they do with them?

'Sell them to the homosexuals,' says Roderick.

'Put them in your burgers, more like,' says Rice.

With this ribald talk, thoughts of Stickerhand recede, drift back into the shadows. Rice expects to sleep tonight; he is wise enough not to have bothered with the rancid burgers. Paul alone will be taken into the custody of the stinking lavatory, forty-one Card Road's very own convalescent room.

5.

The sun has long been in the sky when Rice rises from his bed. The clock on the wall tells him it is seven-fifteen, early morning, there is a sporting chance it is true. His dog won last night, the least fancied in the race. The unlikely happens now and again—a bit too often in his life—last night was a welcome deal. Many times, the hands he finds himself holding are pure dross. Impossible. He puts on his light-blue trousers, there are a couple of stains—spilt tea or coffee—on the left thigh. His other clothes all look worse. Down the stairs he goes.

'You're up early,' says Roderick.

'You too.'

'Always, Rice. I listen to Radio Four every morning.'

'News? I can't stomach it, Gloucester.'

Rod Stone turns back to the table. The landlord has a small radio in pieces in front of him as he listens to the only functioning one which mumbles away from the kitchen side, the room into which Rice drifts. He rifles through a cupboard, finds an unopened packet of biscuits and then goes to the front door, handles a couple of shoes, quickly hitting on a pair. The lucky streak continues.

'Off somewhere?' says Roderick.

'Working, aren't I?'

Rod Stone holds his tongue, narrows his eyes at the transistor board he has removed from the radio. A smile of disbelief crossing his lips.

* * *

Rice is surprised by the warmth of the day at this early hour. He has a handkerchief in his pocket with which he dabs the top of his bald head. He walks towards the city centre, surveys the swathes of houses, the distant business premises which sweep down from the crown of the hill on which he stands. As he descends—Totterdown away to his left—he finds a few tears staining his cheeks. He thinks the man was a friend of his. Not sure about it, it just feels like he might have been. Why else would he lend Rice his memories? Not that they have remained friends. Can't have: the bugger's tormenting him now. It might be that Stickerhand took his woman from him, or maybe he never had a woman, those details have all clouded over in Rice's mind. Vanished in the distillery. The other fella could play the trumpet, that's a certainty. It beggars belief that the pasty-looking doctor in the flowery dress asked him about it. As if this man—Rice Bradford, the one who now and again walks across Brislington in the buff—might actually know how to blow down a trumpet. Make it sound decent. Not a chance that he can do that; trumpet or not, they all want to dip in and out of his mind. Every doctor and hanger-on in each loony bin south of Clitheroe. Scoop his brains out like ice cream. The past has little to do with the present, and the other fella's past is nothing to do with him whatsoever. A cleverer doctor would understand that, see that it's the other man who needs examining. Take the top off Stickerhand's head, make marmalade out of what he's got in there. Leave Rice alone! That would be a welcome change. Give the man a bit of peace. Being left alone has become his central preoccupation. Looking at what Stickerhand has between his ears might be worth a doctor's punt. Not Rice's brain cogs, they're all rusted up, jammed. Too much depot injection. Too much and then a couple of barrels more. 'Long lasting calmness in a syringe.' That's what Ken—the daft nurse on Mendip Ward—called it. An up-the-bottom jobby, that's Rice's take on the same. The injections that make mental patients the world over feel like shit. He sometimes thinks Stickerhand might be dead, and then, at other times, he reckons it's him that steals his clothes. Sends him naked into the night. Rice is worried that all his problems are in the nurse's syringe: he thinks it dulls him, understands that doctors try to slow his brain down just for the fear that he might walk into town without his clothes on. It's when he's at his busiest that he forgets. He glances down, white shirt, light-blue trousers and a pair of matching shoes. Well done, Rice, my son. Proper cladding all over today.

He turns off the main road and onto a small business park, wends his way up to a low flat-roofed building, the large roll-shutter door firmly closed to him. He can hear plenty of noise within. The door is metallic, painted a blue that matches Rice's trousers, and it is filthy, rusted near the top. A little ledge above the rusting must hold water, it's made the upper quarter of the door turn a coppery colour. Rice thinks it beautiful to look upon, the red that wants to be brown. Today that little ridge is dry as a bone; no water seen in Bristol in three months without the turning on of taps. Or Rice has slept through the rain, that could have happened too.

Rice slaps a flat palm against the shutter, it makes a loud thud and then rings on at a higher pitch than the initial sound. A door with an accompanying harmonic. 'Are you in there, Parker? Any work for me today?' Rice waits a moment. The voices which he heard before he banged on the door have all gone quiet. Near silence on the industrial park. He slaps his palm against the metal door again. 'Parker, you owe me fifty quid!'

He thinks he hears talking in the lock up, not directed at him. He strains to listen to it. Another slapped palm on the metal door, gentler now. The harmonic never comes. Rice growls, doesn't mean anything by it, it's just what he does.

'Fuck off!' he hears barked in reply. This bit of the conversation is for him. Well-intended advice from the man behind the metal door.

'I will but I'll be back,' says Rice, says it very quietly. He might be speaking to himself so remote is the chance of whoever is within picking up his reflective comment. He spits once at the closed door and turns his back. Walks away.

* * *

Some jobsworth in a suit who calls himself the Care Programme Approach Co-ordinator has convened a planning meeting. Advised Varina that her two most recent discharges went into the community without their needed care plans in place. He has a spreadsheet which proves it is so.

'We can rectify it soon enough,' he told her. He's inoffensive, that is the only positive she can glean, his role in this hospital utterly pointless.

'We don't need a meeting to write up what's in my mind to do,' she told him.

'We need to know that all professionals involved are on board, that it is an agreed plan not just a fudge.'

'Good luck getting Dr Kavanagh to your meeting,' said Varina.

Well, here she is, the tall and awkward Irish doctor in yet another summer dress. This Clarke-guy, the man with the longest job title—biggest name badge—in the Princess Margaret, seems able to pull strings. Sandra Widdecombe is here as ward sister, and a community nurse called Lindsey. The latter doesn't know Paul Norton properly—not his nurse but she visits his house—been giving Rice his depot injection for donkey's years. Casey Taylor is sitting in on the meeting. It's for her learning, she wasn't summonsed by the jobsworth, the Care Programme Approach Co-ordinator. Varina hopes young Casey doesn't regale the room with too much about the home visit. All the frantic head-slapping would sound chaotic, and mentioning the young man caught having a jizz would be hard to live down. It would go over the head of this smug Ian Clarke chappie, pen pushers never see the funny side.

'Firstly,' says the doctor, 'I want to thank Ian for calling this meeting, and to make it absolutely clear—for the record—that the discharges were not unplanned. I grant that we had not committed our planning to paper. How do you want to proceed, Ian? Norton or Bradford?'

The Care-Programme guy, one of some new tier of hospital management which Varina is hoping the Blair government's jovial new health secretary will send back into their hutches, says, 'Mr Norton, please. His case looks the more straightforward.'

'Can I say,' chimes up Sandra, and Dr Kavanagh nods her assent, Clarke chairing little, 'we're not sure that this boy should ever have been admitted to Mendip Ward. He seemed like he might be mentally ill but when the drugs he'd taken wore off— after forty-eight hours—he was his usual self. The only snag is that he's not a full shilling.'

'Not quite medical language but it's broadly my own diagnosis,' states Caitlin. 'The young man has a mild learning difficulty, also an excitability that makes him prone to exaggerate how he feels when he has taken mind-altering substances. He becomes like a child screaming on a fairground ride. I don't think he meets the strict criteria for our services. However, he may always be on the periphery. It is for the best that we are aware of him. Varina?'

'He lives in fairly squalid conditions. We didn't know that at the point of discharge, not until I got a chance to visit. I'm referring him to welfare rights. See if we can get his basics in better order.'

'Casey,' says Sandra, 'you saw his flat too. Do you want to add anything?'

'I agree with Varina.'

'But it's not a flat,' states Lindsey from the community nursing team. 'He's not one of mine but he and Rice both live in the same house. It's all right.'

Varina looks across at the old nurse. 'It's a mess. Really squalid.'

'Oh, that's just three men living together, that is. The house is similar to mine, just I'm on the other side of the High Street.'

Varina scratches her head. Casey agreed with her that the place was disgusting, that Roderick Stone has no standards. A few days later, Varina found out the hard way that his burger business is equally dire. It is odd that this old depot nurse isn't on the same page. 'We'll see what we can do,' she says.

'Oh, don't you think it might all go a bit belly up,' says Lindsey. 'If you go and get him more money through the welfare, from what I've heard off Mr Stone, their landlord, the boy will just spend it on the drugs that brought him in here in the first place.'

Wanting clients to receive less than their entitlement is a novel form of advocacy by Varina's reckoning. She chooses not to argue in this forum, it would only make Clarke feel important. 'We'll be keeping an eye on him of course. Mr Stone said he would help with that.'

'Yes. Thank God for Rod Stone,' says the old nurse. The community syringe.

Together, they draw up a care plan. Ian Clarke asks each professional in the room if they are confident that they can deliver their contribution, although Varina is the only one with named tasks. Even the doctor has no planned follow up appointment. The phrase, fingers crossed, they do not bother to write. 'Thank you,' he says, 'we can be certain he will get a well-co-ordinated service now.'

Then they move on to Rice. Discuss the genuine article.

Lindsey has a lot to say. 'These old schizo's are hard to keep on a straight line. I make sure he doesn't miss his depot, the snag is, I think there are some changes in here.' She taps the side of her head while she speaks. 'It's ageing that does it. Grey matter getting greyer.'

'It is important he keeps to his injection,' states Dr Kavanagh, 'but our tests don't show anything more going on and he isn't so very old. It is a complicated condition he suffers from.'

Varina coughs. 'He might have a wife who is seeking a divorce. It is from the time he does not acknowledge. The problem is, even Mr Stone doesn't believe she is really his wife and I've only spoken to her on the phone. Without the records from Manchester, we'll never be certain of anything with a client as scatty as this one.'

'My word,' says Caitlin. 'A wife. What did she sound like?'

'Plausible, Dr Kavanagh, quite plausible. She didn't want to upset him, it's just that she needs a divorce in order to move on.

Found someone new.' The room takes-in this new information. 'Unless she's crazy as a cuckoo and he really isn't married, of course.'

Every one laughs except Clarke.

Caitlin Kavanagh tells the meeting how interesting a case Rice Bradford has turned out to be. His denial of a great part of his life is most unusual; his fluctuation between states fascinating. Dr Okafor's pre-admission questions set in motion a mystery which they have yet to fully unpick. 'He makes strange reference to "another man" who seems to be his younger self. I've read of the like before but he is the first of the type to be my patient.'

When Ian Clarke asks what they in St Margaret's Hospital Trust can do for Mr Bradford, the good doctor becomes flustered. 'These treatments will help to stabilise him. Schizoaffective disorder does not have a known cure.' She smiles directly at Ian, clearly wishes him to hear the complicated truth.

'And will this plan help him out of the cycle of admission and readmission?' asks Clarke.

Dr Kavanagh is shrugging her shoulders, lost for words it seems, when Varina Pope answers for her. 'Might do. Or he could just keep taking his kit off.'

* * *

In an independent café on a Bristol side street, not quarter of a mile from the hospital in which that small coterie of professionals discusses him, Rice Bradford has, after an aimless traipse around the city, entered and purchased a mug of tea. A burger too. The latter is not yet with him, it braises upon a griddle; a woman in an apron attending to it periodically. Rice sits at an old wooden table, nursing the warm beaker, awaiting the food.

He puts three sugars in the tea. He likes the unpredictability of this element of the tea-drinking ritual; one to four are the number of spoonsful he may direct into his drink. Dave Brubeck can take five, Rice will do no such thing. And nor would Stickerhand, Rice is certain of it. Wishes he didn't know.

The tea is hot upon his lips, he thinks again about the girl who called herself by the cowboy-name: Pamela in disguise. It drops into Rice's mind that she will have left something in his room, must've manoeuvred her way in for a reason. It might be to incriminate him, give him no choice but to agree the divorce which an unmarried man cannot possibly use. Time has robbed him of a wife. Time and the loss of income from whatever job he used to do before all the stripping off started. Must have known him from somewhere. Stickerhand had a decent job and Rice might have worked with him. Not the trumpet playing. Rice never could have had a musical career. Shoes or handbags or cutting up paper trails. Whatever it was, it's slipped away now. Stickerhand was a skilled if flawed man. Rice might have played second fiddle to him. Could be what this Pamela-wife malarky is all about. Rice not married but working as a stand-in if Stickerhand was in hospital. Or playing the trumpet in the next town along. The trouble is, that saintly Nurse Fiona laughed at him about that. Said the stand-in business wouldn't work. And taking to the streets without clothes is unlikely to be appreciated by wives the world over. One's own or your best mate's. Could there be a culture somewhere that gives it a thumbs up? Not one Rice has ever heard anyone speak about. A big fat no at the proposal stage, all the way from the arctic to the Serengeti Plain, that seems the most probable. Wherever psychiatrists roam, they certainly put the mockers on it. They put accidental streakers away, put them in the bin until they recant their nakedness—take the serum—dress on demand. If Rice does have a wife, unlikely but there is a woman out there who thinks it's her, then divorcing her will put him out of the picture for good. No second chances for mental patients. Either she is crazy to want a divorce from a man she isn't married to, or—and it is only the teeny-weeniest of possibilities—he has a wife of his very own. And that could have a plus side: he is far too old for all this wanking.

'Here you are, sir,' says the waitress.

This one looks like a proper burger; nothing rancid about it. The serving woman wears a smile on her face when she says her piece. She smells of cigarettes like that social worker, and she called him sir like he was smart, learned, and he knows he's only last week's washday ahead of a tramp. Doesn't judge him, this one, there aren't so many like her.

'Looks like it's a good one,' says Rice.

'Fresh mince,' says the waitress.

Rice picks up the brown sauce, squirts it generously inside the bap. 'Here's hoping,' he says to the woman. Biting on the bun, he has to breathe a quick intake of air, so hot is the burger. The boiling fat glistening upon it jumps as if it were still cooking.

The waitress has no other customers, she hovers, reaches a hand inside her top to ensure the folds of her blouse are resting evenly. Nods at the customer.

'Bye heck, this is a top burger,' says Rice. 'Miss, did you ever hear of Double Gloucester? It's a van, serves cheeseburgers at different events. Motorbikes and dog racing mostly.'

'I don't go. It's not better than ours, is it?'

'Better? It's a million times worse. Absolutely vile.'

The lady laughs, feels the top of her blouse once more. 'Why did you raise it?'

'Warn you off, madame. Avoid! Avoid! Avoid!' Rice lets out a belly laugh, projects a little spittle of food towards the woman. Falls just short of its target.

'Thanks. What's your connection to it? The Double Gloucester.'

'I sell the burgers, miss. Would you credit it? Our Paul eats nothing else and he's had the runs for as long as I've known him.'

The woman frowns, darkness wiping clear her smile. 'Right,' she says. Turning away, she adds, 'Enjoy ours all you can.'

Then he is alone again, picturing the other guy, remembering what he can of how Stickerhand lived. There were no burgers sold like this back in those long-gone days. Wimpy bars were similar but this is American food. Rice knows this although Stickerhand may not, could be unaware of the country's transformation: the sad little war-torn mess turned into the fifty-first state. Rice doesn't know about Sticker-boy, if he passed away before any of it happened. Then it comes to him that Stickerhand caused it. Worked in the backroom behind every change.

The wand that cast the spell is advertising. Those messages on billboards, some on the telly too, they can get to a man. Turn his head. Make him imagine he is living where he isn't. As if a particular food cannot be done without, although it was not so very long ago that no one in this country ate any such nonsense. Rice thinks he could never have figured this out for himself. Stickerhand must have told him the cause of the change; a telepathic warning.

The advertisements put the phrases in our heads. We cannot forget them, even when the product is gone. For mash get smash. Who knows why anyone would do that? Pour boiling water upon some bogus medicament—fluff up a bowl of facsimile food—pretend it is worth eating, when it is really dehydrated human brains. The emperor's new spuds. Stickerhand used to have tunes floating around his head like jolly visitors; a little something in a minor key transposing itself into the major. He handled that stuff a treat did Stickerhand. Music might have been his job but he definitely did another one with scissors too. Snipped for a living. Rice can't hone in on the details. Sticker knew all the ins and out—treble clefs and swing time—while Rice hasn't the first idea. Can't even whistle properly.

While he continues to masticate upon the pleasing burger, two Chinese men enter. Talk quietly, heads together, standing just inside the door. Menus in their hands, glancing them over, waiting for the waitress to seat them. Stupid, you can pick your own table in a place like this. A snack bar, nobody's dining at The Ritz. Rice is no mug; the Orientals don't fool him. They are not even Chinese: this pair are Japanese. Rice is wising up quickly. He can see through their Chinese disguise before they even offer it to him. They must work for one of the corporations, one which makes all the electrical appliances that their countrymen have cornered the market in. Televisions, video cassette recorders. These blighters must think he is Stickerhand too. Miss Pope seems to. That's what Rice has figured. They all think it's him. And these Japs know full well that the other man's head is full to bursting with jingle-jangles which could sell every pointless gadget they churn out. An eight-note line, variations upon it repeated across a six-line stanza; it could hypnotise listeners, give them to think a Rubicon crossed, the necessity of their bowdlerised junk apparent to all. Buy, buy, buy. Only the tunesmith would feel the insincerity of it. You can fool all of the people some of the time. That's just enough for these corporations; that's how advertising works. It convinces the stupid. Piss-Paul, Gloucester and Rice: gullible as any crowd at a wrestling match, those three. Paul is the worst. The social worker's husband was a bit of a sucker. Ox dumb, losing all his money on the dogs, eating a Double Gloucester. His house must be full of electrical equipment, Rice can picture it. Every time you watch TV, it watches back. It's a Newtonian law, that one. If you can see it, it can see you.

The waitress is hovering, with a piece of paper stating how much he has to pay, although the food is far from eaten. Is this Jezebel in the pay of the Japanese, he thinks. He knows no tunes, couldn't remember them even if Stickerhand has long ago hummed them to him. Rice doesn't get music, never pays it any mind. Someone else's bag.

'It's given me the runs,' he declares.

'I'm sorry...' the waitress says to him as he rises from his seat.

The balding man dashes straight out of the door. 'The runs,' he shouts. A jogging fat man calling it over his shoulder. 'The runs.' All words are very, very similar when you think about them hard enough. Everything means shit.

6.

'Back again,' says Varina.

It is the first day of September and this absurd social worker has come around at lunchtime, acting as if nothing has changed, although Rice knows, fathomed with those slim mental skills he has retained, that it was Miss Pope's younger colleague who had Princess Diana killed yesterday. Cowboy name, cowboy nature. With her gone, Caseling, or whatever name she's calling herself these days, might get her own face plastered all over the magazine covers. Rice expects that she will use such sorcery to sway his mind, maybe to agree the divorce that her lackey, Miss Pope, talked about. Or more probably she is after his progeny, the consummation of whatever so-called marriage she has contrived. He thinks he may ask Norton to stand in for him on that one. Miss Pope is bad enough and, the more he dwells upon her, Rice finds the young sidekick terrifying.

'Tea?' asks Rod Stone.

'Not today, thanks,' says the once-bitten social worker. 'Is Paul in the house too?'

'In bed. Sleeping off a hangover.'

'Do you know if it's only beer, Mr Stone?'

'Oh yes. I'm keeping my eye on the other stuff. Just a few tins.'

Rice looks up from his seat on the sofa, blinking himself out of his catatonic stupor. Tries to stop mulling over the machinations of the absent girl. 'A few dozen tinnies, eh Gloucester?'

'We shifted a few between us,' he replies.

'I should probably let him sleep.' She turns towards the sofa. 'Rice, would you like to go to a coffee shop so that we can have a talk?'

'I hide nothing from Gloucester, here. Nothing wrong with talking where we are.' She is not going to weasel her way around him, getting him signing stuff he shouldn't. Rice has purpose if little energy.

'All right, and I am hoping to get as much history from you as you're able to recall.'

That's it, is it? He knows this game. 'No secrets from me,' says Rice. 'I can tell you everything so long as it's only me you're trying to turn inside out.'

* * *

The dining room table is clear and Varina has her black bound ledger, the book in which she writes her rough notes, visit by visit, laid out before her on the table. She has already written herself some prompts for this task.

'You were born in Manchester somewhere. Is that right?'

'I was little. Don't remember it. My mum was there. Ask her.'

'Is she alive, Rice?'

'No. She died.'

From further down the page she tries, 'Where did you go to school, Rice?'

'Oh, that'll be primary first, then big school.'

'But where, Rice?'

'There were some nasty bastards in my school, Miss Pope. I don't really like to think about it.'

'Do you remember your first job.'

'Jobs and me don't get on. I've done a few but they let me go. Keep letting me go.'

'Rice, we're not really getting very far. I'm trying to build a picture of all that you've done in your life...'

'I've not done anything. I don't know what you're accusing me of. Your friend should be chasing the other fella, not me.'

'I think you're upsetting yourself about something. I'm only trying to help you. Just me, not my husband.'

Rice sinks his head into his two flat palms, decides not to look at this liar again. Husband! She might mean the funny man who gobbled up a burger a week or more back, she knew who he was referring to. It's not complicated. Cowboy Caseling is orchestrating this, probably stuffing his clothes into some dark corner where he can't find them, doing it every few months for the amusement she can take. 'Can you go!' he says, louder than any other comment, delivered without raising his head from his hands.

'Rice, I'm sorry if this has upset you. I took another phone call from Pamela Bradford. I've not told her about you because of confidentiality but I wondered if you could tell me anything about her? Where she fits in?'

'The other fella knows!' shouts Rice, suddenly bolt upright. 'Find him. Ask him. Keep him away from me while you're at it.'

'And the other man was married to Pamela, was he?'

'I expect he stole her from me, flash bastard with his slick hair, blowing on a fancy jazz trumpet. Her or some other girl, I don't remember girls so well these days. People like me have no chance, Miss Pope. No chance in this life.'

There is a story here for Varina Pope's notebook but she doesn't write it down. Pens only the barest facts, the absence of knowledge or refusal to answer. She doesn't like to write about how crazy the man sounds; it feels disrespectful, and Dave Thompson would only go and tell Caitlin to bring him back into hospital. It did the man no use last time, although his night time stunt on Brislington High Street made it unavoidable. Varina wants what's best for the unfortunates on her caseload. Figuring what it might be, that is a more difficult question by far. Not a column of answers on the spreadsheet of a single Care Programme Approach Co-ordinator in the country. Certain greyhounds can never be coaxed into the trap.

Chapter Three

Down the Cutting

1.

He was good at what he turned his hand to, anybody would have to grant him that. This is the other fella I'm talking about here, the real Stickerhand, the man whose plan ran aground some time back. He told his little missy he was working late and she believed it all right. It's worth calculating back the who's who of this one. Before Pamela there was a nice young lassie called Jane. She did him no harm, and a hell of a lot more good than he appreciated. Stickerhand was the fickle one. Jane was from Rochdale, just the same as Stickerhand. And, I have to tell you, Stickerhand also called himself Rice. This is not my tale; the bloke is another Rice entirely. I'd forget it if I could. Manage it for months at a time. But back it bloody comes. Somebody or other can get into my noggin, can't they? Plopping other people's memories in where they don't belong. That might be the cause of all my difficulties: having an insecure brain, one that's open to the public like a museum. Or it might just be the nature of the memories the other fella plants. Nasty stuff that can make a man feel exposed. That's my opinion and I'm the one whose brain has been saturated with his damned thoughts. All Stickerhand's memories and I wish he'd kept them to his-self.

'I'm working a late one,' he told Jane. And the man who said those words, told that lie, well, I'll say it as I see it: nobody had even called him Stickerhand yet. They would but they hadn't, if you follow my gist. It was him all right but the naming, the nicknaming, had still to occur. It was nineteen-seventy-something-or-other. Callaghan didn't even look like a Prime Minister—barely been at the Foreign Office five minutes—Tony Thingumajig, yet to be born. Well, certainly not born into the public consciousness. Smiling his way through a sixth-form debating society, doing that or thereabouts, I expect.

'See you later, sweets,' she said. There you see! Sweets, a pretty stupid name for a man who snipped fabric in a clothing factory. Endearing enough if you don't mind those saccharin names. The Jane who said it was a nice girl, top to bottom. Sweets, as she called him, was not yet Stickerhand. That came later, like I said.

Being a nifty sort of slippery whatsit, he was peacock confident that Jane wouldn't check up on him. She trusted him, you see. Thing was, Jane is the one who left Rochdale with him, came down the road to Ancoats. And all this when Stickerhand used to fashion himself with my name. Rice Bradford. If people asked him, 'What's your name then?' that's exactly how he replied. The bloody cheek of it. He put my name on all his documents—job applications, rental agreements, the lot—although I am adamant that he is far more of an Eric than a Rice. And Bradford sounds like Bad Blood when you think about this fella while you're saying it. There he was, exchanging a few pleasantries with Jane from Rochdale. Life going swimmingly so that proves it wasn't me. You see, everything fell into place for Stickerhand. It was my dad who couldn't spell, I've no idea about his. Never met the man. He had a nice girl, that's gotten lodged into my memories, and then it wasn't enough for him. His job was a good un, too. Not a top of the pile job, just a hell of a lot better than packing. Packing crap into boxes when the goings good and doing nothing at all when it isn't. That's this Rice for you: me! If they paid him cash in hand it was on account of nobody having bank accounts back then. Not the likes of Sticker and me. Cash was king in the nineteen-seventies, if you didn't know. We had need of nothing more highfalutin. Not that I'm actually acquainted with the bloke I'm telling you about—with Stickerhand—nor with people like him. His memories have just got into my head. That's the nub of it. Probably on account of the confluence of national insurance numbers. I might need to explain it all to that woman, the trick cyclist. Dr Cavernous. She might know the syndrome. I wish his memories weren't in here. My loaf. It's like finding used chewing gum in your pocket. Used but not your own. Very messy and no one wants to touch another bloke's spittle, do they? And if Stickerhand remembers me like I do him, then we're both buggered. Well, I wish him nothing less.

Jane liked to hear him play the trumpet. Hear Sweets, maybe-Rice. The jazz-infused horn blowing of Eric Bad Blood. He would be doing a bit of that on this outing from which he declared only that he was working a late one. And the work referred to was the snipping of cloth, not the blowing of musical notes through a piece of moulded brass. It was not the fact of the trumpet playing that motivated the conniving sod to deceive the poor girl. It was far more complicated than that. The parp-parping into his mouthpiece was not to be a public performance. Not the paying public but he wasn't to be alone either. It would take place in the jazz club. The one down on Church Street, dimly lit, smoky; not that the descriptors distinguish it from any other. Jazz music saunters slowly out of cigarette smoke. Always has, always will. Those northern clubs were dark; that sort of music fades into silence if it's exposed to bright light. If you don't know that, you can only have heard it on record. Not let a live performance take you up a plane or two. I've heard a bit in my time. Can't stand it these days.

The meet up which my namesake had in mind was at Cellar Number One. Where his little combo usually rehearsed. And they had a singer coming, auditioning for them. Turner had let it be known that she had a lot of promise. Good pipes.

The catch for him—and why Stickerhand was maybe-silly not to tell his Jane—is that a decent singer would help the band no end. More bookings, more money. And you wouldn't be wrong if you guessed that Jane would have appreciated a few extra readies. Who doesn't like some of that? A few pounds could have spruced up the flat, curtains or whatever she thought shabbiest, wanting for replacement. Working in the garment factory didn't pay special. Sticker worked hard, even I have to grant him that, but it was just a job. Textiles never really paid anything more than keeping the worst of the bills under control. Groceries, rent, the town gas. Jazz certainly doesn't pay. Not unless you're the hottest in town and wanted in London, New York and New Orleans too. Jane had a café job. A nice café, right beside the fanciest hotels, but it paid worse than what her no-good boyfriend got for snip-snipping. Her boss kept all the tips. André Laporte. Not a Manchester name, that. A thieving name; the tips should have rightly been hers. So, you see, the reason this other Rice didn't tell Jane about the audition is because it was a role that she'd coveted for herself. Jane had sung with the jazz band—crooned her heart out for Smoking Cool—a handful of times. Turner, the self-styled band leader, had said she wasn't good enough. Said it to her face which probably stung. Jane had berated Stickerhand the evening Turner did that; she told him he should leave the band too. He prevaricated. Let it be known they'd have struggled without the few quid his playing brought in. The fact is—and he was never going to give it voice—Sticker couldn't wholeheartedly disagree with his pianist's appraisal. Jane had a lovely voice, only she sang like a choir girl. And churchy isn't jazz, not close when you get down to it.

He wasn't sure when he would mention that they had a new girl doing vocals for them if that became the way of things. This was just the audition. He'd figure it all out when it couldn't be avoided. That was Stickerhand's style. Thinking something would turn up. Might work, might not: it was how he went about everything. An improviser.

When he left the garment factory—trumpet taken from locker, walking the mile to save the bus fare—he was whistling tunes to himself. Sticker was already a bit of a composer, most soloists are. The tunes ran in circles inside his head. Sometimes he thought of a few words. Not to sing out loud, he was never a true lyricist, just the odd phrase that fitted the melody. Reminded him of this girl or that.

* * *

The audition went well. Turner said it first and it didn't even need saying. The girl had presence, depth to her voice. Stickerhand—as nobody yet called him—even enjoyed a bit of musical interplay with her. He held the last note, vibrato effect, and the girl would come back onto it. Scat up or down from the note he was holding. Then he might mimic that. Copy her vocal on his trumpet. Funny, cool. She knew the band's sound before they started although he didn't recall seeing her at any of their performances. The rooms can be dark, smoky, although he thought he would have remembered a girl like that. Most men spot the lookers, don't they?

The singer had her hair in ringlets. Must have taken her hours winding them over some kind of curlers or other. Sticker wasn't one for bothering about his own hair. If he owned a comb, it was an occasional friend. He liked looking on the black hair that fell across the eyes of this girl. A toss of the head revealing the set of her face, the sweet but firm features. Narrow nose. A smile alit it now and then. Not all the time, this was jazz not pop. And this new singer could look lost or angry when she was crooning out something blue. You might think such emotions—being at sea, at the end of one's tether—would sound unpleasant, but truly, she made them alluring. A mood you wanted to fall into with her. Sang bright or sang desolate. She had the lot. Smoking Cool had just found themselves a new vocalist. Pam Becker was in the band.

She crops up a bit often, that one, doesn't she?

2.

Varina agreed to meet her before she told Dave Thompson about the possibility. And now he insists on being in on it. She is cross about that. He can ruin even the simple stuff. This particular meeting could be a far cry from that.

Varina is determined to learn more about Rice Bradford, fears it will be very painful. Something has made him flee all memory of whatever shared past he and Pamela have.

Dave's reason for joining in is chivalrous if misguided. 'What if she's another manic? You said his carer doesn't believe he ever married.'

Varina tried to explain that Mr Stone is not really a carer. He owns the house but they all rub the tops of each other's heads like lunatics. Shout out a moronic phrase as they do it.

'But he keeps an eye on them,' Dave explained.

His simplistic analysis is annoying. Adds nothing to her understanding. She knows her clients far better than this suit-wearing man, the social worker gone to golf. He has a rank and a confidence that allows him to wield authority in the hospital psychiatric social work team, say how they should do what they have to do. He's never set foot in number forty-one Card Road.

And here he is hoping to be judge and jury at the Pamela Bradford show. Varina Pope takes her job seriously. Leaves a little of herself in the room at every client meeting. Worries that her manager muscling in will detract from her performance. He can be a stultifying presence. Frowns on the sunniest of days.

She sets a jug of water in the middle of the table, three glasses. Varina has asked June, the team clerk, to make teas and coffees when they start. Pamela has come all the way from Manchester, it is the least that they can do.

* * *

'I didn't catch that,' says Varina. 'Your name is Jan?' She says the name with a soft jay, pronounces it as she understands the Dutch do.

'Wye, a, en, dee,' says the young man, 'Yand.'

'Thank you.' Varina writes it into her black book—Yand—keeps to the spelling he has just given her. An odd name. She'll ask around, see if it's Dutch or what. He and his mum both speak with accents as northern as Rice Bradford's. Manchester people, she'd guess.

'Yand has come to support me,' says Pamela. 'He didn't want me doing this on my own.'

Varina sees the sense in this, taking a familiar face into the fray, although the boy looks no more than twenty. Unlikely that he knows how to comfort a woman seeking a divorce from a man with a long history of mental illness. It's a rare skill. Varina would have liked more support from her own son, when her family went through its far smaller wobble. Brian on long term sick. He suffered from depression and Varina should have understood this well enough. She's made a career out of helping others through the same emotional weather. It turned out to be exceptionally hard when it was her own house beneath that cloudburst. Her once-reliable Brian staring blankly back at her across the breakfast table. All has dissipated, the man is back to normal. An approximation of it at the very least. It's her working assumption that Rice will never pull that off. Not close.

'You've come a long way today,' says Dave Thompson. 'We can see how important it is for you.'

'The train tickets cost me something rotten,' says Pamela, 'but it feels like the right thing to do.'

'I'm sorry,' says Varina, 'will you be staying down here for a day or two?'

'We plan to. I don't know if...' She smiles at Dave, looks less than worn down by life for the first time so far today. '...well, we both hope Yand can meet his father again. If it's all right?'

'Pamela,' says Varina, 'we cannot prevent you from visiting but there's a lot to talk about first. It might not go well. Mr Bradford is not a well man. Not well at all, I'm sorry to say.' Her own head is swimming as she speaks this small caution. She wants to take Yand to meet the father who declares he was never married. Everything has fallen out of a clear blue sky.

3.

'You'll have a drink with us, Pam?' said Turner. All very matter of fact. A very satisfactory audition completed, so now she was one of the guys.

Stickerhand noticed, as Pam dipped her head, glanced at her own fingernails before mouthing a quick 'Yes' that her earlier confidence was only part of the act. Hadn't rehearsed for a drink with the boys.

As they walked up the stairs, she fell behind Turner. In step with the man who played the trumpet, borrower of my name. 'Is he married?' she asked. The question didn't surprise Stickerhand. He'd seen Turner put a proprietorial hand on her back two or three times. Pam Becker checking out the lie of the land seemed like a pragmatic next step.

'Four kids,' said Sticker quietly. A softer voice than his own. Put on so as not to carry to the man about whom it spoke. 'If his Maureen knew the half of it, eh?'

They were side by side on the stair, Turner already up and through the door, when she stopped and he did likewise. Looked into the man's face with her drink-you-in eyes. The rarest shade of green. 'Are you married?' she asked him.

What do you think the conniving whatsit answered to that one? He said it lightening quick, I'll grant him that. Not a beat missed, not so much as time to tap a cymbal. 'No. Never married, me.'

True in its own way, Stickerhand was not telling a lie. Not with the word no. He was omitting to say he lived with a girl. Had been doing so near on three years. No mention of that, when it might have been salient to do so. A girl waiting for him back in his flat, neither him nor her twenty years of age when they first left Rochdale for the greater anonymity of the city. Not a lie by the jazz trumpeter but a sneaky hop over an opportunity to keep the order of things clear. If that wasn't a wrong turn, I can't tell you what is. Not that Stickerhand thought it a mistake. He was most likely proud of his little deceit, that one. Out-Turnering Turner, that was his game. Not a hand he had ever played before, not according to the memories he's magicked into my brain. It was just something he tried that night—an improvisation—going up those stairs to the bar of Cellar Number One. And it was probably then when things started to cleave apart. That's what I reckon. Not that I was there, you understand.

* * *

The stupid fella didn't have one drink, or two drinks, and that had been his behaviour many times after a little practice. A meet-up with the band. Not one or two, he had seven or nine. A number of that ilk.

Turner was there about forty minutes. When it became clear to him that their new vocalist was only interested in singing to his piano, not lying upon it in a state of undress, the frustrated philanderer left. The bassist had been and gone also, while Electric Guitar never went for a drink. Never ever. He got a super sound out of his Gretsch, stayed all the while the audience were applauding, then took himself home. The audition was business for him, nothing more. Wife and kids and none of Turner's pushy charm. No audience to bow and smile to and never a wish to cheat. Electric Guitar still wore Brylcreem like it was nineteen sixty-two. No point in him hanging around single lady jazz singers in the early nineteen-seventies.'

By nine o'clock it was just Pam Becker and Stickerhand. She came close to giving him his nickname around about then. 'That thing you do,' she said, 'the note goes on and on. You stoop like you're running out of breath but never do. I think it's brilliant.'

'Funny hand,' I call it. 'Concentrate on the hand with my eyes. The trick is in the diaphragm. I can go on as long as I like, make it sound like I'm wheezing my last while I'm at it. Good, isn't it?'

'Beautiful. The way you waver the note, never change it but change how it sounds. I thought your hand was stuck...' There, you see! She said his hand was stuck, and Funnyhand wouldn't be much of a name for a jazz musician, would it? A puppeteer could run with it, never a trumpeter. '...couldn't take it off the keys...'

'Ha! Their buttons, Pam. Buttons or valves on my blowpipe. Keys are strictly for keyboards. And jail. I'm never stuck on the button—could go up or down if I thought it fitted—but why change the note if you've struck a good one.'

Pamela Becker laughed with the talk. Put a hand on his forearm more than once. It might have been the way she was putting back the Bacardi. She was nervous before the audition. Told Stickerhand as much. Told him, 'I hope I keep this down,' when he bought her a third. 'I had a funny tummy before I even got here, I was that worried.' After Turner left—a polite 'Well done on the audition,' before taking himself down the stairs and away—she moved her attention on to getting pie-eyed. Tummy doing fine, one could have inferred. It must have felt safe with this nice young unmarried man. And the danger was surely to the show-off-trumpeter, girls with Pam's good looks are always going to land on their dancing shoes, aren't they? Well, the pair of them drank so much that he lost all self-control. Started touching her like he was Tommy Turner and the girl was just as drunk by this time. Didn't object to a bit of pawing. When the time came that they couldn't speak without slurring, outside they went. This was April, not the warmest, and it wasn't Bristol either. This was northern England. Nineteen seventy-four is what it was.

He found an alley they could pop down. He thought she was going to let him do it all, there and then, but she whispered stuff about needing a condom and he didn't have any. So, it was just a bit of putting his hands where he shouldn't. Really, really shouldn't when the daft bugger had a perfectly good girl waiting for him at home. I don't think he had a plan in his head. You might think I should know, one way or t'other, but it's not like that. If it had been me, I would have felt ashamed, and all I've ever felt about it is embarrassment. That a man using my name—

although it never came close to suiting him—could do what he did to Jane. Betraying, two-timing, carrying on behind her back. It embarrasses me as a man. I don't really know any of the people—jazzy Rice, Pam Becker or young Jane—not sure how the story's got itself into my head. It's only there at all when I get in this mood, you see. It might be the Japanese who put it there, think I'll cave in and write them some jingles. And that's the nub of it. Even the crafty Japanese have got the wrong man. Tunes I wrote couldn't sell a ha'penny chew. Sticker might have plonked the memories into my head just to throw them off the scent.

4.

Varina feels that she is making progress. The lady has not only confirmed Rice Bradford's date of birth, she has confirmed it is precisely one year different from the date recorded on every record she has seen. This insight should enable them to secure the records from the Manchester hospitals, the ones about Rice from years ago. And they'd been close to giving up.

Pamela Bradford has also told them the story about the origin of his name. The same broad facts that Rice told the doctors and nurses at that first ward round. If they'd called him Eric, the world would be a marginally different place. It was not to be. His father couldn't spell and he has schizoaffective disorder. Bears a food staple for a name.

Yand is silent throughout these exchanges. Pamela has stated quite clearly that Rice is his father. And that she has had no contact with him since shortly before their son started school. Hasn't taken their calls for many a year. Yand is silent but attentive.

'I knew where he was,' Pamela Bradford told Varina and Dave, 'it's just that back then he was bad news in the house. I couldn't cope with him and a little one.'

When she was saying this, Varina heard Pamela's voice break. She has had enough heart-to-heart conversations with families of the chronically mentally ill to be prepared. Varina pushed the tissue box to the quavering lady, then saw it pushed straight back. 'No. I'm all right. It was all too long ago for me to be bothered by it after all this time.'

Varina is very up front, says that she is happy to help Pamela in her moves towards a divorce, but it might mean simply confirming that Rice's refusal to engage is a symptom of his illness. 'The court will want to hear it from Dr Kavanagh, not from a social worker. We don't have the same clout.' She also asks if Pamela is happy to help her gather a full social history, having had no insight into his illnesses back in Manchester. The early days. Her visit could be a great help, if she doesn't mind.

Yand looks a little pained by the prospect.

'It'll be good for you to hear it,' says his mother, and the young man reverts to the supportive demeanour with which he has spent the majority of his time in this room.

Dave Thompson then rises. 'Mrs Bradford,' he says, 'I'll leave you in Varina's capable hands. I only came in because we weren't sure how straightforward this might be. It's been a pleasure to meet you.'

Pamela must be clever. She raises an eyebrow. 'You suspected I was another nutter, didn't you?' Yand looks crossly at Dave Thompson; his mother taps his arm in contradiction. 'I've told you about the landlord, Yand. All your dad's friends are probably no better than him. Not these days. Rice was a brilliant man once, can't see how this lady could have known that. All the signs have been pointing the wrong way since before Rice came down here. Down to Bristol.'

Dave leaves the room and Varina watches the door close behind him. What use is that man, the social work team manager who volunteers himself as the hired-heavy. Psychiatric social work is about healing, that has always been her belief. Relief from the symptoms of illness; distance from the trauma that precipitated it. Neither come easily, she's learnt that. How a bouncer, a bodyguard, or a crack team with a syringe full of go-to-sleep play a part in any of it has always been beyond her. There is actual social work to do here. Through the pulling together of Rice's past experiences she may build a helpful picture of the fragmented man. Help Rice to recover lost time. And for this very reason, Dave Thompson makes himself scarce, goes back to signing off expenses. Completing Clarke's Care Programme Approach spreadsheet.

* * *

'No sign of it at all before we got married.' Her tone suggests it was obviously so. No way would she have married him if those tell-tale signs were present. She looks a little exhausted but she's a good-looking lady. Might have turned a lot of men's heads back in the day. She could have done better than an off-kilter husband. Still can, hence the need for this divorce.

'But you said he drank quite a lot?'

'We all did in the jazz clubs. Pretend I didn't say that, Yand. I wasn't a mother then, so no harm in it. Not really. The spotlight was on me as the singer but, I swear, Rice was the real talent. The one who made the band a bit special. I suppose he drank more than a little. It's a way of life for jazz musicians. Never stopped him getting the most wonderful sounds out of his trumpet. Beautiful noises, interplay with the others. Improvisations. He was never so far gone he couldn't play like...'

'Can I stop you a moment, Pamela. How old was Rice when you first met?'

'Twenty-two. Or twenty-three. I think twenty-two.'

'And you met through jazz music?' Varina can see it all coming together. Dr Okafor had told the ward round the funny tale of Rice asking about a trumpet when he was starkers in Brislington. It may not be the random madness it appeared. Pamela confirms that it was his chosen instrument. He used to be a very talented jazz musician. And there aren't many of those coming in and out of the Princess Margaret.

'I met him when I joined his combo. Well, it wasn't really his. There was another man thought himself top dog. The organiser was a chappie much older than Rice. I fell for the trumpeter. Stupid me.'

Varina notices Yand flinch when she says it. She's finding Pamela quite hardened. This might be what time has done to her, married to someone for years and years who has given her nothing but a son to raise. Not even an easy out.

'Your dad was a trumpeter,' says Varina, hoping to take the edge off his mother's negativity. Yand says nothing. 'And your mum, she still sings?'

Yand does not answer. Listening in, but he is no more than an observer. Pam speaks to the question. 'When I'm peeling potatoes or cleaning up in the bathroom. I've not fronted any sort of a group for years and years. A lifetime.'

'And when you did those things, playing jazz—you and Rice first together—was he a moody man? Did he have ups and downs? Could he cope with stress? The stresses of everyday life.'

'No one's perfect, neither him nor me. He...' She stops mid-sentence, twists her face into a grimace and then glances at Yand. '...we had invited all my family and the part of his that was still speaking to him, I couldn't really back out then but I nearly did. I was going to cancel the wedding. He went off for a day—in the week before—wouldn't tell me where he'd been. I wouldn't even have known but he didn't bother to clear it with work. His supervisor came round to our flat looking for him. Worried where he was. I thought they'd sack him and what have you. But not so. Rice was too important to them.'

'The garment-factory work?'

'That's it. Well, I thought he was at work and this lady who came to find him knew that he wasn't. Not a good sign with our wedding coming up at the weekend.'

'And did you learn where he went?'

'Not to this day.'

'Did you speculate?' asks the social worker.

'I speculated he had another woman but he swore on his grandmother's grave it wasn't that.'

Varina looks intently at Pamela, waits for her to offer a second possibility. She does not. 'Are you certain he went out with clothes on?'

'He wasn't barmy back then. I've already told you that.'

5.

After the dirty bastard nearly got his way with Pam Becker in a back alley—so nearly, it wasn't heavy petting, animal bloody husbandry, it was: a pent-up bull having an off-day—he went back to the flat like he'd only worked a late one at Puttock's. That was the name of the garment factory.

Jane was not a stupid girl. Not a bit of it. I don't expect she ever guessed he'd turn out like he did. She laughed and said, 'How much extra work did you do, Rice? Working down the pub, was it?' There you see. This fella had nabbed my name, gotten all those close to him using it like it belonged. And Jane Winters never called him Stickerhand. Not once.

'I did the hours, then a bunch of us went on to the Bird in Hand. A few beers. Sorry, Jane.'

'Aw, don't be. You've been working extra. Who went with you, Rice?' He named three or four of the men in the factory. They worked in maintenance for the most part, he wasn't close to them. It was women on the looms, women doing the cutting. Women plus Rice; he always did the initial outline, the first cut. Worked from stencil, a bit creative and a lot of discipline with it. 'That Louisa didn't go too, did she?' asked Jane. Louisa was likely just a name to her. One that her particular Rice had dropped into the conversation a few too many times to be coincidence, Jane must have worked out for herself that he liked the look of her.

'No, not Louisa. None of the women actually. Just us blokes.' The dirty liar. Louisa wasn't there but still the man was a dirty, dirty liar. And even though Louisa used to smile back at him, she was never the sort to let him put his hand down her knickers. He would have done it if she'd let him. You don't have to be Albert Einstein to work that one out. She simply wasn't the sort; not from the same mould as Pam Becker. The half-an-hour-a-go sort. Jane shouldn't have been fretting about Louisa: pretty girl but not one for stealing other women's fellas. Becker was the vexation. Becker and Sticker and the velvet mist that rises like hot steam, making its way through every lust-filled mind. Condenses up there and then falls down like autumn rain, through brain and breast and groin, right down into the bollocks. That's human biology as best I've got it figured out. Cats and dogs and ferrets too, I expect. All at it.

Jane had cooked him a meal which had long gone cold. He was back home later than any late shift would ever make him. His drunkenness—the pub backstory—actually worked as cover. She quickly reheated the sausage and mash for him in a frying pan. The beans in a saucepan. He wolfed it down in double quick time. The man was still in a bit of a stupor after what had happened between him and his new singer. Once he'd gobbled up his food, he took poor Jane to the bedroom and started to push her onto the bed. She was surprised, acquiesced anyway, didn't know that all the images rushing through his mind as he pulled off her knickers, put himself right inside her, were not of her at all. Not of poor little Jane Winters. He was virtually laying with another woman, one with a better singing voice and curly hair. Jane moaned with joy for how he was going at her. Not fake moaning, at least not as far as any fella in the room could tell. Soon-to-be Stickerhand was the fake though, wasn't he? His passion still in that dark alley round the corner from the jazz club. Dirty, dirty liar. Filthy, dirty bastard.

* * *

The following Saturday Smoking Cool were rehearsing at the club. Giving the girl the feel of the tunes, you might say. And the dirty fella who all this is about, he had already talked about it with his girl, Jane, the girl who, if you want my opinion, he no longer had a right to stake a claim to. Not that she knew it yet. He'd talked about the rehearsal, kept her in the dark about the new vocalist. Deceitful bugger. She was going to catch the bus to Rochdale to see her mum and kid brother. Jane didn't expect him along on that trip anyway. Birthdays and Christmas, yes. Otherwise, she went back home alone. 'It'll be eight o'clock before I'm back,' she said.

'I might go for a drink with the boys after.' Probably buy himself a packet of three long before he even arrived at the pub, that's what he was thinking. Pub, back alley. Pam's place if it was practical. My name, that's the one the heartless shit was using. Rice, he called himself, like it isn't unique. I'm the one who's Rice. I wouldn't have been thinking along the narrow gauge that this one did if Jane had been my girl. Brings shame right up to the name, doesn't it?

When Pam Becker came into the rehearsal room, a cool couple of minutes late, she was wearing a hat. It was really a man's kind of hat, like a cricket umpire might wear, floppy white atop the black ringlets of her hair. Anyone could tell you Pamela did not look like a man for even a split second. Any fella you care to name. Funny hat, clever choice.

'We're raring to go,' said Turner, a dismissive tone of voice for the late girl.

'After the intro, I'll walk out from behind the drums, thank-you,' she told him.

Stickerhand kind of laughed at that. This novice in the band putting down the high and mighty bighead. Coleman on the drums gave his high-hat an inviting brush stroke. 'Come and wait here,' he coaxed the girl.

'Thank you kindly,' she said going to where he beckoned, ducking down, making the point that they could start the act, riff about, as if there was no female singer in the band. Pamela hidden from view.

Turner shrugged, started rolling notes around his electric piano. Coleman picked up the brushes again, the bassist started going up and down. A neat inflexion in the timing, fluctuating between driving and meandering. They were a decent combo back then, the nineteen-seventies. Electric Guitar searched out Pamela with his eyes, nodded, two quick chords and he was straight into the funny riff he'd devised. They were playing My Wedding Day, the weird song that Dario Renzo made famous in the sixties, a proper opera singer vocalising over Dario's dreamy guitar. Stickerhand was not looking at the others, making a few faint notes but this was not his part. And having a girl singing this one shouldn't work in normal times, in real life.

> *I ricked my back when at a funeral*
> *Of an old friend of mine*

She looked miles too young to sing that line.

> *Back when I dated*
> *The girl in the coffin*

She never even changed the gender. It barely made sense her crooning over a lady-love like this. However, Pam Becker could sing the phone book and you'd believe it was the revelation of God. She had the feel for jazz. There was no predicting which notes she'd hold and which she'd pass across with the barest acknowledgement, so light could her step be. She meant it though. Had some extraordinarily loving feelings for this dead woman who had snubbed her lifelong. And for the key change, the line about the presence of her ghost, Pamela moved around the stage quivering each note. Stretching and bending them. With that, the talented but dirty-minded trumpeter blew in off the ocean. Let a quiet note grow into a roar and then whipped it into a melodic repeat of the chilling words Pam had just sung. He ended it on that long note, middle finger holding down the valve. Cheeks blowing, wavering it a little, then a lot, then not at all.

A jazzy eerie funeral, capped off with Becker singing the repetitive last line.

> *This is my wedding day*
> *This is my wedding day*
> *This is my wedding da-a-a-ay*

Smoking Cool had never sounded better.

While she was still singing the chorus to a close the piano man came in for a solo, Pam humming the melody; next Electric Guitar went a bit crazy—a bit Cajun crazy is what the man who misappropriated my name used to call it—terrific improvisation. All in the lee of the new vocalist. The bassist even did a couple of riffs in opposition to the guitarist, before Stickerhand did his solo again, second time around he went half speed. The notes sounded free, out there because they wanted to be. Pamela was back singing, 'This is my wedding day,' over and over. It sounded mental, being a funeral of a past lover with whom the singer never made-up, and sounded astonishing, being played so loose, diffidently, a big departure from the original record. They turned a four-minute song into ten, not a moment wasted. As it finished, some staff behind the bar, preparing for the evening—the place wasn't open to paying custom during the afternoon—burst into spontaneous applause. Turner grinned, possibly unintentionally. He always thought that he was Smoking Cool, that the name described him. This singer had brought something new. Brought it out in the trumpeter too.

'Your hand keeps sticking on that note,' she told him. Her tone was one of telling off, a reprimand. That's how cool she was, at least when she was playing the role of jazz singer. The trumpeter took it as a compliment. He'd got her measure. Felt her vibe. Felt it a few days earlier, too. Only the pair of them knew that; the rest of the band not in on their back-alley stunt. There never should be more than two involved in a mucky fumble. I sometimes think that's one too many.

* * *

When they were drinking a few beers together after the rehearsal, the drummer told him there must be glue on his right hand. It was not much different to what Pam said in rehearsal. Fingers sticking to buttons. 'Stickyhand suits you far better than Rice,' he told him. The trumpeter shook his head, didn't like it one bit.

Turner was acting aloof. Jealous as hell, you can bet. Cold shouldered by the pretty woman, and he thought he was the ladies' man. 'Sticky from putting it down his trousers,' he said. Barked a laugh at his own joke. To Pamela, to Coleman the drummer. Stickerhand ignored it completely. This kind of talk happened when it was just the lads. It felt of a different order with Pam Becker in the room. Next to his right arm. The hand that pushed the trumpet buttons. The man could think only of the back alley of a few days earlier, although it wasn't his own hand that needed the tissues.

'Sticky sounds like kids sweets,' said Pamela. 'Our trumpeter is Stickerhand.' All the boys seemed pleased enough with this nickname. Laughed about it. Pam leaned into the man she'd just christened, whispered in his ear, 'You can stick your magic finger on my button later, Stickerhand.'

He looked around at the lads. Not one of them had heard it, Pam had excellent control of her voice. She could choose when to send it warbling across the city and when to keep it snuck in bed at home.

* * *

I think you've got the picture now. Stickerhand was a dirty bastard. The sort who could forget about young Jane because she sang a bit too saccharine for jazz, and he'd only gone and let this curly haired vixen fill his mind as a better alternative. Didn't know yet that singing isn't everything. I shan't be telling you what went on between them: if you've thought it, they probably did it. They were each as bad as the other, that pair. And I'm not a prurient sort, it's just that I always think about everyone in the room. Like when I tried to comfort crazy Cheryl in the Princess Margaret. Not that she was easy to coax out of a rotten mood, I just see it as the thing to do. To try. I don't aim to set them off, I'm not like the mad constipated one. Nothing like that made old bat.

Poor Jane Winters.

6.

'I never had a dad,' says Yand. Varina is nodding as he says it. Knows how many different ways these stories can pan out. 'Don't remember him. Never knew him. Mum has told me about the first years like they were good. That his leaving was a shame and his not coping a catastrophe for him; not for us, Mum and I are all right. I never know what to think about a man I've no recall of. Stories of utter madness. That's as much as has stuck in my mind.'

Rice's wife or rather, ex-wife—she's the latter now, whatever the paperwork says and however rich a whirlwind romance they once enjoyed—cuts across her son. 'There's beauty in music, Yand. It isn't madness. There may be no obvious reasoning to it. Rhythms that raise a pulse or set us feeling almost tearful without explanation of why we feel what we feel. It's not madness, the feelings it invokes are too real for it to be that. He was really something when I met him. My Rice, your dad. Before he started coming apart.'

'Did you learn much about his early years, Pamela? Did Rice tell you about growing up?'

She looks at the social worker, then quickly at her son—Rice's son—eyes no longer focussed. Thoughts running backwards. Varina scrutinises her, the silent Pamela Bradford, guesses she is picturing something important. Dredging up whatever measure of answer she knows to that most curious of questions. Who is Rice Bradford?

* * *

'Rice was born in Rochdale and I've told you already how he came by his name. It's a funny story, hard not to like him for it. I understand that he had an older sister. I only know this from a conversation I had with his mother, not something he ever told me directly. His big sister and a boy were both killed, Rice only eight or nine years old at the time. Many, many years before I knew him. She was riding on the back of the lad's motorbike. It's a tragic story, little girl never saw her fifteenth birthday and the family were ashamed because the lad was seventeen. Mrs Bradford said to me that she and George—the illiterate George Bradford—fell out over the funeral of the boy whose fault it was. When she told me, Sadie Bradford said, "George and me, we were both heartbroken, just I felt like two kids had been robbed of their lives. I hadn't known she was seeing the boy but I wasn't cross about it. George was different. Angry. He said the lad murdered our daughter and used her for a slut before it happened." When I asked a question or two it was clear to me that neither George nor Sadie really knew if they were a couple. The ride on the back of the motorbike might have been a first. The closest they'd ever come together. I guess Sadie's forgiving nature and George's nasty streak came out with it all. Apparently—and this marries up with the dates Rice gave me although he never mentioned his sister—his parents split-up within a year and divorced in two. Rice told me about the horrible rows that went on between them. His dad was the mad and angry sort. That came across in the tales he told.'

'Mad?'

'Angry-mad, not in any other way. Looking back, I'm sure it was all grief that put the family through this upheaval, looking back because Rice never told me there was anyone to grieve over. Never told me he even had a sister. A dead sister. The day I married him, I still thought he was an only child.'

Varina listens intently to the tale. Barely notices how bored Yand looks by it all.

'Mrs Bradford said that Rice had been "out of sorts" for a couple of years after his sister died. That it was like he couldn't accept she was gone. Threw a fit when she and George redecorated the dead girl's bedroom; offered it to Rice as an alternative to the box-room that he slept in. I understood that soon after the divorce, Sadie's own father died. Mother had been dead a while before, and she came into a little money. It wasn't a lot but it was something...' Pamela looks levelly at Varina who is making only the occasional record in her bound notebook. It all has meaning to the social worker, a jigsaw falling in to place. The never-ending puzzle of a life, every final piece a gravestone. '...and it was Rice who told me this part. His mum decided to spend some of it on him. He was still a little lad—not teenage—just into secondary modern, and she bought him his first trumpet. Got him a few lessons too. He spent about half a year learning some basics and then joined Rochdale town band. Easily good enough to be there and all happening so early in his playing. Blowing down it in the parks; Sunday afternoons on the bandstand. He only did that while he was little, finished with brass bands by the time he was fourteen. No time for four-four time, if you get what I mean.'

'Is it usual,' asks Varina. 'It's your field of expertise, not mine, but a boy who didn't pass the eleven plus being such a musical prodigy? As you describe him.'

'Oh Varina,' says Pam, 'he would have got to grammar school if we were only civilised back then. A poor kid grieving his sister for two years. They didn't get the counselling and what have you back in those days. Nineteen-sixty, by my guess; there was nothing for the likes of Rice. The trumpet was the therapy. I've always thought that. Music does it for a lot of people, Mrs Pope. Always has.'

* * *

Yand is looking bleary eyed. Not crying tears but he's on edge. He nudges his mother and whispers something to her. Whatever he says it's inaudible to Varina.

'I know,' says Pamela, 'I should have told you all this before; I didn't plan on telling it here. It seemed disrespectful when I first thought about this, telling tales on poor Rice now he can't remember a darned thing for himself. It's just that I've seen how you ask, Varina. I think you want what's best for him.'

'Definitely, Pamela. I was worried that we'd be at loggerheads because you want to divorce him, but I can see that you've not troubled him with this for as long as you were able. It must have been extraordinarily difficult having a husband whose whereabouts—whose mental state—were unknown to you almost all the time.'

'I never thought of him as a fragile man, not when we were together. He was a musician and they're a funny lot, could be volatile and he drank too much...' She glances once more at Yand. '...I did that too. Jazz clubs had a drink-too-much vibe, if you didn't then you couldn't really count yourself as present...'

'Pamela, did you drink before you played, sang? I'm just curious.'

'Some jazz musicians did, some didn't. We were Smoking Cool, every member had something before we started and most stayed for a lot more before the place closed. Not Johnny on guitar, everyone else.'

* * *

'I've not really told you about his other job, at the factory...'

'No. I suppose jazz is more interesting than factory work...'

'...not entirely, Varina, he was a genius. Quite incredible. They never gave him the credit...'

'Sorry, Pamela. What exactly did he do in the garment factory?'

The crease lines on Pamela Bradford's face turn into the happiest smile, and then her eyes narrow as if to drive this joy from her own face. 'He was indispensable. Told me when we were first together that he was a cutter. I thought he meant repetitively like you said, and perhaps he had been once. Told me he started off there just sweeping up the floors. But Rice back then—whatever he looks like now, dresses like now—he had an eye. Puttock's was the company name but by the time Rice was working there a family of whatsits had taken over...you know...the cotton industry thing. And this was back then, fewer rules...'

'Can I stop you, Pamela. Whatsits?'

'Owned by one of those Bangladeshi's who just rip off whatever's selling well in mid-market fashion...'

'Pamela, it might have happened. I don't imagine that approach to the garment business is uniquely Bangladeshi.'

'You weren't there,' says Pamela. 'I don't think Rice was the only one, I'm certain he became the best. One part of the job was doing the first outline. Finding out the way the garments they were copying were best cut. How best to make it so they wasted as little fabric as possible. He was a man who would always say, "We can do better than this." His designs weren't startlingly original, didn't try to be, but the owner quickly liked that they were similar rather than copies. Improvements you might say. It meant that there could be no challenge on the design. No legal challenge. And Puttocks' dresses became very popular. Dresses and skirts that my husband designed. If he was from Italy, instead of Rochdale, Rice Bradford might have become a household name.'

'Rice designed skirts?'

'Embarrassing isn't it,' Yand tells the social worker. 'My dad making skirts and dresses. From what you've said, it sounds like he can't even keep his own trousers on these days.'

'The last part, yes,' Varina emotes in her social-workese, 'that must be hard. But Yand, the ability to design clothes, men and women study this for years and I doubt that your father studied it at all.' She glances at the ex-wife. 'He just had the knack.'

Pamela smiles, must see that Varina wears grey slacks, a blouse that is the same colour while being far enough different in shade not to match at all. She isn't wearing a Mao suit but her attire suffers the same absence of chic. While she, Pam Bradford, has on the stylish dress, the summer wear with a splash of colour. Creams and blues against her lightly tanned skin.

7.

Everything about this name-stealer bugs me. From ten o'clock until long past midnight he was in her flat. Miss Sings and Strings the Men Along. That's the her I'm talking about. In her little one room, half a block from Hulme Playhouse. While they were at it—him giving her what for, drumstick down the trumpet hole if you get my drift, her enjoying having him put it there, I expect— they were nattering on and on about Smoking Cool performing in the neighbouring venue. Playing the Playhouse. And that was all a foolish pipedream cooked-up by this pair of cloud-nine lovers. Never happened, never could have. Those proper theatres were far too big for a jazz combo. These weren't the nineteen forties. Jazz no longer wanted a high ceiling to reverberate around. It liked them low. A fug of cigarette smoke attaching itself to the barely metred sound.

It was very, very late on that Saturday night when he walked back across town. All the way from hers to his. The girl—Pamela Rose Becker—had told him earlier that he could stay over. She didn't care about appearances and quite frankly nor did many people. Not by then. The swinging sixties had been and gone, this was nineteen seventy-Wilson. I think it was. One of those years. Of course, Sticker knew he had to make up some blather to tell Jane. Where he was after the practice; what he did all evening into the small hours. The longer he stayed, the more outrageous his explanation would need to be. In the event he turned up at two a.m., let himself in and never heard her rouse in the bedroom. He slept on the sofa, kept his day clothes on all night.

This was the end of April and when she—Jane of Rochdale, the one who had thought she was his girlfriend for something along the mark of six or seven years—arose from their bed, everything seemed normal. On balance it did. When she walked through to the lounge-diner—the only other proper room in their little flat—she would have seen the man asleep. Must have heard his snores already. Audible in the bedroom, kitchen, bathroom too. Why would it bother her? It wouldn't. Jazz trumpeter sleeps off beer on sofa. Doesn't even bother to undress. Nothing new in that tale. Nothing at all. Not unless he cared to tell it and Stickerhand Bradford was keeping schtum. As closed-mouthed about what he'd been up to with Curly-Haired Becker as a man can be.

* * *

The Tuesday after Sticker and Becker first did all the dirty stuff— and I mean all—Smoking Cool played before an audience with the new vocalist taking centre-stage. The duplicitous trumpeter had talked around the houses with Jane, never mentioned the new singer once. Advised it was to be a regular night, a pub on Sackville Street that they had played many times before. The girl had said, 'Do you mind if I don't go? Work in the morning and...'

'No, of course not.' He might have jumped in too quick but she didn't notice. Truth was, Jane never seemed to enjoy watching Smoking Cool after it became clear that she was never going to be a part of it. Sang nicely but not jazz. When Stickerhand—this was his name by this point in time, not that Jane ever applied it— practised in the flat, she would listen reverentially. She understood what he could do. Thought him good. Better than good. I think Turner was the one Jane couldn't stand. The decision maker, judge and jury. He might have been right that she wasn't the greatest for fronting a band like Smoking Cool. Too disciplined, her voice control sounded forced when she tried to jazz it up. Thing is, Turner was nasty with it, the way he treated people. Especially a girl who was so obviously off-limits to him. Sticker's bird. And if Jane disliked him, the rest of the band probably thought the same. They seldom said it, of course. Pretty good on the ivories and fixed up all the bookings too. In other circumstances, she might have enjoyed learning that the new girl, Pam Becker, had put Turner's nose a tad out of joint. That he'd have to settle for the wife at home this time. As it was, this little detail was too complicated for the trumpeting Rice to tell. And the new singer sang like a brandy-swilling, cigarette-puffing nightingale. She had to be in the band, could be no stopping her. Hard to say what Jane would have made of it. Turner saw the potential, the musical truth that Pamela added right from the off. In other circumstances, Stickerhand would surely have told Jane about her, about the new singer. They might have become friends. Jane still had more of them in Rochdale than she did in Manchester. Instead, he only went and did his back-alley prodding and probing and everything that followed had to be hush-hush. Every twist after that finger-smelling moment. The man was improvising in his relationships every bit as much as he did when blowing down his little brass mouthpiece.

Apart from being a great success there were just two other small things to mention about Tuesday in the Queen's Arms. The first of them was that a reporter from the Evening Clarion was listening and later talking to Tommy Turner and Pam Becker. He tried to have a word with Electric Guitar and Stickerhand, but the first was too shy and the second a tiny bit flustered about it going in the paper at all. When Jane learnt that the band had a singer—the following tea-time unless her reading habits changed pronto—she would find it odd that he'd neglected to tell her of the development. After the reporter left—a few scribbles in his notebook—he and Pamela spoke at the bar. She told him that the guy loved everything he heard. The write-up would be the greatest publicity. I expect she never understood why he seemed to be in a huff about it.

Pamela wrapped herself around him at the bar and this might have done a lot of things. It got Turner to leave early, so that was a result for the pair. Pam was whispering in Sticker's ear about going back to his flat. She knew it was closer than her place in Hulme. Didn't know there was another young woman living inside. Stickerhand didn't take the opportunity to educate her. He took her outside, promised he'd take her soon but not tonight. She was a little funny about it, asking why not. He said that after their next performance, which was only Saturday, it would be back to his. She shrugged and said, 'I guess I can wait until then.' He gave her a squeeze, touching places on her that most wouldn't. This was on the street, late at night, and the pub they played was a bit of a dive, middle of the prostitute's district. God knows what people thought but Pam Becker was probably as filthy-minded as Sticker. Didn't give a pair of dirty knickers for what anyone else thought.

They did most of what the dirty tarts did, except for Stickerhand keeping all his money. Got the fun without parting with a shilling. With a five-penny piece. Did it on the canal towpath, the dirty low-lives.

* * *

He drank four or five the night before, still rose at six-thirty on the Wednesday, a half hour earlier than his usual. Jane was up minutes later. That was her habit because the café opened at seven-thirty. An hour before Sticker had to be at Puttocks.

'Up with the larks,' she said to him.

'Sit down, Jane.'

'What is it?' she asked, then added, 'Look at your face.' She smiled when she said it, they weren't an argumentative couple. Couldn't have guessed he was for starting now. Happen she was surprised by the funny turn her fella's features took. Clueless about where it might be going. Poor thing.

Rice Bradford—if you'll believe that this was the bugger's name—and Jane Winters had been together since they were young. They'd known each other virtually as long as they'd known themselves. Cecil Street, Penrith Street. Their parents had been neighbours give or take a few terraced cottages. A few of those factory workers little houses. They played together when they were kids, the nineteen-fifties, with broken bicycles and skipping ropes for toys. Chalk marks on the pavement, hopping games. Someone's older brother passing around a lit cigarette, this pair both too scared to put it to their lips. Primary school scared that was; the fear that doesn't last.

They both went up to the secondary, Jane one year behind, but by this time they weren't really knocking about together. Boys play with boys, and girls play with girls, when they get to that age. Young Stickerhand played with neither for the most part. Played with his trumpet. Then, him fourteen, her only months shy of it, they started walking about together again. It was easy to see the attraction for the boy. Slim, pale, blue eyes and an honesty that might be a jazz singers ruin. She was straightforward, a contrast to Rice even when they were first getting together. Teenage together: school choir. Still living a stone's throw apart. Not a difficult throw, an underarm chuck.

They were still in school—it was barely a hand-holding affair—and Rochdale never really latched onto the swinging sixties. The hemlines rose up on every girl's skirt, mind you. Not swinging but a decent imitation. And the trumpeter with my name had left the town band. Couldn't have stayed once he'd blown the cobwebs off their turgid wartime tunes. Other, better, songs giving him those tingling feelings by this time. Back in those nineteen sixties, a boy being musical might have helped him attract the girls. Quite a few made hay with a lot less flair than that lad had. But Rice was stuck with his teenage awkwardness even when he started glancing over the girls. Awkward didn't stop him wanting one, and the lassie already holding his hand seemed a natural. For a year or two they were a couple who talked, kissed and danced a little bit. Jitterbug, they could do it. That was the limit. Jane once asked the young Stickerhand, who wasn't yet called by that name, about taking things further, about buying some thingies from the barbers on Lincoln Street. The lad coloured up in his cheeks, this was forward talk and he only out of school a few weeks. It wasn't only his face that the blood rushed to. He'd thought about it often enough. Thought about it whenever he wasn't doing something else, and a teenage boy's bedroom is pretty much a shrine to thoughts of all that palaver. Bodies rubbing up close; round and round and up and down go the thoughts of the all the teenaged boys.

They continued to be a couple, and with a closer physical bond than they let the adult world know about, for near on two years before Sticker said he might move to Manchester. He was playing jazz with a few Rochdale lads, not anything that matched his talent yet. He said the moving thing very casually to Jane, he might not have made it clear if he was suggesting that they split up or move in together. The girl was smarter than the boy at that point in their coupling. At every point is my assessment, but I only say this because some sorcerer has stuffed my ruddy mind with it. These are not my memories. The pair of them went on the bus into the city weekend after weekend, sourcing jobs and cheap accommodation. Sticker took Jane to a couple of jazz clubs, took his trumpet too and one let him join them for the six o'clock rehearsal. Must have liked what they heard. This was before Smoking Cool existed. Electric Guitar was in that band: Storyville. And they took on Sticky Rice, he did melodies and impro. No one but him and Electric played in both of those bands.

It was only when they moved in to Cotter Street—their own front door—that the fella coaxed Jane back to singing. They enjoyed those sessions, just the two of them. Practicing a few standards in the bedsit. It was Sticker who insisted Jane try out for the band. Not for Storyville, only for the one that came after. She played with them more than a dozen times. Musically, Jane was the weakest link. Nice voice, it's just that she wasn't a jazz singer. Music isn't everything, you know. It might be nothing. Most things are when you analyse the arse off them.

And there she was, laughing at his serious face so early in the morning and he just said, 'Can you be gone when I'm home this evening. It's not working.'

That was as cruelly heartless as it was untrue. Nothing wrong, not with Jane Winters. For three years Jane and the man who shouldn't rightly be called Rice—not in a world that makes any sense to me—lived together in Manchester. If it had been a proper Rice—me—I'd have treated her right, I really would. I'm not a bastard, that's the other fella. So now you really must start believing me: these are the memories of a crueller man than I've ever been. No idea how in hell they got themselves crammed up here in my sorry brainbox. Can't explain where they're from beyond there being a fella out there who's taken on my name. I wish I knew the long and short of it but all I've got is this residual distress.

Down the Cutting

Tragic isn't it. Jane and Sticker: a couple for years before they ever moved to the temptations of Manchester. A young and chaste couple, then a pair who did that which came naturally. Two lost kids in a cottonless mill town, making life better for each other with their presence. Then another three in the shining city. Good years as I've thought about them, his thoughts, but they seemed pretty good as I've had them laid out. He owed that girl so much more.

'I don't know what you mean,' she whined back at him.

'Of course, you know. You're holding me back.' This is the implausible excuse that the skirt-chasing bastard told her. Don't know how a man can treat a girl that way.

'What's gone wrong? What's...' Jane was blubbing now. Nobody could blame her. And don't ask how I know this, but the nasty man who had my name stitched into half his clothing didn't mean a word of this blather. He just thought it was how it was done. You find a sultrier girl, then you've got to dispatch the runner up. No two ways about it. He remembered how Turner had ejected Jane from the band. Remembered how Turner had seen off a couple of lady-jazz-fans after he'd poked them a time or two and then got tired of the doing it. I think, from the wise position of all this happening a long time ago, that in his ball-dropping excitement, brought on—aroused, goddammit—by the curly-haired coquet, he never quite did the calculation that Turner had always done. Blasting some kid into the water who'd only been on his shoulder one or two nights took only a little pretend anger, faked derision. That's all it took to make them turn and go. Tommy Turner never tried to eject his missus, the woman who'd borne him all those children. Jane hadn't gotten around to babies but she was always good to him. Twenty-two years old is all that girl was when this horrid conversation was spewing its lava.

'Don't cry like a baby when you're not even happy being here, being in the city. You're small town, Janey. Can't hack the jazz, don't like to see me blending into the whole scene. Not really a part of my life any more, are you?'

Jane sat and cried as the man arose from the seat, went and took his trumpet out of its case. Started to blow some bluesy notes as if to demonstrate this angry conversation was not affecting him, happening to her while being of no consequence to the trumpet player. Stars Upon the Sea rippled the air in the flat. A few weeks earlier they'd sung it together. A sweet version, Jane's voice was spot on for a tune like that. Then he suggested it for the band, got the Becker girl to sing it in her cruel see-you-never voice. Some twinkling twilight friend this lying shit turned out to be. It's like he heard the tune and not the words. Felt something to the core when he was playing on his shiny instrument and then it was just an act. Nothing in his heart when the bugger stopped blowing.

Jane came and stood in front of him. 'When did you become so fucking mean!' she demanded.

Sticker shrugged.

'André can go fuck himself,' she said. That was the name of the manager, the boss in the café where Jane worked. 'I'm going now. Going back to Penrith Street.' All of this she shouted at him.

Stickerhand blew down his trumpet.

'I should never have come here.'

Our little boat is bobbing on the sea, lied his trumpet. He was almost getting the consonants out of the instrument. He was as good at playing the trumpet as he was ornery in his manipulation of the poor little girl who'd given him everything.

'You're not normal!'

So you see, the girl was knocking one or two rabbits bang on top of the head. Knew a nasty piece of shit when it reared its head. Not like me, the proper Rice, I'm normal top to bottom. Apart from the clothes thing. Forgetting to affix them properly to my person. I'll give you that one, I'm still fairly normal, in the range. A regular bloke.

8.

'Do you know what I think, Pamela?' says Varina.

The lady glances at her. Shrugs. 'What?'

'The point you made, Rice having an older sister who died—who sadly died—you'd expect he remembered it all too clearly, you said he would have been eight or nine. But Rice didn't tell you, never acknowledged the reality of it. Kept it down. That's what he's done more recently with the last twenty years. I need to talk to Dr Kavanagh. She understands brains better than I do...' The social worker gives a small smile at this, her foray into layman's language sounding a little daft but there's little else to use. The doctor's big words hide many a career's worth of uncertainty on the same subject. '...he clearly started then, started young. You've heard his diagnosis, I take it?'

'No. Or was it that thing you said on the phone?'

'I think I did, Pamela. Schizoaffective disorder...' Varina looks at the son of the man being labelled. '...it sounds like schizophrenia, I know. It is quite different. Really. He seems to have the capacity for delusion, it's mostly at the extreme end of emotion that this happens. This other trait, way of conducting himself, disowning or forgetting memories that the rest of us can't imagine anyone getting confused about...' Varina brushes imaginary hair out of her eyes—hers cut too short to require the action—looks directly at Pamela, eyes meet. '...he does not admit he has ever been married. Convinced me completely until you began explaining so much, Pamela. Our Rice is a very complicated case, that much is as clear as day.'

Yand pulls himself out of a slouch in his plastic seat. Sits upright for the first time in fifteen minutes. 'Why does he take his clothes off then?'

Varina takes her time thinking over the correct reply. Tries to find the sympathetic warmth in her voice that she struggles to feel for this young man. It is the wife's testimony that has brought her close to tearing up. 'I know it sounds like he's ever so disinhibited—and it could be that he is—yet I'm tempted to take him at face value. The man says he forgot. So far, I've learnt only of summer admissions to hospital. Sleeping in the buff, unclothed, is not so uncommon. Rising and leaving the house on an errand so important you forget to put your clobber on, well, only a very manic person could do that, Yand. Very manic indeed but I don't think there is any wider meaning. He doesn't seek people out or pester them. Not as we've ever heard about.'

Yand seems to be taking this in carefully, slowly. 'And he won't go to court for it?'

'Not at all. When the police attended, they knew he was one for us, here at the hospital. They could tell that straight away.'

The boy nods. She seems to have tucked away a fear she'd not known was floating around inside him. 'Pamela when did...'

Varina stops talking. Pamela Bradford has the strangest look on her face. Open mouthed, perplexed. 'He came home with a black eye. I think I'd forgotten it; not like him to get in that sort of state, you see. Never a fighter Rice, never. And he wouldn't tell me...'

'When was this,' says the scribbling social worker.

* * *

'We lived together in Cotter Street for over a year before I fell pregnant...' She glances at Yand. Something about the look, the way he took her eyes to his own, suggests to Varina that he is embarrassed by it. She expects that he has long known the order of the marriage and the pregnancy. It's the same order she and Brian chanced upon. '...I was really pleased to start a family. He was making more than ever, both at Puttocks and in the jazz clubs. We were both still doing the latter, only I couldn't picture myself continuing to sing while I was carrying. It's a full-diaphragm thing, doing jazz. I was overjoyed to be having Rice's child, always thought I'd get back to music another time. And I think my fella was happy about it too. I really did think that. He patted my stomach, talked to my stomach. To Yand who was inside. Yet to meet us. All good. Then we got hitched...' Pamela Bradford wriggles in her seat as if in discomfort, straightens her dress upon her thighs although neither Varina nor Yand can see below the table line. She pauses before continuing. 'It was odd too but I expected that. I'd still to meet his mum at this stage, and Rice never saw his dad. Or only once in a blue moon. He didn't want either of them at our wedding. Their divorce was the only reason he gave. Told me that he would talk to them both. Square everything with them. He didn't want my family there really— that was clear to me—but I insisted. John Tinsley was best man, the guitar player. Him and his wife came, nobody else from the band. We couldn't really afford anything big, so we did the opposite: a registry office and a few drinks.' Again, she looks quickly at Yand before further straightening of her dress. 'No honeymoon,' she adds.

'Pamela,' says Varina, I'm confused by some of the timings.

When did you learn about Rice's sister, her untimely death?'

'Much later, lovey. I didn't know his mother at this stage, never met her before all the trouble. Separation, illness. I met Sadie Bradford three or four times after he took ill. In those four or five of months. That was when she told me about all that.'

'And you told her it was the first you'd heard of his wee sister?'

'I did. I've got to tell you, Varina, she didn't seem a bit surprised.'

* * *

Varina has heard a million hard-luck stories in the course of her career. Behind every tale of chronic mental illness, lies another. A life divested of potential. It's always in the mix. The jazz clubs give this tale a certain feel, an excitement above the usual. Rice Bradford's ex-wife's admiration for his trumpet playing twenty years after the fact is the rarest thing. Squaring it with the image of the man she saw shaking his landlord's head, shouting, 'Yes, my son,' that's very hard to put together. The shell that is Rice Bradford must once have been a quietly impressive man. Pamela tells Varina that it was a marriage of love. They clicked from day one; music filled their flat and later their house in Droylsden. She admitted that she wanted the man who walked out to walk back in, wanted it for over a decade before she put him into a place in her mind reserved for the permanently afflicted. Consigned him to the certainty of no recovery. Tragedy and realism, thinks Varina. All for the best, and still bolting that door shut must be unbearably painful. Heart-breaking, she can hear it in Pamela's voice.

'I didn't think on it. I did when it occurred, during those days when he was walking around the flat with a big black eye. Events move us along, don't they? I had this one to squeeze out...' Her eyes gesture towards her son. '...and a house move to organise. I suppose I accepted his version. Set upon after hours, wouldn't go to the police because he was too drunk to remember a thing. I didn't buy it. I let it go but I didn't buy it. Still don't to this day.'

'What was it about this injury that made you think that way? Not trusting his story.'

'Nothing. No, something...once, right at the beginning he said to me, "I might have had it coming." Then, when I tried to drag it out of him, exactly what had happened, what he meant by the comment, he said he was set upon. That never added up. Only that. Not a lot, and plenty if you let it sit in your mind.'

Varina feels puzzled by this tale. As a new wife, Pam forgot about her husband's black eye for years and years, and yet she still looks so troubled remembering the event after all this time. 'Did Rice not get along with his parents?' she asks.

'He'd go to see his mother once in a while.'

Varina looks directly into Pamela's lightly made-up face. Expects her to say more but nothing comes. 'He wouldn't take you?'

She laughs self-consciously. 'I think that's the size of it. I asked him once if he was ashamed of me. It wasn't a row, might have been the nearest thing we had to it. He got all flustered. Said he was ashamed of her. I said he shouldn't be. I take people as I find them, always have. He insisted I couldn't go. "It would only put her in one of her moods," he said. I let it go. Never knew her; never needed to. It was only when I met her years later that it didn't sound like the genuine reason. Nothing moody about her, not as far as I could tell.'

Rice was similarly troubled way back when, thinks Varina. He might have expunged all thought of his sister from his life as he now has done his entire life in Manchester. She wonders how to ask this. It's a wild hypothesis. 'Have you any contact with his mother still?'

'No. I don't know that she's even alive yet. Wouldn't know where to look. She's no longer on Cecil Street, that's as much as I'm certain about.'

'Was it strange when she told you about the death of his sister?'

'Not as strange as it sounds. It made one or two things fit into place.'

'And do you know what the sister's name was?'

'I'm sorry. I don't recall that. It's long seemed sad to me not to have a name for a story. It never lodged up here, that's all.' Pam Bradford taps the side of her head, finger upon dyed black hair. Nobody has a brain that meets every demand made upon it. They can be temperamental, anybody's and everybody's.

9.

I know a lot about him, don't I? The slippery trumpet player who booted his childhood sweetheart back to Rochdale for no reason that makes good sense. Not unless you're made of stone. He lived in the same place—little flat on Cotter Street—with the Becker girl. She did a little bit of work here and there but singing was her thing. I think she was older than Stickerhand, not that it's any kind of an excuse for his behaviour. He was a man not a child. Not a decent man, not upright: that's a fact. A miscreant by any proper reckoning.

I'm not sure if Pam Becker had lived with a fella before. It strikes me as very, very likely. She was uninhibited in the department which you know I'm talking about. The stuff that hypnotises randy young fellas like the boy who stole my name. Piss-Paul too but girls run from him like he's wearing a get-your-gonorrhoea-here T-shirt. And the poor sod has never had the chance to catch it. Then, for whatever reasons rattled around in the Becker girl's unmoored mind, she started insisting the two of them get married. Most of the ladies seem to have a few of those guy ropes in there. Peg 'em down and keep your clothes on, eh? And if you do as they ask, your life might run a course better than mine has managed. There must be worse fates than hitching your gurney to the right girl. Not that my namesake picked the right one, I wouldn't have stood for Curly Top for a second.

I find it odd that Jane and Sticker never thought of doing it— the matrimony thing—a bit like they were both too young when they moved down to Manchester and never thought to change how they were once they got there. What Becker wanted by marrying the man is beyond my knowledge. Maybe she thought he'd make a fortune in the rag trade. It must happen for some but not really to the likes of him.

Shame about Jane Winters. I only know her because my brain gets hijacked now and then, and I can tell you this: I'd have married her—the Rochdale girl—if I'd been in charge of my name when the possibility was abroad. And I don't doubt that I'd have jizzed myself once or twice thinking about sexy Pamela. It's what men do. A little of what no one need know about. Liking the look of a girl isn't an excuse for feeling her up the back alley. Not when you've already got a girl, and a better one on many a measure, if just a tad mousier.

Stickerhand only went and fell in with the singer's plan. Marrying, all that. Making their attachment a matter of public record. Did it because he was hypnotised by her voice, that's what I think. He only argued about the detail. No church: the only time he ever went to one of them he absolutely hated it, loathed it. Felt the hand of death upon him, and on all the family he had with him. He determined on that terrible childhood day that he wasn't going back to a place like that. A church. Not in this life. I don't go to them either but I have different reasons. I'm not partial to vicars. Shirts on back to front, they look ridiculous. Can't tell if they're coming or going.

No family. Stickerhand insisted on that, and Pam Becker was as resolute about the opposite.

Her mother came and one brother. She had a second one living in Vancouver who couldn't make it. The two that did, plus Electric Guitar, his best man, comprised all the guests at Manchester Town Hall, where the registrar did the necessary. And all as went on to the Abercrombie for drinks afterwards. The registrar chappie missed that part. It wasn't a high-life wedding— far from it—that wouldn't be jazz. Stickerhand put on smartish clothes, no tie. She was a picture if you like that sort of thing. Yellow and blue, a dress designed by her husband-to-be. Not white, not after what that pair had already got up to in her place, his place, their bedsit. One or two city ginnels too.

A pair of taxis ferried the guests from the flat to the Town Hall. They could have walked if they'd been so minded, not even a mile. Down the pub, it was pints of mild for the fellas, barley wines and sweet martinis for the ladies. Mr and Mrs Stickerhand. He wore a white flower, not of the right type. The guests might have gone on to the Wimpy bar or something when it was all over. Three drinks were enough for him, for pretend-Rice. Like an ordinary Saturday afternoon except he wasn't single at the end of it. No longer a freeman in any sense that a bloke could recover from.

I don't know what the married pair did after they left the bar. Sex, I expect. They had a flat for it. It was one of just two things they had in common, from what I can gather: jazz music and rutting for England.

* * *

Stickyhand, Stickerhand. Like Turner said when a name in the vicinity of it was first floated, it does sound like a fella who puts his hand down his own pants a bit often. I've always thought that. About fifteen years ago, in the John Connolly—which is a funny name for a hospital, a loony bin—there was a chappie also called Connolly, he went on and on about it. Simon was his name best I recall, not the John who'd got the whole hospital named after him. You can bet your life that John Connolly was a Lord or a doctor, certainly not a nutcase. A philanthropist, probably, so much money he gave some to the likes of me who don't even care for it. Gave it so we could have electro-convulsive therapy and other such wonders. I didn't see any straight-jackets in the John Connolly, didn't check all the understairs cupboards. I can tell you for nothing, Philanthropists paid for hundreds and thousands of the ruddy things in their time.

Simon Connolly—no relation I'm sure, whatever cock and bull he tried to spin—was a bit older than me. Proper bats in the belfry, that man. Far worse than just forgetting to put his clothes on now and again. He lectured me on and on about not playing with myself. It sounds embarrassing, I know, me being in my thirties at the time, but he lectured all the patients about it. He reckoned that he was proper sensible, nothing wrong with his mind at all, until he overdid the thing I'm talking about. Pretending you're with a girl when it's just your own hand giving you a bit of loving. He must have got to me, his incessant talk on a subject we never spoke about back then.

I asked the trick-cyclist in the ward round, 'Does playing with...you know...the sausage in your trousers, make a man's brain turn to mush? Send them around the bend, so to speak.' It was another of those lady doctors who I asked. Normally I'd have been too embarrassed but the Connolly bloke had got the notion lodged so firmly into my head that it felt important to get to the bottom of it. Find out the truth of it then and there.

I forget her name. She was doughty, severe, older than they let doctors work these days. That or she aged quickly. Grey-haired.

Lines on her face like somebody had been flaking off icing with a toffee hammer.

She laughed at me, which wasn't of itself nice, but was actually reassuring. 'Three patients have already asked me that today. None of them was Simon Connolly; however, I do detect his handiwork. Please don't trust a word he says. Simon is a patient, not a doctor. It's a silly old wives' tale. Something parents say to youngsters, to teenage boys, to stop them from playing with themselves. They really needn't bother. It's normal behaviour. Completely normal. Everyone does it. There is no correlation to brain function. None. Masturbation is not a cause of mental illness, I can assure you. I've studied it.'

So, there you have it. I don't suppose the women working in the hospital laundry were so keen on her message, but that doctor said it to any who asked. Stickerhand, me, we're all allowed the odd hand-shandy. Well, if you do the maths, it's probably the odd five thousand, maybe ten of the damned things. Paul Norton will have done twice that and his twenty-fourth birthday is still a few weeks away. You'd think he might be brain of Britain if he hadn't, stranger things and all that. Not so: I asked Doctor Grey-hair about that one too. It doesn't even turn you stupid: some of us are, some of us aren't; the wanking has no bearing on it. It isn't those stolen dreams that drive us nuts. Carry on boys!

* * *

I've gone on a bit about the wedding and it was a miserable affair really. Those two making a public declaration of a coupling they should only have been ashamed of. And I should have said what happened before, it might be what got Stickerhand into the glum mood that even getting wed to sultry Pamela and drinking a few pints of mild couldn't shift.

One day, while he was working at Puttock's—and this was after the notice was posted with the registrar in City Hall saying that him and her were to be married, but before the not-so-big day had happened—a supervisor named Doreen called him into the office. The man calling himself Rice was not worried about it. No reason to be. His work was always good. Doreen worked closely with Mr Haque, you see, and Haque was in charge of the whole place. The biggest boss who showed his face. Rumour had it that there were others involved, dealing with sales and marketing. Turning rags into riches. Not that any on the shop floor came into much money through their endeavours. That's never going to happen on this Earth, is it? Workers getting what they're worth.

'What's the matter?' asked that Rice.

'Telephone call for you. I can vacate the office if it's personal.'

He thought that was a very nice offer by Doreen. You could see how far he'd risen up in Puttock's those four years. From being a dogsbody all the way to taking private calls in the office.

'It's all right,' he said, picking the handset off her desk. 'Hello.' Stickerhand was not very familiar with telephones. He'd used them of course, just that it was a now-and-again experience for him. Didn't have one in the flat and he'd certainly never taken a call in Doreen Mathers' office before.

He didn't recognise the voice that spoke to him, a voice he should have known but hadn't talked to for months and months. A couple of years at the outside. Mr Winters, calling from Penrith Street in Rochdale, telling the dirty jazz trumpeter that Jane—the girlfriend he never should have thrown over—was dead of an overdose. Anti-depressants from a doctor and she only went and took the lot. Her father used the word suicide. That made all the juices in Sticker's stomach turn sour. Ashen-faced he went. It was not a word said often back then, not about an event, a death. Not in a Roman Catholic family. But the poor girl's father gave it to Sticker with both barrels. 'Suicide,' he said. 'She took her own life on account of how low you made her feel.'

Doreen Mathers couldn't have heard the words, so it must have been the look on his face that let her know the gravity of the situation. He couldn't hide it. Might have liked to, he simply couldn't. She disappeared out of her own office, as she'd originally offered. Left him on the phone with the grieving father.

'She was that broken-hearted over you, Mister Bradford. She didn't understand what possessed you to push her out like that. Not at the time. We loved Jane, didn't want her going off to Manchester like she did, but that's young people. When she got wind of this marriage that you're getting yourself into, it cut her to the quick...' Old Winters went on and on, never quite laying into Stickerhand, just telling him how it was. That a girl he'd known his whole life had ended hers over the love of him. Over how he treated her. His failure to reciprocate, to be who he had been every day until the morning of that mean conversation. Over his taking Pam Becker to be his wife when it should better have been the homespun girl. They neither mentioned the curly-haired one, by name or description. She was haunting the telephone talk though, wasn't she? Pamela and Jane never met. Not unless she sat at the back of a smoky jazz club once or twice listening to the singer and the trumpeter. Their musical interplay.

I hope she never did that; it could have happened, of course. Many, many months over which she had the chance. Rochdale's only a bus ride from the city centre. I fear she did, went and heard them, that she pictured the couple when she was swallowing down those damned tablets.

Doreen came back into the office with a mug of sweet tea. Put it down in front of Sticker. Made eye contact enough to make it clear that he should drink it. Then she was gone again. A decent sort, I expect. Not trying to pry. For my money, she should have brought him hemlock.

He finally asked a question or two. Offered some kind of sympathy to Mr Winters although he was feeling too wretched in himself to put much more than perfunctory courtesy into it. He understood responsibility even as he was sealing up the doors to it. Asked when the funeral would be. The call came fully a week after her death and he learnt that she was to be buried the next day. Learnt also that he should not take himself to the service, Jane's father quite insistent on that point. Rice Bradford—the other one, you understand, none of this had anything to do with me—would not be welcome at the church of St John the Baptist, the interring of his childhood friend. Not remotely.

10.

When mother and son have left the office, Varina goes to the kitchen. This is a tiny room in which hospital social workers, community psychiatric nurses and assorted occupational therapists may make a cup of tea. Nessa, another social worker, already has the kettle on.

'They were extraordinary,' she tells her colleague. 'Ordinary in a million ways and so at ease with being in the middle of Rice's madness. Even the boy, Yand, who couldn't remember his father while living his whole life with him at the centre of a million contradictory stories, seemed moved by the end. Acted a bit indifferent while alert to every word. Needed to know. And I really think the whole jazz club scene was part of the picture. It was easy to visualise the mother singing in them, smoky little night spots, audience as rapt as I've been. And she stopped when he was born. She was...' Varina searches for the term not making it onto her tongue, looking into the freckled face of her younger colleague. She cannot explain why a matter-of-fact interview, gleaning a life history from an ex-wife who is a decade beyond knowing the man she once loved, should bring tears to her eyes. '...a bit heartbroken, not really over it after all these years. Not over him. She didn't say it directly, that just came across between the words, all afternoon long.'

Nessa pours hot water onto the bags in the mugs. Tells her colleague to sit. 'Is there something at home upsetting you?' she asks.

'No. It's this job. Not that it's wrong, it's just so sad. We can learn about people who've left the rails. Can only speculate what has pushed them down the cutting. Biology, says Dr Kavanagh...' Varina slows her speech down for the doctor's name, smiles a small aside for Nessa. '...while I know that it's their social circumstances. The weight of a hard-to-live life. She's lived with the heaviest burden has our Pamela.' Varina explains the who's who of it. 'The boy, Yand, he must be terrified he'll go the way of his father. That he's genetically programmed to do so.' As she speaks, Varina is laughing at herself. Laughter for her own stupid tears. They deal with similar every day of the week. The sectioning and the self-harm. Relatives denying their husbands or wives are ill, or denying they are well for fear of all the tribulation arising from looking after a loose cannon outside of the hospital. This supposed place of safety. It's a washing machine and only a few come out of it any cleaner. Very hard to shift oil and paint and schizophrenia.

11.

He went to Rochdale, to the crematorium, on the day of the funeral. Stayed in the graveyard, stood a distance away from the door. Fifty yards or more. He didn't recognise who was who when they were carrying the coffin from hearse to chapel. Not from where he was standing. He felt a burning sensation in his stomach. The weight of what had gone on. Sticker always knew he was acting, playing a part, a year or so back when he'd told her to go. It was what he had to do if he was going to bring the new girl into his flat. Wanted the floozy, had no true desire to bring any upset to Jane. A means to an end. It had crossed his mind when he was doing it—dispatching her to Rochdale, applying the kind of sympathy he might offer a blue bottle with a rolled-up newspaper—that deep inside himself, he believed she would be back. Have him back. Him and the Becker girl only ever felt like a fling, simply not one he wished to confine to back alleys on dark nights. The hussy was offering more and he was for the taking of it, couldn't help himself. Should have but couldn't. Sending reliable little Jane home—laid off until the outlook picked up—that seemed the way of things. The despicable man's perfect life spinning every way he wanted and him picking the fruit from the trees while he spun around.

The money at Puttock's got better and better as he mastered more ways to cut cloth into pleasing shapes. Putting a swing on the hips of the girls in the city. He could do the same with his trumpet, let out soulful, doleful sounds or let it rise up to praise the god of possibility. He took his little tunes up higher and higher. Far above wherever they seemed to belong. The first notes were a tease, he never let them get away, rise up like the later ones. The anticipation built before the deliverance of beauty. And taking Pamela higher, sex mad the bloody pair of them. Even after they were living in the flat, they did it in an alley one more time for no greater reason than an inability to wait until they'd walked the mile back home. A right pair of dirty reprobates they were, the Sticker-Becker couple.

Perhaps he left some of his filthy-mindedness there in the

graveyard in Rochdale. He was watching from the boundary with unease inside him. Not sure if this was a burden he could carry through life. When he thought about Jane, it was not of her nagging, which could happen but he lived with it long enough, it was not of her complaining, although she'd have liked to go back and forth to Rochdale more than they ever did when they were together. He remembered carrying her bag home from school and the girl giggling. He was daft-old-fashioned when he was a kid. No one but him ever showed such chivalry. And that, the young Rice, being so obliging to a neighbour's girl, it was a better quality than the cloth cutting or the jazz playing. A simple something which he did only for Jane. And he only managed that when he was really quite young. Before he let himself swell up with all the tangential thoughts that jazz inspires; back when he knew nothing at all about the geometry of a skirt.

* * *

'I spoke to your wife...' He looked at her like she was mad. '...went to your flat. It's so close. We all wondered where you were. You've never missed a day before, Rice...'

'I'm not married.' It was the truth but he was only a couple of days away. This was before you see. Two days after the private call in the office. It all happened before that sham of a wedding that he went through the very next weekend.

'It must have been your wife; she was in your flat.' Doreen Mathers was concerned that her star cutter and designer—plagiariser too, but they never spoke about that—had taken a day off without notice. Not turned in and no explanation before or after. Any other worker would be sacked for the same. This one was a bit too far over on the useful side of the ledger for that to happen. She might have been concerned that he lived with a woman he wasn't married to, didn't really take it in. A bit like me not spotting I've left my clothes off. It's all in a day's muddling, that's all that was.

'Something came up.' That was as much as he would say. Funerals get sympathy, might have paid him for the day if he'd said why he didn't come in. He wasn't talking about Jane Winter's death to anyone at Puttocks. It might sound like he was using his position, his talent with chalk, knife, scissors, thread and needle too, to make a point. He was not. Stickerhand simply wasn't able to let in the darkness he felt in that Rochdale graveyard. Couldn't let it roam the streets of Manchester alongside him. Finish him, and it really could have done that. He knew it instinctively, you might say. And we do all behave on instinct, animals that we are.

'Mr Bradford,' she said, 'we cannot put up with you or anybody else deciding when they will and will not come into work.'

He ignored her. Completely ignored her. Doreen Mathers bashed the keys on her typewriter more firmly, banged paper files on her desk more loudly. She probably thought the young upstart was taking the Michael Crawford. And yet, if he really did have license to do what he liked that wasn't the way of it inside his head. He was running out of sense in this life. A girl from his own little corner of the world was dead and he could no more talk about it than he could juggle with chain saws while walking a high wire. Everything had become that precarious.

He worked the full shift, nothing wrong with his hands; the pieces that he fashioned came in around par. Sorted all the cuts and lines. Made clothes that drape just so, enabling all the boys and girls who are too scared to walk around in the nuddy to feel assured that their clothes won't fall off.

But they all do just that in the end. Everything falls away. I'm the living proof of it. That's what I am.

*   *   *

Stickerhand and Pam talked music, talked a lot of jazz. Pop a little bit, although Sticker was sniffy about most of it. Not the proper song writers—Ronnie Prousch—but he hated all the seventies chart nonsense. Men with glitter in their faces. Pamela told him what was going on in and around her family. She had two brothers and a mother still alive. Her father was a goner long before she met Stickerhand. Jane used to talk about her family when he and she were shacked up together, and that might be why he found it so hard to listen to Becker. After a little while he didn't. Stopped listening altogether.

He could blow on his trumpet and she'd roll the words around the room. The lyrics. They had a little electric organ that he played too. Not in the band. Wouldn't play it except in the flat on Cotter Street. Later, the house out on the east side. Keyboards were strictly Tommy Turner's domain. Sticker could pick out tunes he heard, made a few up in the bargain. He called some of them jingles, laughed about them, I don't expect the Japanese were laughing, were they? They were making notations, figuring what fitted where in securing their hypnotic hold over all the consumers in this land. On this Earth. I think they were only doing it from the shadows then. The mind stealing was a trick they hit upon later.

'It's not different just because we're married,' she told him, tried to reassure him. Coax him out of whatever blues she thought were running through his veins. It was obvious that something or other had erased the vigour he'd had before.

He didn't answer her questions. Answers exhausted, no longer had in stock.

* * *

When he emerged from Puttock's quite late on a Thursday—just a few weeks married—there were two men waiting for him. He recognised the smaller of them, nodded, said, 'I'm sorry.' As he began to walk, they fell in step and he felt more uncomfortable than he had done even at the funeral. 'I'm sorry for your loss,' he said more directly, properly spoken this time. Said it to Jane's brother. Man to man.

'Fuck off,' replied George. I think you can guess what came next.

The pair of them pushed him into a side alley, not one he'd ever been in with Pamela for his willy-work. Not as came to mind, anyhow. Back streets in the northern quarter are all of a muchness. The big bloke punched him in the stomach straight off. Winded him. He bent forward trying to breathe and the lad gave him number two in the same place. The brother then grabbed his hair. Sticker didn't wear it stupid-long like the hippies but it was over the collar. It was nineteen seventy-five. The brother pulled his head down, brought his knee up into this Rice's nose. The lad mashed him up but there's many get worse on a Friday night in Manchester. A light leathering; the principal thought going through Rice's head was 'fair enough.' He had this duffing-up coming and he knew it. He might have had a lot more coming if there was any justice but none of us know about that.

137

About the hereafter. He got a right good smacking about by those two fellas. One tough but careful not to break anything, one soft but cross. He offered nothing in return. When George, the brother, was kicking him as he lay on the ground, Stickerhand shouted, 'Kill me. Send me to Jane.' The two men looked at each other and left. Something in those words had satisfied them. Job done.

What could he do? Sneak back in to Puttock's was the best he could come up with. He went around the back, always a window left open somewhere. Cleaned up. Clothes off, brushed, back on. He went back to Pamela. Stayed there. It wasn't the same though, was it?

And he wasn't really off his trolley, either. He was atoning for who he'd slipped into being; needed to slip out of if he was going to make it through his twenties. And when he started to struggle, started to act the madman, people said he was having difficult times. Pam Becker said it but she was calling herself Pam Bradford by then. A doctor or two said it but that was not for two or three years yet.

I think the difficulties began when he tried to out-Turner Turner. When he flirted with Curly Hair while a plainer, sweeter girl was waiting for him at home. Think about that before you put your hand down a girl's knickers, eh boys? It can come at a terrible cost and jacking off is free of charge. It won't send you crazy like all the other might, I have that on good authority.

Chapter Four

Babbacombe Beach

1.

After a short period of aimless chat, and Sandra Widdicombe complaining about the new admission, Dr Okafor goes to phone Dr Kavanagh's secretary. Find out why she has not arrived for her own ward round. When he returns to the meeting room, he tells the assembled that Caitlin Kavanagh is sick. They speculate briefly whether it might be a gastric problem, flu or might she suffer from a nervous disorder. All agree her staying away from the psychiatric hospital is the right call whatever the cause.

Sandra asks the junior doctor if he can chair the ward round. They should discuss the new admission. 'He needs a change of meds,' she says. 'That's my opinion, he's not settling down at all.'

'All right,' says the doctor. 'We won't do them all. Just him, plus any others who are playing up.'

Varina thinks it a funny basis for a ward round, not a pursuit of mental equilibrium but of peace on the corridors. A hospital for the wellbeing of the nurses. It will be an achievement if they can pull it off.

The student nurse is in today, Casey. Varina thinks she has applied herself more seriously to her role since the visit to Card Road. Whether the squalor and infantility of the three living there has done this, or Casey's own reflection on a half-brother long passed away, she cannot guess. Paul, Rice and Roderick form the oddest house-share Varina has ever come across. Only Rice is truly mentally ill. Varina dredged up Paul's social history: he used to be in care and his drug problems go back ten years. That's an awful long way for a kid of twenty-three. The psychiatric service can't do a great deal for a lad like that but no one else will either. It seems right to give it a go. Paul has only drugs to look forward to, that is the sad truth. Drugs and having the hand of an older man upon his head, wobbling his scalp. Yelling out the mindless yes-my-son phrase, beloved of that household and no other.

When those gathered in the small room discuss Mohamed—the new patient who has yet to emerge from his bed space into the ward proper and who predictably refuses to attend this meeting—Dr Okafor talks about how difficult phobias are to treat.

Varina is impressed when Casey questions this. 'Or is he scared of all the other mental patients?' She has the strength of mind to query if his odd behaviour is phobic at all. Sandra Widdecombe stares open-mouthed. Nurses shouldn't question doctors; they should nod their heads and mimic the meter of their speech. 'A lot of people can be scared of them, and he's the only black person on the ward. It must be very strange for him.'

Varina nods, a small smile finding her face. Might tell Casey to consider social work if the nursing hierarchy proves tiresome.

The ward round finishes more than an hour earlier than it does when Dr Kavanagh is in the chair, fewer than half the patients have been discussed. The pace of the conversation was slicker, no laboured diction initiated by Dr Okafor. Nor did he wish to interfere with his senior's ongoing plans. Some new tablets for Mohamed, everyone else will stick to the script.

When the formalities are over, Varina asks Casey if she is free to discuss the Rice Bradford situation. She agrees before clearing it with Sandra. Her charge nurse then says no, they have to follow up Dr Okafor's plan for Mohamed. Try once more to coax him from his lair.

'No worries,' says Varina, 'shall I see you in the canteen at lunchtime?'

* * *

The queue snakes out of the refectory and a short way up the corridor. Varina beckons the young student nurse—in light-blue jeans today, a thin cotton sweater above it, lovely shade of red—to jump many places forward, to join her close to the serving hatch. A couple of old nurses tut in disapproval as Casey obeys the instruction.

'It's a working lunch,' Varina tells them.

They pick wooden trays off the metal stand. The food in the Princess Margaret is acceptable. The staff access better fare than makes its way down patients' gullets, that's common knowledge. Varina picks the hotpot, not summer fare, just cheap and filling. Casey takes a prawn sandwich and a plastic bottle of orange juice. There are a few hellos from those they know as they head for a corner table to talk about Pamela Bradford. For Casey to learn of Yand's existence, a man older than she is and he cannot recall his father except through the prism of his mother's verbal conjuring.

'I saw the ward file,' Casey tells Varina. 'It doesn't say anything about children, or even a wife.'

'No. They came out of the woodwork, didn't they? Everything we've had in Bristol is from Rice's mouth, what he told Dr Okafor and other junior doctors before him. He's a bit of an iceberg, a great big hidden underbelly. I don't know what to expect when we finally get the files from Manchester. Pamela told me he was taken into hospital there, she was very vague about his symptoms at the time.' Then Varina dips her head, lowers her voice to a conspiratorial level. 'Do you think he's kidding us, Casey? Knows the lot, everything in his past, and just won't tell us.'

Casey Taylor looks a little scared, as if this social worker is speculating about mystical powers. Shaman Rice. 'I often think they should just pull themselves together, but then I see they would if they could. Mentally ill is no fun, Varina. Nothing in it for the patients. I'm not clever but I can see that much.'

Varina laughs, touches a friendly palm on top of the student's hand. 'You are clever indeed. I've been letting the whole jazz-musician story get to me. Hoping to hear him play his trumpet.'

'Are they all like that?' asks Casey. 'The houses where the patients live.'

'No. None of them are like that. I've not seen patients rub each other on the top of the head before. It's a new symptom. Usually, they live like you and I. Many of the younger schizophrenics have a kindly mum doing everything for them, a house that I'd happily live in. The ones who have left normal life behind, well there aren't that many of them and then we went and found two under one roof. It's like winning the lottery, except the prize is chronic.'

'Three,' says Casey. 'Ten pounds.' Varina nods and smiles.

'Do you want to come along when I next visit. I've to put the divorce matter to him. Need to tell him if he doesn't agree to Pamela's request, Dr Kavanagh and I will have to offer our evidence to the judge. Make the case that Rice can't contribute, doesn't know his own mind. The judge will grant the divorce regardless, so it is better for him to be there. Acknowledge the truth of it. Patients always feel that things are done to them against their will, and then they can be their own worst enemies on that front. Some of the time they can be.'

'I don't think Sandra will let me come. She tries to keep students in their place.'

'Ask Cindy. She's your supervisor, isn't she?' It'll not be until Friday afternoon.'

'It's nice that you think of me. I like getting away from the ward.'

'Aye. Patients and nurses alike.'

2.

'Rice!'

The shout comes up the stairs and through the tiny gap under his door like a call to arms.

'Rice!'

It is Friday lunchtime and the man has not moved for fully forty-eight hours. Roderick has brought tea and coca cola, both of which he has sipped only a little; a piece of pie but it is uneaten on the cluttered bedside table.

'Rice!'

The call is loud, urgent, of the type intended to stir movement. It could be that the house is on fire, an earthquake wrought on Brislington. A visit from a graveyard ghoul.

'What do you want, Gloucester?' he shouts in reply as he stomps his way to the bedroom door wearing only underpants and a string vest. Down the narrow staircase he comes, heavy of foot. Unhappiness written on his flagging features.

'Bloody hell, the dead have risen,' says Paul, on hearing his housemate. The return of Rice after his two-day retreat from the world.

'Robson's here,' says Roderick.

'Grrrr. Well, he bloody shouldn't be,' shouts Rice, an animation that had not been there just the moment before.

Robson knows when it's giro day, when he might tempt Paul to purchase pills or papers, smokes or a little vial with a washed-out old syringe for company.

'Nothing to do with the old fart,' says the man on the doorstep. The pusher. And the said Robson is quite old himself, stick thin, dressed in a pair of jet-black trousers, loose cotton threads where he has stitched up a couple of holes. Left leg and one on the arse. Above the trousers, a white shirt sports the initials P and R on the left chest pocket. A company logo, highly unlikely that Robson has ever been on the payroll. Charity shop clothing most likely.

'Grrrr. Leave Piss-Paul alone!' shouts Rice, rushing the open door.

Paul Norton is sitting on the sofa with a view of the front door through the angled pane of the bay window. Roderick had raised a steadying hand to keep him from rising, taking whatever this man might offer. Rice is the attack dog.

'Steady on,' says Robson. 'I'm not fighting you.'

Rice kicks out, takes the legs from under Robson, whose backside finds the pavement. 'Leave him be! You hear me!'

'I'm not arguing with you,' says the prostrate man. 'I'm here for Paul.'

'No. You're here for money and there's none of it for you in this house. Wicked, wicked man.'

Although he has fared worse in the brief skirmish, Robson is laughing at Rice, the bald fatty in the white underpants. Fearless but a million miles from athletic. 'I can send boys round who'll break your legs,' he tells his assailant.

'You haven't any friends, Robson. You prey on the kids who a better class of drug dealer would leave be.'

Paul has risen, come to the door. 'Sorry, mate. Not today,' he says.

'Hear that, Robson,' says Rice forcefully. 'Now go back to whatever snivelling hole you crawled out of.'

'I've got the purple ones that you like,' says Robson, picking himself up.

'Shove 'em up your arse!' shouts Rice, pushing the man hard enough that he falls straight back down again. Then, more gently, he presses a hand into Paul's chest, compels him to step back into the house and Rice follows, pulling the door shut behind him. Rice looks at Rod Stone. 'Now, Gloucester, can I please go back to my nervous breakdown?'

The landlord laughs. 'Have a cup of tea and a biscuit, Rice. You've done the lad proud.'

Paul is looking through the gap in the curtain. 'He's going, Robson is. He won't come back and hurt me, will he?'

'That's all he's ever done since the very first time you started buying all that rubbish off him,' says Rice. 'It's me and Gloucester who don't hurt you. Every bugger else does. That's the truth of it, Paul. Stick with your pals.'

* * *

'He's back,' Roderick tells his tenants a couple of hours later when they hear someone outside the front door. 'Ready Rice.'

'Bloody hell, not again,' he moans. His first words in over an hour. Another two cups of tea drunk and he has remained in the living room since dressing. A more sociable Rice than he has been for the last two days, still very withdrawn on the scale of things.

Paul gives Rice's head a rub. 'Yes..s..s, my son,' he says, speaks it softly. There is a little tension expressed in that inane phrase.

Then they hear the sound of ladies' voices, a light rap on the door. Roderick walks into the hallway, opens it to them, then he turns back to the room. 'Your girlfriends are here.'

'Mr Stone, don't confuse them, please,' says Varina, as she and Casey enter the narrow hallway, step through into the dining and living areas, partition open today.

'We thought you was Robson come back again,' says Paul.

'Who's Robson?' asks Varina.

'Drug dealer, Miss. Rice knocked him for six this morning.'

Casey is once more in her dress of cream and roses, her community attire, and it is far smarter than anything worn in this house since her last visit. Rice is thankfully better clothed than he was for the doorstep wrestling match. A pair of corduroys hide his underpants. An old white shirt covers the string vest.

'What did Rice do?' the student nurse asks of Paul.

'If he's out, I buy the drugs, but if he's in, Rod sets him on to Robson. Rice can fight better than young ones. Can't you, Rice?'

He has his head in his hands. The flourish of a physical tussle rallied him from his stupor, and now the energy has left him as quickly as it came. These visitors have dampened it completely.

'Rice, are you all right?' asks Varina. 'Are you hurt?'

Without looking up he addresses her. 'Miss Pope, why do you bring her here again.'

'Casey is a student. Here for the learning. Are you not happy with her being...?'

'I told her to go away on Wednesday. She's for the other fella, not for me.'

His assertion confuses Varina; she turns to her student colleague. 'You came here on Wednesday?'

'I didn't...' Casey looks scared. '...I've only ever been here with you, Varina. Honestly.'

From behind Rice, Rod Stone is shaking his head at the social worker, tapping his temple with a single forefinger, indicating that Casey is correct and Rice is mistaken. Casey normal and Rice bonkers, judging by his excessive eye rolling.

'That other lady was here though,' says Paul.

'It's her,' says Rice, waving a hand at Casey without lifting his head to meet her eye. 'She goes this way and that, doesn't she?'

'No,' says Paul. 'The other lady was much older.'

'She can be any age she likes, this one,' says Rice.

Varina asks the room who visited them on Wednesday. Rice harrumphs for not being believed and Roderick answers. 'Her that thinks she's Rice's wife. The telephone woman.'

'Did Pamela come here, Rice?' asks the social worker.

'I don't know any Pamela. The other fella might.'

'Rice, are you happy to talk in front of Paul and Mr Stone.'

'I will but I'm not happy. I'm not happy in this world, Miss Pope.'

'You just compose yourself. I am pleased to hear you've looked out for Paul—well done—but it sounds to have been dangerous.' Then Varina looks at Paul Norton. 'What happened?'

'He comes to sell to me. Robson knows what day I get my money. Gloucester called him down...' Paul points at Rice as he speaks. '...and I hadn't seen Rice for days. He'd taken to his bed, like he does, but he came down for me. He should teach me to fight, except I'd probably just take the drugs anyway. That's my problem.' Then he lowers his face to look directly into Casey's. 'Do you do drugs, Miss?' he enquires.

She lowers her eyes to her shoes, takes a second before saying a hurt, 'No,' and even Varina wonders if she is being truthful. It might be a wise lie, or maybe the world is different than it was when Varina was Casey's age. She smoked a little pot on many an evening in her early twenties. Wouldn't have been shy about admitting it, such were the times. 'Did you call the police?' Casey deflects the question that troubled her.

'No need,' Rod butts in. 'No police here. We sort out our problems as they arise. Police aren't much use around here.'

Varina tries to take notes in her book as she is standing. 'What did you say the man's name is? The one Rice fought off.'

'We don't know it,' says Roderick.

'Phil Robson,' says Paul.

'He's scum is Robson,' says Rice. 'Proper scum.'

'No police,' reiterates the landlord. 'Please?'

That is a rare courtesy in this house. Varina senses a need for discretion without having a clue about the relationships between the players.

'Now, Rice, can you tell me about your visitor earlier in the week?'

Rice simply hangs his head forward, jaw open. It is inaudible but he appears to be panting.

'If it's any consolation, I have met her and I advised that she shouldn't visit. I'm sorry that she did.'

'Oh, she should do as she's told, shouldn't she, Rice?' says Paul. He remains stubbornly silent.

'Rice,' says Varina, 'we really need to talk about Pamela because of what she's asking. Do you understand?'

He doesn't so much as raise his head.

'What does the mad bitch want?' asks Roderick.

Varina gives him a withering look—squinting and wrinkling her nose in distaste—mouths the word, 'Divorce.' Perhaps the landlord has more sway than she does with Rice. Got him to see off the drug pusher, quite something.

'Impossible,' he announces. 'Rice never married, did you?'

Rice turns his head slowly. 'Shut it, Gloucester. You've seen me when I start fighting. Just shut it!'

'Rice, would you like us to leave. And don't fight with Mr Stone. He's looking out for you in his own way. I simply don't understand what happened, what you and Pamela spoke about.'

'She says the same as what you say, Miss Pope—the married rubbish—but it's mistaken identity. I know a little bit about a woman called Pamela but I don't know her. She thinks it's me that she's married to and I'd certainly know if I'd done that, wouldn't I?'

'What were you doing twenty years ago in Manchester, Rice? Are you sure you haven't simply forgotten a lot of the past? Like you occasionally forget to put your clothes on?'

Now it is Rice's turn to deliver a withering look. 'Everybody forgets the small stuff once in a while. The clothes. I know what I did twenty years ago, I'm not stupid.'

Varina waits, Rice doesn't speak. Paul beams a grin around the room, eyes quickly coming to rest on young Casey. Roderick coughs. Then Casey asks, 'What were you doing, Rice, Mr Bradford? What were you doing twenty years ago?'

'I was married to you, weren't I, Mrs Bradford? Daftest bloody thing I ever did. Why do you ask, when you're the one that knows very well what I was up to? Have your divorce. I can see you no more want me than I want you. And I'm not giving you any money. I've got none and I wouldn't if I could.'

The room falls silent again. Casey looks at Varina, her face a little paler than when she asked the innocent question. Eventually the social worker puts a toe in the water. 'Do you remember your son, Rice?'

'Look at her!' he snaps, turning to Casey once more. 'You've not dropped no kiddies have you, Pamela? Not one.'

'I've not...I'm Casey. I met you for the first time on Mendip Ward, Rice.'

Varina has a hand on Casey's arm, cautioning her to await the man's response.

'See,' says Rice, 'even she doesn't want a divorce now. It's all madness, you coming round here trying to tell me who I am and who I'm not. All ruddy madness.'

* * *

'I think I was part of the problem,' says Casey as they talk in the car, Varina driving them back to the Princess Margaret.

'Well,' says the social worker, 'he's latched on to you in the strangest way. I think your being there helped, however strangely it came about. He's agreed to sign the papers; all I have to do is get them to him when he's in a similar frame of mind. How are you bearing up? That was the most curious visit.'

'I couldn't imagine him fighting. And then he only did it to help Paul, who's far bigger than him in the first place. He's nice but mad, isn't he? Rice.'

'Paul Norton is the biggest mouse I've ever met, Casey. A mouse a foot taller than you. Standing up for himself is an outlook he's yet to adopt. And it isn't Mr Stone who helps him either, that's plain to see. Our Rice is the hero in that house, poor soul that he is.'

3.

It's more than a week since the house on Card Road saw that quick succession of visitors. The drug-dealer has not returned; Rice went to the Princess Margaret at Miss Pope's request and then refused to sign a anything under the sun. She took him along the corridor for an outpatient's appointment with Dr Kavanagh, only to find she was not there. Still sick, as she had been the previous week. The doctor taking time to heal. Dr Okafor stood in, offered Rice a bed, a readmission back onto Mendip Ward; the would-be patient pointed out that he still had his clothes on. The whole hour and a half felt to Rice like another mental assault. They are coming thick and fast, that is how things have been feeling every day since the brief admission that brought on this meddlesome social worker.

Paul Norton is up at six o'clock. Ante meridiem. He has never seen such an hour before. The tall crooked-nosed young man is excited, pouring milk on his second bowl of cereal. He shouts up the stairs for the older men to come down and join him. From Rice Bradford's room, the sound of snoring, from Rod Stone's a short, sharp shout. 'Shut it, Piss-Paul.'

It is two hours and four more bowls of cereal before the two older men arise. They have cold tea by their bedsides that Paul made but neither man drank, and now they enjoy a warm one in the cluttered dining room.

'We're setting off,' says Paul, trying to hurry them along. 'It's time.' All three men packed cases yesterday evening. A promised holiday is to take place, Roderick-of-Gloucester proving good to his word. For Paul Norton it is his first such escapade since living in a children's home. The promise of a hotel raises his hopes of a higher life than any he has yet enjoyed. Roderick has determined that it will be a working holiday: Devon by burger van. Rice, meanwhile, is fleeing his responsibilities, vacillates still in his belief about his marital state. Of the trip to Torquay he says, 'If I meet a nice Devon girl, I shall marry her. Miss Pope be damned.'

When they have drunk their teas and Paul's pleas to depart have raised his voice a notch higher than either of the others have before heard it pitched, they load the van. 'No more fucking Brislington, eh Gloucester?' he squeals. 'We're going, Rice. We're really going.'

Stone locks his house and jams himself into the driver's seat. Turns the engine over, sparks stuttering life into his vehicle and business. The traffic out to the motorway is slow, crawling. Paul bashes a nervous hand on the dashboard and Rod tells him to give over, to desist.

'Sorry, Gloucester. I just want to get there.'

Rice has a packet of cigarettes with him, neither a new habit nor a regular one.

'Not in the van,' says Roderick.

'Pull over then,' says Rice.

'One for me,' says Paul.

The three men smoke at a layby close to Easton-in-Gordano, their progress towards Devon temporarily at a halt. As they stand facing the oncoming traffic, Roderick asks Rice if he was married to the woman who came by over a week ago. 'Not the young one, I know you were just winding her up.'

Paul interrupts. 'They're both lesbians, Gloucester. They don't marry because lesbians don't need to.'

'Ignore Piss-Paul,' says Roderick. 'The northern girl...' He is staring at his lit cigarette, as if noticing it in his hand for the first time. '...with the fancy hair. That lady, did she used to be your wife?'

Rice pulls on his own ciggie before speaking. 'She was somebody's wife, wasn't she?' Then he hunches his shoulders, turns aside the merest quarter of a cheek. Roderick Double-Gloucester won't be learning more than that particular nothing.

When they are back in the van, the traffic inches along for another five minutes and they are able to join the motorway. Southbound. The vehicle belches out a bit of black smoke, simpers its way up to forty-five miles an hour.

'Fast lane,' shouts Paul.

'Slow lane,' Rice retorts.

The vehicle will obey only the latter, no choice about it for this clapped-out old bus. As they make their way south, Paul asks question after question. Will they see the sea; are ice creams are sold in Torquay; morning breakfast will be better than Gloucester's shit, won't it. Even the landlord concurs with a toothless smile at Rice's third affirmative answer in succession. Passing Bridgwater, Paul manages to read the sign, shouts at his driver to leave the motorway.

'Burgers, Gloucester. They sell burgers.'

'Daft ape. I'm not buying burgers when we've got a couple of hundred of the damn things in the back.' Paul is full of shredded wheat and bran flakes, not an impediment to shovelling further food down his throat.

*   *   *

'Petrol,' says Rod Stone as he pulls off the carriageway when the name Ashburton appears on the road sign.

Paul is going frantic. 'You've passed Torquay, Gloucester. Missed the holiday.'

'It's near Torquay. No signs for Babbacombe yet.'

Rice is in a trance.

'Stop and ask the way,' says Paul.

Roderick pulls the burger van up on the edge of town, a main street of shops stretches out ahead of them. Rice snaps open the van door, feet on the pavement, heads in that direction at a determined pace.

'Keep your clothes on,' shouts Rod.

'I used to work here,' says Rice. The landlord taps his head, Paul Norton grins. An air of disbelief inside the van.

Once Roderick has parked properly, not an easy task with this lumbering vehicle, he and Paul set off after Rice.

The man in the lead passes a group of pensioners on the road side; the one in front has a clipboard, wears a lanyard around her neck with a facsimile of herself within its plasticated display.

'Where's the leatherworks?' Rice demands of the lady.

She looks flustered. 'I don't think I know you. I'm leading this tour...'

'A tour of the town? Then you must know where the leatherworks are. Tell me where it is then, missus.'

Paul has caught up. 'Miss,' he asks, 'is Babbacombe around here?'

'That's on the coast. I'm sorry but I'm working. I haven't the time to be answering these questions. You're not on my tour.'

'See, Gloucester, it's not even round here. You've ruined the holiday.'

'What are you wanting with the leatherworks?' asks Roderick.

'Got to get my old job back. Get my life back on track. I could skin donkeys in the old days but I don't know if I was really me then. Leather is what I do. You work it in the dirty water, you know. It's a proper job. I used to smell of leather when I was him.'

Rod Stone exchanges a look with Paul Norton, a look of concern.

Paul worries only about his evaporating holiday prospects. 'He's been taking what I like taking.'

'It's not that,' says Rice. 'I'm not for cadging and freeloading, never have been. I can do what I did and there's not many of us left.'

'Get your job after our holiday, Rice.'

'No, Gloucester! You're not controlling everything I do. Not any longer. I'm my own man. A proud man. A tanner. Leather might be my middle name, mightn't it?'

They have walked some way up the High Street, the gaggle of pensioners on a walking tour of Ashburton now far behind them. Rice steps into a newsagent's and looks through narrowed eyes at the man behind the counter. 'Where have you put the leatherworks!'

'Steady on,' says the shop worker. 'What is it you want?'

Rod Stone has entered behind Rice, taps a knowing finger to

his forehead while making eye contact with the man behind the counter. 'We're with him. Not to worry mate.'

'The sign said...' Rice is talking very slowly, treating the world as the place in need of explanation. '...the sign off the fast road, for the turnoff here says, Ashburton Tannery Town. Where's the leatherworks? I'm a tanner. I can do it.'

Paul has come into the shop too, tells the man and a couple of other customers that this loud man, Rice Bradford, can skin donkeys. Other customers in the shop stand to the sides, one lady leaves. They might think three madmen are amongst them, although only Rice is not himself.

The newsagent's face drains of all tension and he begins to laugh. 'He can skin donkeys but he can't read signposts.'

Paul and Rod join in the laughter, although neither can have the first idea what is funny. Paul puts a big hand on top of the glummest head in the shop, wobbles Rice's brains back and forth. 'Yes..s..s, my son.'

Roderick shushes him.

'Tannery town,' says Rice. 'I saw it, I'm not stupid.'

'It says, Ancient Stannary Town,' says the shop man, emphasising the additional letter Rice neglected in his telling of the signpost. 'Stannary. Sssssssstannary.'

'Yessssss, my son,' says Paul, hand back on Rice's head.

'Stannary, tannery. It's just Devon talk, isn't it? Leather is leather whatever you call the place they dry it out. Has it closed down?' asks Rice.

'Tin,' says the know-it-all newsagent. 'Tin mines were along here. That's what stannary means. They worked tin mines around here for centuries. Not anymore. That's the history of the place.'

'Shit. I don't know anything about tin.'

Roderick nudges Rice, laughs. 'Daft bugger,' he says, while wobbling the man's head again. Doing it in the style long fashioned at forty-one Card Road.

'Tin mines,' laughs Rice. 'Happen I'll have to find a job after the holiday then. And I won't be going down a flipping tin mine. Can't cut that stuff with pinking shears.'

The bemused newsagent tells Paul and Roderick how to get to Babbacombe; Rod learns that he has missed the turn. Must go back the way they've come, head for Newton Abbott and then the coast. They can't miss it, they're told, although Roderick has already done it once. 'Not unless you mistake it for a tannery. For a leather-works.' All three men laugh at that, Rice with a small intake of breath in the middle of his forced chortle.

* * *

The sun has created a furnace out of the brick and tarmac of the side road on which they park. St Marychurch, an outpost of Torquay. The street runs from north to south, bakes in the scorching heat of this summer afternoon. Rod Stone has guided the van into the only available space. No others in the vicinity, cars are bumper to bumper around here. The hotel he sought is on the neighbouring street. This is as near as they can park.

'Is there a beach, Gloucester?' asks Paul.

The houses here—a few of which sport Bed and Breakfast signs—are an improvement upon Card Road but only by a couple of notches. Terraced, three storeys high. Some newly painted, some impatiently awaiting such a makeover.

'It's that way,' he points up the street. 'There's a beach nearby, so it must be up there.' After a short time, he adds, 'Or down there,' pointing in the opposite direction.

Paul stares and stares but no sea or sand come into view. Not up or down.

'Let's get into our rooms, unpack,' says Roderick.

Each man carries a case. Rod Stone leads his people to the promised hotel. When they have rounded the corner, found the right place, Paul rings the bell. Martin's Guest House says the sign; a lady answers the door. She looks a few years beyond retirement age, smells of smoke, wears a denim dress. A jeansy-looking skirt with a bib front. Sports a plain white blouse beneath it.

'We've booked rooms,' says Roderick.

'Have you, now?'

'Stone, Bradford, Norton.'

They are at a small desk which has been jemmied into the understairs recess, the wood of the adjacent banister reeking of polish. The lady looks at them through narrowed eyes. 'I've got you. Well, you'll need to sign my book.'

'Excuse me,' asks Paul. 'Is Martin here? It's his guest house, you see.'

'That's my husband. He'll cook you your breakfast, I expect.'

'But what's your name?' Paul continues, looking back and forth between his two older friends.

'I'm Brenda. Mrs Peters if you prefer.'

'Brenda's all right. Why isn't it called Brenda's Guest House. Or Martin and Brenda's.'

'It was his baby when we first set up...'

'Or Brenda and Martin's Guest House. That sounds best to me.'

'Be quiet, Piss-Paul.'

'We'll have none of that language...'

'Sorry, missus.'

'Mrs Peters.'

'Yes, that. I'm afraid our young lad is a bit excited,' Rod explains.

'He's not young,' says Brenda Peters.

'I'm only twenty-three.'

'I was married with children when I was younger than that,' she says.

Rice has carried his case halfway up the stairs. 'What number?' he calls out.

'Come down,' says Brenda. 'You've to sign in first.'

'Gloucester knows my name,' says the bald man, continuing on his way.

'You've no key,' she shouts up, then turning to the others, she says, 'Is he always like that?'

'Oh, we're mentally ill, Brenda,' says Paul. 'At least, me and him are.'

'Oh, no,' says the landlady, 'I don't have them in my guest house.'

'But your husband might,' says Paul. 'It's his guest house really.'

'They're both well, Mrs Peters,' offers Roderick. 'I've known them both for years; never been better.'

'And him like that?' says the woman, gesturing towards Rice on the upstairs landing. 'Oy,' she shouts, 'this one says your mentally ill.'

'I've been harassed by a woman and had a bit of bad luck with my jobs,' he says, a strength to his voice for the first time since the disappointment at the newsagents in Ashburton. 'You wouldn't deny a man a bed for the night for so paltry a reason, would you?'

'Come down,' she calls. ''I've to speak to Martin about it. That's for the best.'

Rice relents, makes his way back to the foyer. As Mrs Peters leaves through a door at the back of the corridor, a door marked private, he hisses at Paul, 'You've a big mouth, haven't you?'

'I was making conversation. You're the one who was acting funny.'

'Calm down,' says Roderick. 'Martin will put a bit of sense into her.'

Minutes tick by. A brass bell on the worktop, in the shape of a flying saucer with a button like a miniature trumpet key protruding from its pinnacle, outstares the men. Paul and Rice reach for it at the same time, the younger man's hand arriving first; the bell sings its high chime, only to be muted by Rice's flat palm.

'Give over,' says Roderick, annoyance seeping into his voice. 'They've not said we can stay yet.'

A girl comes out of an upstairs room. 'Has someone answered that?' she calls from the landing.

'They were just messing about,' Roderick tells her.

She comes down the stairs quickly. A thin blue overcoat upon her, a dustpan and brush in her hands. 'Mrs Peters hasn't booked you in?'

'You can do it. Who are you?' asks Paul.

'I'm Sarah. Just the cleaner, really. I don't do the booking-in.'

As she speaks, Brenda emerges from the flat at the back of the ground floor. 'Are these men bothering you, luvvy?'

'No. I was just seeing what they wanted.'

'I'll sort them, Sarah. Get back to your jobs please.' She turns to Roderick. 'Martin said you can stay, seeing as how you've booked, but no funny business.'

'Keep your clothes on, Rice,' says Paul.

'Shut it,' replies the sometime-streaker, putting a hand on Paul's head, wobbling it as he growls, 'Pissy-Pauly-sunshine.'

'Oh no,' says Brenda, then she shouts, 'Martin!'

There is the sound of a couple of doors banging, an old man emerges wearing trousers, a string vest above it and a pair of red braces holding his trousers up. They embed themselves in the fat upon his chest.

'I said they weren't too strange but they are. They keep on swearing.'

'Right,' says the man who must be Martin. 'We've other guests to consider, you know? You've got to leave right away. Got that?'

'I've paid up front,' says Roderick.

'I'll post it back to you.'

'I need it for tonight.'

The half-dressed man exchanges a quiet word with Brenda. A few words and phrases reach Rice's ears. '...the normal one...saying the rude wee word...completely crackers.'

'You two outside,' says Martin. 'I'll refund you.' He points at Roderick. 'We're not thieves here.'

As the two ordered out are leaving, Rice speaks in a sombre voice to Paul Norton. 'I knew we were cursed when the leatherworks vanished into thin air. It should have been there by rights, then I'd be back on a proper wage.'

* * *

When all three have returned to the street the two former patients of the Princess Margaret look to their landlord for a lead. After the short trek to it, he starts up the van and drives them all about two hundred yards where he parks outside another Bed and Breakfast. It looks like Martin's Guest House, give or take a pastel shade of window-frame. Another three-storey-high mid terrace. This one goes by the name of Pelican Hotel and the sign in front tells of vacancies. They tumble out of the van, walk up the four steps to the front door.

'Leave all the talking to me,' says Roderick. 'Not a word from you two clowns.'

At the reception desk a man in a ruffled suit asks if they have booked rooms.

'Not as such,' says their de facto leader.

He looks in his ledger. 'I can do you two doubles, it's all I've got.'

'You'll share won't you,' says Rod Stone.

Paul beams, Rice groans. It is going to happen.

Roderick pays—using his returned deposit—books them in for

four nights as planned. The three men climb the stairs, up to the rooms, carrying the cases. Paul bumps his repeatedly on the banister. Rod says, 'Very nice,' as he takes himself into the larger room.

'Hey! You're on your own, Gloucester' says Rice.

'It's me that's paid for them, remember.'

Rice goes into his room and throws himself on the large bed. There is no happiness in his determined flop.

Paul jumps onto the other side of it, crying out the single word, 'Holiday!' When he hits the mattress, the bed moves to the side, its legs crumble and the entire frame shifts down ten inches to the floor. 'Cheap!' adds Paul, sounding no less thrilled by the truth of it.

'We'll have to fix that,' says Rice.

'I can't do it.'

'You'll help. We just need to knock the legs back in. Gloucester can buy us a bag of nails.'

* * *

In the evening they take the van to the marina down in Torquay. Paul wants to buy chips; Roderick tells him to have a burger. He asks Paul to wait until there is a crowd, and then he must pay for one and say it's good. Shout out its finer qualities to all who walk the streets. The passing trade. A routine they have done several times before, a sham happy customer. It's pathetic, Paul Norton a piss-poor actor.

Rice tells them he has to leave. Must look for what he needs.

'Not another leather-works?' says Rod and he gets a V-sign for his enquiry.

It is a troubled Rice who goes past the closed-up shops, ones that sell ice creams, yacht accessories, paintings by local artists. That is their function in the day time, all doors closed this evening. He whistles dolefully to himself. He knows that the events of recent weeks have unsettled something within him. Twisted his gut. He'd not really thought about the girl who killed herself in a long, long time. That kind of carry on never made any sense to him. Life is pretty shit but we keep going: that's long been his experience. Perhaps it was different for her, the girl, whoever she really was. The state of being which she endured may have had a greater importance than he can any longer believe plausible. The weight of wanting more pervades the best of times, that can be a curse. Go long enough without and you give up the aspiration. Right now, Rice would like a job, like to send his giros back to the government which he thinks very stupid to give them out in the first place. Callaghan was, Blair is, that bloody woman who gave them out so begrudgingly was the worst of the lot. Put a smear of shame on the envelope they came in. Paul and the likes of Paul need the benefits if they're to get by, shouldn't be giving it to Robson. Any of it. Rice doesn't really know if he can manage without them, a hope not a belief. Parker, at the packing job, seldom gives him more than a twenty. Often shuts him out. He wonders if the Japanese did invade his brain— his or the other fella's—steal the catchiest tunes for their nefarious purposes. Might have used them to sell stereophonic sound systems or promote sumo wrestling. If they have, he never got a penny, and he doubts if the other bloke did either. Stickerhand was close to skint in every memory that's been spliced into Rice's troubled brain. Passed from one Rice to another. This Rice would have been good at sumo if he'd had the training. Slapped out the pest, Robson. Did it in sumo clothing near as dammit. The trouble is Rice has forgotten what job he used to do. He told a few people that he skinned donkeys but he has no reliable recollection of it. He suspects the trumpet to be a trap, a bait, not an instrument he has any skill on. Working with leather sounds like the right ball park, not so the skinning of donkeys. Poor little donkeys need to keep their skin on, couldn't get through winter without them. It could be that he cut leather into sporrans or shaped it up like a squirrel; these are activities he could relish if someone would just pay him for the doing of them. Momentarily he wonders why they might, then remembers the giros. It seems he must only take his clothes off periodically to get them forever more. Daft, dafter, daftest. He'd like to have seen Nurse Fiona take her clothes off—worth a fistful of giro's, it really would be—knows she wouldn't pay anything to see him. Told him to get dressed sharp.

He walks up a residential road away from the marina, up the hill where the properties overlook the bay. Square-shaped properties with Spanish arches leading into side gardens.

Manicured lawns, palm trees. A man in a crisp light-blue short-sleeved shirt is buffing up the bonnet of his sportscar. Beavering away in the fading evening light, on the drive of his box-like house. White-washed walls, flat roof.

'Excuse me,' Rice addresses him, 'does your wife wear leather.'

The man steps towards him. 'Are you selling something?'

Rice sees the shammy in his hand. 'Can I have that,' he says stretching out to take it. The man passes his cleaning cloth across as if hypnotised by Rice's request. The recipient stares at the light brown square in his hands, lightly squeezes out a little of the water it is holding. 'I can cut this into a little bikini thing for her, if that's what she'd like. If she's big upstairs—you get my drift now, don't you?—happen you'll have to give me a couple more shammies.'

The man snatches it back from him. 'Get out of my garden!' he shrieks at poor Rice.

'I'm not in it,' he answers. 'Not really; it's probably the other fella.'

Rice heads on up the hill. The man beside his sportscar mutters something under his breath, yet another phrase of the fucking-nutter variety. It doesn't carry in full to the walking-away man. He's long been able to divine what people say about him.

'The lady doctor agrees with you,' Rice shouts over his shoulder, remembering how thin his psychiatrist is, how her flowery dress lay across her like lettuce stuck to bacon.

Further up the hill he can see the open sea to the east. There are yachts at anchor in the near water. Rice can make out people upon them. Imagines they are drinking wine, men in smart clothes entertaining ladies. Posh men wearing cravats and captains' hats and ladies sitting beside them, white wine spritzers in their hands. The sails bob this way and that on the gentle waves.

Rice is starving hungry, decides to go back down the hill for one of Gloucester's crappy burgers; at least he gets his money back once he's praised the God-awful food in front of a few disinterested bystanders. Quite the promotional campaign. He walks down the road, gives his friends a wave when they come into view. There is a customer in front of him, a man without fear of food poisoning.

When it is Rice's turn, Roderick says, 'What can I get you, young man?'

'The works, please,' answers Rice. 'Brown sauce and mustard whipped up to a paste.'

* * *

It is ten-thirty in the Pelican Hotel and the three men from Card Road, Brislington, are the only ones in the tiny bar excepting the hotelier, a man who has introduced himself as Bill and still wears the ruffled suit in which he checked them in. He bends down to grasp a further trio of Mexican beers from the bottom of the fridge; once more he asks Rice, Rod and Paul if they would like a slice of lime in the neck of their bottles. All refuse, have little truck with such frippery.

Paul is trying to tell the others a joke but there seems to be no punchline, only speculation on whether the young trainee doctor—as he thinks Casey Taylor to be—wears knickers.

'She's not a doctor at all,' says Rice. The other one's a social worker but that young one was married to someone who thinks he's me.'

'What line of work are you in?' asks Bill, clearly puzzled by Rice's cryptic words.

'We're spies and he's our batman,' says Rod, pointing at Paul, the skivvy.

The younger man appears to savour his given occupation, beams from man to man. 'Look at him, Gloucester. He thinks you've called him Superman,' says Rice.

'No really,' says Bill, 'are you professional men.'

'He sells burgers, I'm in leather.'

'I'm batman,' says Paul.

'Is that your van out there?'

'It is,' says Roderick.

'Fiddlesticks,' says Bill, 'I reported it.'

'How do you mean?'

'You see, it shouldn't be parked on that stretch of road, by rights. There's a sign.'

'The sign says it's for guests.'

Bill explains as best he can that he had mistakenly presumed it was a commercial vehicle. He has never before had guests staying at the Pelican Hotel who came by burger van. 'There's always a flashing light on the wheel-clamper's van. When I see it, I'll put him straight,' says Bill.

Roderick's face turns a little redder. Hackles raised by the thought of his van being nobbled. 'It's my livelihood. What if I clamped your hotel?'

'The drinks are on me,' says Bill, taking three more Mexican beers from the fridge behind his little bar.

'Not for me,' says Rice, 'I'm off to bed.'

* * *

Rice changes into the pyjamas he has brought with him. Pops down the corridor to use the toilet. Once back he takes the window side of the bed which is upon the floor, two legs splayed out horizontally, the other two folded beneath the frame.

Ninety minutes later he is snoring intermittently. Sounds like a television on the blink. This is when Paul and a belly full of Mexican beer join him. The younger man removes all his clothes and slips between the sheets. Even snuggles into the snoring man for such comfort as it might bring. Rice is out of it. A shedload of medication injected up his bottom every three weeks. Reciprocates nothing and Paul might like it that way. It is surely the knickerless young doctor which Paul Norton dreams about in this bed. Imagines for want of a better bed-mate than Rice Bradford.

4.

A few hours earlier on this self-same day, Varina Pope took a telephone call from Pamela Bradford. She is in bed now, Brian snoring as haphazardly as Rice does, although they are some one hundred miles apart. Her clients whereabouts unknown to the social worker. She ponders the call, staggering content, strange turn of events.

'I've thought and thought since meeting you,' said Pamela, 'and I can't go through with it.'

At first Varina did not pick up the point Pamela was making. 'Do you think it was terribly wise to go round to Rice's house? You know I advised against it.'

Pamela told the tale of meeting the three men. Said that for all the changes time has wrought upon Rice, he is still the man she once loved. The only one she ever truly loved.

'He is,' said Varina once she understood the point of the conversation, 'but he won't return to functioning as he used to. He is still in denial about who's who.' Varina tried her best to explain Rice's odd fixation with Casey Taylor. 'He believes she is you. Young Casey might be the age you were when the pair of you were first together.'

Pamela asked questions about this. When she had established that Casey is a pretty girl she said, 'Should I be jealous?'

Varina knows it is bad form to laugh at a client, or their family in this case. Never belittle a living soul: first rule of the profession. This was different. Was Pamela simply worried that Rice has an eye for the younger girl? Varina would feel flattered if anyone thought she may once have been as good looking as Casey is now. Or she might section them, so far from reality would the conjecture be.

'If you mean does the girl reciprocate the feeling, it's a very definite no,' she told Pam Bradford.

Then the talk took another unexpected turn. Pamela asked if Dr Kavanagh would allow her to take Rice back to Manchester. Varina thought the very idea was madness. She could see no reason why Rice might go. He believes Pamela is another man's wife, although he acknowledges it is a nameless man who he knows surprisingly well. 'He's not a chattel,' said Varina, and then had to explain the oddly chosen term. Again, she felt she might be inadvertently putting Pamela down, belittling her, when Varina had truly warmed to the lady. 'What does Yand say to all this?' she asked.

'He never knew his dad. I don't think what he has to say matters.'

Varina thinks about this, finds it strange. Pam Bradford has given her life to raising Yand. Rice contributed nothing. As she lies in bed, Varina realises that it was more than nothing; Rice has given her memories and these must be very real things. Limited utility, present as a gallstone.

'I'm going to have to move down to Bristol and win him over.'

'I thought you wanted to divorce him in order to marry again?'

The social worker felt annoyed with her own question. Never usually speaks so directly.

'I've told him it's off. He's not half the man Rice is.'

That was the phrase which threw Varina. She has heard the story of the fine jazz trumpeter, the skilful dress cutter, the lover even, for they clearly had a romance that—in its first months—swept both away. These were tales of the nineteen-seventies. Whatever he once was, Varina cannot think Rice Bradford is any longer those things. That Pamela can, that it is the vital man she still sees, surely has little to do with the shell—bald, overweight and thin-skinned—to whom Varina is the assigned social worker. Rice must once have been somebody so bewitching that this husk is a worthwhile consolation. She looks beside her, where Brian snores in the bed they share. He was once a strong man. Once is a faded photograph. Firemen are brave and that is the occupation that consumed her husband's life. It is four years since Brian last went out with a crew, two since he retired; sick leave and desk duties marked the days of two idling years on full pay. All fires are out. Those that used to burn did not stir a passion that can breathe life into their marriage now. They both loved the dog racing those years back, loved each other. For a few years it has been little more than a source of embarrassment to Varina.

Pamela has her Rice, in memory or in flesh; Varina has her job. Visits across Bristol, checking the wellbeing, the social conditions, the correct benefits, for those afflicted with psychiatric illness. It gives her life meaning. She has built a decent working relationship with Dr Kavanagh, and the lady psychiatrist is one of the politer ones. Still Varina adjudges her own role to be a cautionary one. Ameliorating the meddlesome interventions of the learned Caitlin. The Irish doctor is a strong advocate of a brain-mind duality—which Varina does not believe in—she speaks at symposiums. Everything we think and say is a chemical reaction, and if the balance is disturbed, the right concoction will redress the matter. Medication from teaspoon or pipette. A bucket if needs must. Varina imagines the mind stretches further than the doctor's uninspired supposition. Pamela Bradford is proof. Everyone is mad but some stay out of the clutches of the syringe-wielding professionals. Varina scarcely cares how small the difference she makes actually is, needs only the certainty that it is so. That she has helped someone in a small way. The doctor's drug regimen is like felling a forest. She wonders if tonight's insomnia is because of Pam's unexpected call, that pleasant woman's wish to be Rice's carer. The store that she puts in her shared past with the trumpeter has brought an unwelcome perspective on Varina's own role in his life. She believes the lives her clients led before illness deserve recognition, dwelling upon them reminds all that these are more than the barking mad people they may currently appear. She knows it from a textbook, and from listening into the trembling and tearful accounts when Pam Bradford and her like tell the stories she records in her leather-bound notebook. Abridges it on to their hospital reports. Varina has never played the trumpet, never blown passion or artistry into anything she can bring to mind. She believed she could empathise with the lives of others, and now sees she is only imagining that such a mental feat might be done. Living through others is not really living at all.

Brian Pope snores a loud one, a funny whistle on the end. Sounds like a kettle; the Popes are not musical at all but they do like a cup of tea.

5.

'Your room stinks worse than mine,' announces Roderick. He is fully clothed, including a brown tweed jacket and a dark blue tie. They match not at all and comprise odd clothing for this hot August day. He has performed a morning shave, not a daily event for him, nor an essential one in the pursuit of burger sales. It is after eight o'clock and his words seem intended to rouse his companions.

The two men in the lower-than-expected bed start to stir. Rice raises a hand from under the covers. 'What's this?' he exclaims. 'Oh! Piss-Paul, you've only gone and done it again.'

The man grins sheepishly. 'Can't help it. That's the Mexican beer what's done that.'

'You drew the short straw,' laughs Roderick.

'We'll have to wash the bedding in the bath,' says Rice. 'And I need you to buy some nails, Gloucester. It was young 'un who broke the bed.'

'Did they take the wheels off?' asks Paul.

Roderick takes a moment to understand the question. Paul Norton is not cognisant with the way wheel-clampers operate. 'Never came in the end,' he says. 'Never came.'

Rice leaves the bedding soaking in the bathtub down the corridor while the three now-dressed men go to breakfast.

'Look at the little cereal boxes,' says Paul.

'Full English?' asks Bill.

Two take the proprietor up on his offer, Rice opts for a simple boiled egg.

When their food arrives both Paul and Roderick have a plate full of blackened sausage, bacon that snaps under the pressure of a fork, fried bread that swims in fat, an egg that is running nowhere and baked beans which appear admirably heated through. They love it.

Bill comes back to their table and says to Roderick, 'When do you need your van?' The three men stare at him, do not answer his question. 'Wheel-clampers came in the night. I never heard them. I've put in a call, a hundred pound to have the contraption removed, I'm afraid.'

'I don't have that sort of money.'

'It's all right, sir. We'll go fifty-fifty.'

Roderick looks a little flustered by this. 'I suppose so,' he says while taking out his wallet. 'What have you got, boys?' he asks his companions, clearly short of the fifty pounds he is in sudden need of.

'Why are you paying it, Gloucester?' says Rice 'This fella's caused the problem. You're allowed to park where you are.'

'Don't listen to him, Mr Gloucester, he's mentally ill. You said so yourself last night.'

'But I think he has a point,' says Rod.

'No. Mentally ill people make no sense.'

'Once in a while they do,' says Rod. 'Same as the rest of us. What do you reckon, Paul?'

'I don't know anything really. I think you should ask him to fix the bed while he's at it.'

'Will you shush it,' says Rice.

'What's with the bed?' asks Bill.

'It's faulty,' says Roderick.

Bill walks out of the dining room, shoulders raised, a frosty look occupying his face. Rice berates Paul for raising the issue. 'If I'd mended it, he would never have found out. Now he'll make us pay to have it fixed.'

Roderick also tells Paul that he's thick, that he should have kept his mouth shut. Paul doesn't argue, no disagreement with either man's assessment, he simply didn't spot it until they explained themselves. Paul finds his own stupidity a source of constant surprise.

'And did you really have to wet the bed,' hisses Rice on hearing footsteps coming back down the stairs.

'I couldn't help it. We drank a lot of beer, Rice. I expect Gloucester did the same.'

'I'm not having you staying here any longer,' says Bill on his return. 'My bed's completely broken.'

'But we like it how it is,' protests Paul.

'Call it quits,' says Rice. 'The van, the bed; quits. And we can stay.'

'No. Leave. The van's nothing to do with me.'

'You liar,' objects Rice. 'You had it clamped. It's got everything to do with you.'

'No. We're quits. The van, the bed.' says Bill. 'Now leave.'

'I've not drinked up my coffee,' says Paul.

'Leave!'

* * *

The three men are once more in the burger van—their cases behind the front bench seat—on the road outside the Pelican Hotel, when a bright-orange van pulls up next to their hobbled vehicle. The name, Parking Solutions, is emblazoned in bright red lettering upon the otherwise yellow van. It blocks all the traffic on this narrow street, the continuous terracing of hotels and residential housing. Cars parked nose to tail along the kerbside, left and right.

Roderick starts talking to the van driver about burger money, how quickly he can accumulate some, Rice talks across him. 'I'm Bill,' he states, 'the owner of this hotel. I requested your services in error. Foolish of me to make insufficient enquiries. Subsequent to my call, I have learnt that the vehicle belongs to these esteemed guests of my own establishment. Please unclamp his wheel and invoice the Pelican Hotel, full cost, all the taxes. My accountant will have it all paid up in no time. All right, my man?'

'I guess so,' says the wheel-clamper. He picks up a bag containing several large ratchets, screwdrivers too, walks around to the driver's side of the burger van. Gets to work. A few deft turns open up the clamp. Off in seconds. 'A hundred for cash, one-thirty if I'm billing you.'

'The invoice please, my good man,' says Rice. 'I shall claim more than thirty back from the Chancellor of the Exchequer. That Scottish fellow. I'm a hotelier, you know? It's what we do.'

The clamper gives him a funny look, snorts and leaves.

Paul whispers to Rod, 'He's gone funny again, hasn't he? Might need to see the doctor, might Rice.'

'I'm not sleeping in your piss tonight,' says Rice. Mentally ill or not, he has standards.

* * *

When they take the sign to the beach, the road is a surprise to Roderick. He's never been here before. Not this part of Torquay. Narrow and windy, it quickly dips away. Leaves the high clifftop to slalom down to Babbacombe Beach.

'Bloody hell,' he says, from behind the wheel. The lane is far steeper than any road in the environs of hilly Bristol. A succession of hairpin bends; signposts warn of its treacherous gradient.

'It should have steps,' says Paul. Sections of the pedestrian walkway have exactly those. Rod is virtually standing on the brake. The Double Gloucester burger van inches its way down to the sea.

'Good luck getting it back up,' says Rice.

'You boys are pushing,' says their perspiring landlord.

A sports car is coming up the hill and Rod brings the van to a juddering halt. It's very narrow on the bends, not easy for the vehicles to pass each other; the outrageous incline tests everybody's driving skills. Rod signals that the sports car may come around him.

'You first,' shouts its bespectacled driver.

Rod releases the brake, as he is adjacent to the vehicle

Stickerhand

rounding the bend, his rear wheel hits the curb and this startles all inside. Rod breaks heavily, the van judders, they must all hear the displeasing tin on tin—not loud, a scrape—and they are past. Rod lets the brake out, quickly reins it back in, so steep is this hill; still the van rolls forward.

'He's shaking his fist,' says Rice, sounding more amused than at any other time this stumbling holiday. His comment is about the sports-car driver, the man is out of his vehicle now. 'He's not happy with you, Gloucester. Looks like he's hopping mad.'

Paul laughs along with Rice. Only Roderick not getting the joke.

Rod pilots his burger van around bend after bend, down to the small car park at the bottom.

Paul is the first to release his seat belt. 'They're swimming,' he says, pointing across the beach.

The sea is a mesmerising shade of turquoise, green in the distance, vast and tranquil with tree-lined hills cascading down to it. A spectacular coastline stretching out before them. The sun is warm—not yet noon—the dark-sand beach, laden with sunbathers, beckons.

'We're here to sell burgers,' says Roderick. 'The lunchtime crowd is the best.'

He puts his apparatus on. His small gas grill, a pan of ready cut onions. Rice starts to help while Paul tells them he is going swimming.

'You can't actually swim though, Paul,' his landlord reminds him.

'Just trying. Sink or swim.' He is naked inside the van, serving hatch already down. It is a small car park, a café across the way. The height of the hatch hides his tackle.

'Put these on before anyone sees you,' says Rod, handing him his navy blue trunks. Paul does as he is asked. There are no customers at this time, no takers for his unplanned strip show.

'I'll swim later,' says Rice.

'He's good at it,' says Paul. 'Swims like a fish, does Rice.' Then he leaves the van, walks with more purpose in his stride than is ever seen in Bristol. Holidaying becomes him and he has known none better than this debacle.

As the two remaining men butter baps and turn burgers from

168

one side to the other, a man in glasses comes to the window. He is panting. 'You damaged my car. Look, that's my paint on your old van,' he says.

'It's knock for knock, isn't it?' says Rice. 'If you're paint has found its way onto this van, you're probably the one to blame.'

'That's scurrilous talk,' says the man. He is short of stature, no more hair on his head than on Rice's, an expensive tennis shirt clings to his fat little body. White legs angle out of beige shorts; he stands like a starfish. 'I wasn't moving. Stopped for you. I'm taking down your numberplate.'

'Would you like a burger, sir, call it quits.' Roderick is more conciliable than Rice.

'I'll see you in bloody court,' says the little man.

'He's a fool,' says Rice loudly, 'turning down a free burger. If he starves to death, it's certainly not your fault, Gloucester.'

A few beach goers have wondered over to try the food on sale. Rice keeps cooking while Roderick collects money, starts to put burgers into buns. They have sold no more than five and no complaints yet received, when a man in uniform comes to the van.

'My ticket's on the dashboard,' Roderick tells the parking attendant.

This man is very tall, he has a Torbay District Council insignia on his white shirt which he wears above crisp blue trousers. His top button is open, although a loosened tie tells of the formality of the man's role. His eyes are electric blue. 'You can park all day; however, parking isn't selling burgers, conducting business. You'll have to stop this. Must close up the shop, I'm afraid.'

'I can't stop this. It's my living,' says Rod.

'Not on Babbacombe Beach. Look...' The man with blue eyes points at the nearby café just fifty yards from the car park. '...they've got a license to trade, you haven't. Fair's fair.'

'What do you mean by fair's fair? You know nothing about what is and what isn't fair. Nothing at all.' says Rice. 'Women can claim to be your wives although you've never set eyes on them; half the doctors in Bristol think I'm mad and he isn't...' Rice gestures towards Roderick. '...even you can see that's nonsense, surely. There's a lady injects drugs up my bottom every three weeks for no reason beyond some crazy experiment she's conducting. Quelling the fire inside every fella who'll lower their trousers for her. What's so fair about this life, smart arse?'

'Rice, Rice,' soothes Roderick, 'save that for another time. This gentleman just hasn't seen our agreement, our permission papers. Did you bring them?'

'No one agrees to us even being alive, Gloucester. We've not been made as welcome as we should have been in this stinking hole.'

The parking attendant lets out a long sigh. Might be getting the measure of the men he must bring to heel and his task looks no easier for the knowing. The penetrating blue-eyes look up at Roderick in the serving hatch. 'Have you really got papers?'

'Really and truly but we left them back in Bristol,' then he leans forward tapping his forehead. 'He left them, he's mentally ill.'

'Not good enough,' says the man. 'I don't believe it, and you can't provide the proof I need. More than my job's worth to allow you to carry on. Shutters down, please. No trading. No more selling of hamburgers until you show me the documentation.'

Roderick lets out a prolonged grunt.

'We'll have to make the best of it, won't we?' says Rice. 'Swim, sunbathe, do like all the other nutters.'

The attendant stays while Roderick shuts down his apparatus. A teenage boy is looking expectantly at the van. 'I'll just serve him,' says Rod.

'You've no licence.'

Rice puts a burger inside a bun, onions on top, a squirt of brown. 'On the house, lad,' he says handing it across. Then he eyeballs the piercing blues of the attendant. 'You'll be paying for that personally when we sue you for malfeasance. Trying to hound poor Mr Gloucestershire here out of his livelihood. What kind of a game is that?'

The attendant tries to hold his gaze, his cheeks are flushed. Rice's tone is full of confidence, the outcome he predicts quite barmy.

'Thanks, mister,' says the kid.

* * *

At the beach Paul Norton has put his tiny hand towel—stolen from the Pelican Hotel—down on the sand, very close to a pair of young mothers. One has a small baby lying beside her on a beach towel, the other has a young child digging in the sand close by. Paul sits hunched up, holding his knees, staring at the swim-suited lady lying on the towel, looking at the tops of her legs, thinking about the same things he thought of last night when only Rice Bradford in the same bed could enter his field of vision. His outline apparent, street lighting filtered through the thin curtain. More of an unpleasant olfactory experience than a sight to savour. He smiles to himself, knows he drank more than Rice, farted more than Rice. The baby starts to make a moaning noise. Paul is surprised by that. Snuggled against this nice-looking young woman, what has the baby got to complain about?

'Come on, Panda Bear,' he hears the young mother say.

She raises the baby from beside her, lays it across her stomach as she lies back, then she dips one hand into the top of her swimsuit, rolls it aside exposing a single breast. Paul is delighted to see it and then, just as quickly, the baby's head has erased the sight. Suckling upon the breast, drinking from where Paul knows she would never let him do the same. Wouldn't matter how politely he asked, still going to be never. He rises from his towel, a couple of paces in the direction of the sea, then turns his head back, looking at the well-formed legs, his gaze falling on the crotch covered by the southerly triangle of her red swimsuit. Turns again and keeps walking. When he reaches the water, Paul wades in. He knows he will have to go quite deep. The lady lying beside him took a breast out. This wank will not wait, he really has to make certain all his moving parts are below the waterline. He feels like he might burst, it could be over earlier than makes for ideal jizzing.

* * *

Rod asks Rice if he's really going to take a swim.

'Oh yes,' he replies, 'back to Bristol, is my thinking. I'm no fan of Devon, I've found. They're stuck up around here. Stuck up something rotten.'

'Swim and then we'll move on. We need to sell some burgers today.'

'You do that, Gloucester. I'm getting myself burger and chips from the beach café.'

'Daft bugger; why didn't you eat one of mine?'

'I'm through with gippy tummies from your rancid meat, Gloucester. Even the cheese sweats. Let's see if Babbacombe's burgers are nicer than the ruddy people.'

'I only make them how the punters like them,' says Rod.

Rice has yet to change for swimming, carries his trunks wrapped in a towel. Heads for the beachside café.

'I'll come back for you and Paul,' shouts their de facto leader. 'Burgers to sell.' Once back in the driver's seat, he fires up the van's stumbling engine.

* * *

In the Riviera Café, Rice is disappointed to find no burger on the menu. A girl explains to him that steak panini is quite similar. She even says it is superior.

'Do I know you?' asks Rice. The girl is wearing a short green skirt and white top, she has a green cap with Riviera Café written in red upon the front. Black hair escapes the cap's yoke. 'You're not going to tell me that we used to be married, are you?'

The girl laughs like he is the funniest comedian. 'Do you want chips with your panini?' she asks.

'You do chips? Nobody's written that on the menu either.'

'We call them pommes frites. They're the same thing.'

The girl gives Rice a little flag with a number twelve on it. 'Choose a table and place the flag in the bucket,' she tells him.

Rice is impressed by this experience. Gloucester should buy flags and buckets. He sits at an outdoor table looking across the sands. The hot sun torches his bald head. Rice is familiar with sunburn; doctors have told him to keep out of the rays on account of the medication he takes. Why make depressed patients avoid sunlight? Double trouble. And a bit of blistering up there is a familiar feeling; discomfort the lot of mental patients the world over. The redness, soreness, on top of his head is not the worst of the effects of the mind-numbing medication. Not as debilitating as a hollow head. Rice scours the beach, hoping to see Paul. Hoping mostly because any prolonged absence may require him or Roderick to investigate, go and find their gargantuan child. For a long time, Rice fails to see him, and then a head in the sea acquires a chest and the entire Norton starts to emerge from the water. Makes his way towards the shore. Rice can see him clearly now, work out that he has been out in deep water and successfully managed not to drown. He gives Paul an unreciprocated wave.

The green-and-white-clad waitress brings his food. Rice thanks her with enthusiasm, tells her that she is the nicest girl in Devon. He has surmised this—hasn't gathered conclusive proof— yet to meet them all.

Paul is on the beach when next he looks; Rice waves again and once more Paul fails to return it, then he sees him stop, stoop down and talk to a lady who is sunbathing. Rice cringes inwardly. Paul has an eye for the girls but no ear or mouth. Rice cannot tell from here how the exchange is playing out. Nobody looks angry; Paul is not putting his hands on her swimsuit or flesh. Small mercies. There is another girl, she stands up, Rice thinks she must have been lying at the far side of the other girl. At first Rice thinks she is naked, then realises her bikini is white and her skin a slightly less shiny shade of the same. She is very close to Paul. In that moment, Tall-Paul looks as though he has a girlfriend—the unlikeliest of sights—and then the girl waves across the beach. Rice watches as a black-haired man wearing only cut-off jeans jogs across in response to the girl's beckoning. He exchanges words with Paul. Rice expects to be seeing a thump, supposes that Paul has spoken inappropriately to the ladies of little dress. No such altercation occurs. He sees the man remonstrate a little, then pass something to Paul. He cannot see what it is, something passed from hand to hand, a coin perhaps. Then Paul is moving towards Rice once more. A pleasant exchange or a lucky escape, Paul may explain it later. Nothing of certainty has been revealed.

Not in Rice's lifetime, he often thinks.

Rice waves and, on this occasion, Paul returns the gesture. Vigour and enthusiasm mark his response. Back from the ocean, from interacting with girls in swimwear. The lad is doing well on his holiday—not in every respect, pissing the bed and breaking its legs off were poor choices—talking to girls his own age without upsetting a boyfriend, that one might be a first.

* * *

Paul sits next to Rice at the outside table, putting his rolled-up towel on his lap. That and his tight trunks are all that he wears. His other clothes remain in the van which Gloucester is driving to a location more conducive to burger sales.

'You've made friends,' observes Rice.

'Brilliant,' says Paul. 'I just thanked the one in red and she was really pleased.'

'What did you thank her for, Paul?'

'She did something for me but she didn't know it.'

Rice looks at the young man, scrutinises him as if he might be able to work out the cryptic comment by studying his face. Paul raises a hand to his mouth, pushes something in and swallows.

'Would you like a pomme frite?' asks Rice.

Paul has to have the term explained, Rice tries to remember what Greenie said. 'It's French for fish and chips.'

'I don't eat foreign rubbish,' says Paul.

'It's better than Gloucester's crap.' Rice takes another bite from his steak panini sandwich, chews upon it while he talks. 'And the other girl, the one in white. She got her fella to see you off?'

'No. She touched my arm. I've to go back in the water soon. I want to think about her next.'

Rice grimaces, starts to have an idea about what has gone on, but not how come they have been so friendly. 'And the bloke?' 'What did he want with you?'

'He gave me some stuff. He knows about the Double Gloucester van; he'll get it back from there later. I said he can have my pay.'

'Stuff. Stuff. Oh, Piss-Paul, you don't mean drugs, do you? Will you give me whatever you've got, please?'

'Too late, Rice,' laughs Paul, sustaining a wide-open mouth for a few seconds. 'Holiday! I've swallowed it,' he declares.

The girl in green comes and stands by the table. 'Are you finding the food all right, sir?' she asks.

'Bloody marvellous,' says Rice, and again she laughs. It's a joyous sound, this girl seems more at ease in his company than anyone has been in years.

'Do you want to order anything?' she asks Paul.

'No money,' he says. The girl looks a little puzzled and turns back for the indoors.

'Bring him a coke on me,' says Rice.

'Thanks mate.'

* * *

Rod Stone's burger van is struggling to make it up the hill, the bendy acclivity between beach and cliff top. 'Shouldn't have come,' he mutters to himself as his vehicle judders and stalls. He restarts it. The engine catches first time and that's something for this knackered old van. Pushes it into first gear and once more he lets out the clutch. The vehicle moves a short way forward before it once more slides to the side and begins to slip back. 'Rice!' he shouts. 'Piss-Paul!' It is habit, he knows they are not in earshot. The road is simply too steep for this clapped-out old rust bucket. The engine turns—rotation, movement—but the noise of it is more death rattle than simple summer grumbling.

* * *

At the outside table Paul is starting to bark like a dog. Rice has seen this before and he has no time for it. Not today. He goes back inside the café; the girl in green leans across a table, wiping stains of a red sauce that Rice imagines must go by a grander name than ketchup. 'Miss,' he says loudly, and she turns around. Smiles at him. 'Can you get the man a doctor. If you know one who rides a unicycle that'd be blooming perfect. No coke after all, can't see him drinking that. I've left the money on the table.'

'Wait,' she says. He is already walking away, down the steps, not minded to obey her. Greenie doesn't even pretend to be his wife.

The girl puts down her cleaning cloth, follows Rice out of the door where she sees he is already at beach level, striding away. Towel in hand, trunks wrapped up within. She goes to collect the plate from his table, speak to the other man. She sees that there are three pound-coins upon it and she puts them into the pocket at the front of her short green skirt. 'Are you all right?' she says to Paul.

He laughs at her with glazed-over eyes. Looks to have been hypnotised. 'Have you got a baby?' says Paul. Then he tries to stand from the chair but slips on the wooden veranda. He tumbles down noisily, legs part in either direction. 'Oh hell,' he says.

'Let me help you,' says the girl as Paul squirms on the floor.

* * *

The vehicle has yet to make it a third of the way up the steep incline, stalls once more. Roderick turns the ignition key, it splutters to life, he releases the clutch, and the hapless van slides back four feet before he can slam on the brake, forgetting his clutch, stalling the engine. Sisyphus the burger van. A large Rover is a short way behind, trying to rise up the same difficult hill. The stalled vehicle impedes the Rover's passage.

Rod puts the handbrake on, opens his door and steps onto the road. 'Can you help me?' he asks the driver of the car behind him.

The windows of the Rover are all wound down, the heat of the day intense. 'I couldn't tow that,' he says, then shrieks, 'Watch out!'

The van is sliding again, this time Rod knows it's not his fault. Can't be since he's not even driving, simply watching from the roadside. He steps out of its way, it is juddering down under the force of gravity, the handbrake has gripped the wheels, they do not turn. Too little tread on the tyres, tarmac like hot treacle. The van moves only a very short distance before its rear loudly kisses the bonnet of the Rover.

'That will cost you dearly!' shouts the Rover driver. The two vehicles snog as they slide together down the hill. The Rover driver does what he can, wrestles with steering wheel and handbrake. The rear of his car comes to an abrupt halt as it squashes itself at ninety degrees to the dwarf wall at this lower bend. The wall holds, both vehicles have come to rest. The disaster is contained.

'Look at the mess you've made!' The Rover driver is furious.

Rod Stone can't be doing with this. He starts to walk briskly up the hill; it is steep and the other man is shouting at him. Rod coughs, spits out yellow sputum, struts away further, takes a handkerchief from his pocket to mop his sweaty brow, his balding pate. He thinks he can hear the man coming after him. He turns his head. 'The parking man will know what to do!' he shouts, then feels a little overcome, the walk uphill is too much. Hot and sticky; holiday stress. He has taken no money today, not proper money. Although the sun is at its highest, a darkness comes across Roderick's vision, the bleakness of a Bristol winter. He feels suddenly cold and slips down to the ground. Sits there. 'Aah, aah,' he coughs, not a productive or a purposeful one, just marking the difficulty he is having with this particular day. With breathing, in fact. The other driver is out of his car, approaching him with angry words initially, then he changes his tune when he sees Roderick slide to the ground. Keel over. The poor bugger has blacked out.

* * *

Rice cannot see the black-haired man from whom Paul procured his drug-fix. Taken on the promise of money to come. He knows where the women are, he is subtler than Paul in his observation of them. In no way is he less vigilant. As he arrives at their two towels he drops to his knees, down on the sand.

'You've ruined it, you have,' he says by way of introduction.

The baby starts to cry and the young mother holds it to her chest as she sits up to attend to this intrusion.

'Leave us alone,' says the other girl, the one in the white bikini. When Rice's intense stare holds her within it for longer than she can bear, she adds, 'Who are you?'

'I used to be a friend of Stickerhand's but I've no time for him now. He never really did your druggie rubbish. Puffed on something once or twice but it was never his thing. Is it a husband or a brother you've got supplying?'

The girl in the white bikini looks bemused. She has straight fair hair, no tan to speak of; today might be her first upon a beach this year. 'You want to buy a few pills? Is that it?' She waves a hand in the air, a signal to someone.

'I don't think he's right in the head, Trace,' says the one with the baby.

'None of us,' says Tracy. 'That's true of none of us.'

'Nothing wrong with me,' says Rice, discreetly looking over the girl on the ground, her red costume, her rich tan. It contrasts with pale Tracy. Squares on a chessboard. 'Do you mind me asking, are you both Devon girls?'

'What does it matter where we're from,' says Tracy. 'I can get you stuff if you've the money.'

The other girl raises her foot, taps Tracy's shin. 'He could be police,' she hisses.

'You're not police, are you?' says Tracy to Rice, putting her feet far apart to get some purchase in the sand.

Rice glances down at the girl's pale legs, the white triangle of bikini that covers what little of her she cares to. 'Do I look like police? Leatherworker, me. And I don't like drug dealers. Is your pal coming or what?'

'Leave off,' says the girl on the ground. 'He gave your son a happy pill, not a big deal. He is your son, I take it. That funny boy?'

'He's not a funny boy, his name's Paul. We call him Piss-Paul because he's funny to us but that's another story. What's your name, love?' Rice directs his question at the girl in red.

'No names. Just call me Jane. Don't go getting the police, right? We don't...' She clutches her baby very closely to her person. Rice has sunk onto the sand; he is beside her but appears to pay her no attention. '...mean anything by it. Drugs are normal for a lot...what is it mister?'

He is not looking at the girl at all when he speaks. 'So, you're Jane, are you? You would have to go and be her.'

* * *

An ambulance pulls up, kerbing the wheels on the steep slope. There is a policeman at the top who stops any other traffic from coming down. Those on the beach are prisoners for the duration of this emergency. The ambulance, prone patient and lightly entwined vehicles have blocked this steep and narrow road for a little time and a lot of head scratching. There will be no going up or down in anything motorised; nothing can pass if it is wider than a pedestrian.

Two men wearing short-sleeved green shirts jump out. Paramedics. They look over Roderick Stone.

'Vitals not too bad,' says one.

They agree to stretcher him into the ambulance. Begin to do so very, very carefully.

'Probable heart attack,' one directs solemnly into a radio attached to his upper sleeve.

The man from the Rover is still here, points at the modestly mangled vehicles, his light green car and the Double Gloucester van. The damage done is not so great, and a bomb wouldn't devalue the van. The ambulance sits alongside the pranged vehicles, the driver of the emergency vehicle touched neither, very skilled. When it moves others might pass likewise. The uncoupling of the van and car will keep someone or other puzzled for a little longer.

'The police have seen it,' says a paramedic.

There will be free accommodation for Stone tonight. In better circumstances, it would constitute a lucky break. This time it's touch and go. Heart behaving like a fish out of water.

* * *

Paul has scraped himself off the floor. He is rocking backwards and forwards on the rear legs of a plastic chair, manages to do so to the point that one of the metal legs snaps. 'Cheap!' he shouts as he falls back to the veranda.

'Look,' says the girl in green, 'they are almost here.' Her index finger spears the image of the ambulance halfway down the hilly road behind the café. 'I don't know why they've stopped.'

Paul continues to rock, chair beneath him, sideways on the veranda, keeps his eyes firmly on the girl in green. Rocks. Stares. 'Cheap!' he says again, this time in response to nothing.

'What's your name, sir?' she asks him.

'I don't know,' says Paul.

'We'll need to tell the ambulance men. Think!'

'It's probably something daft, isn't it?' he says, rocking himself backwards and forwards, knees tucked into his cradling arms.

A male co-worker from the café is standing next to the girl. He is hesitant, sticks around like he might be a support to her in this difficult situation, knows only how to toast paninis, not how to keep a lunatic quiet until the men in white coats arrive. He likes the girl in green—Emma—fancies her in truth. He has spent his last four shifts thinking only about asking her out. Taking Emma on a date. Might she agree to be his girlfriend? He realises that popping the question while awaiting an ambulance could be construed as tasteless. And way too easy for Emma to reject, the girl preoccupied with helping another. No other course of action comes to him. He doesn't really wish to help the mental-case on the deck. Wonders why his colleague attends him so judiciously.

Just standing next to her, glancing occasionally at her tanned legs in the short green skirt, has made his own brains turn to mush. He doesn't think that it's Emma's looks which have sent the tall man lying on the floor crazy. That's not the order of events as he understands them; however, it must be in the range of the possible. Emma really does look a peach.

*   *   *

'What did that mean,' says Rice. 'I saw you.'

'It's nothing, I've got sand in my hair.'

The girl in the white bikini has made an odd hand movement above her head, noticeable even to Rice. Which is something because he's really gone out to lunch this time. Not come back again. Doolally. His suspicion that she has signalled the man who supplied some rubbish to Paul not to venture any closer towards them is a strong one, a correct one. He's pretty frayed at the edges but not as far gone as most were back in Mendip Ward. Or maybe he is, the lady doctor who let him go had no crazyometer with which to measure his state. Draw a definitive conclusion.

'What does it mean, Jane,' he asks of her friend. 'You never lied about anything. Always true. What was Tracy doing?'

'We've never met,' says the girl who is calling herself Jane.

'That's not like you to start playing games.' He looks searchingly at her. She has lain back on the towel. The baby which she holds is once more suckling on a popped-out breast. 'That's not mine, is it?' says Rice.

'What have you taken?' she says.

'Boy or girl?'

'It's a boy.'

'Mine?'

'Of course he's not yours. I've a boyfriend as could punch your lights out.'

'Aye, brothers too. What did you call him, in the end?'

'This is Andrew. Don't be weird about my baby, I don't like it.'

'Andrew,' says Rice. 'I like the name whoever the father is.'

*   *   *

'Come now,' says the ambulance man. 'We can't stop, we've a man needs more urgent attention than you; we'll take you if you pop into the ambulance straight off.'

'Go,' says Emma, taking one of Paul's big paddle hands into her two smaller ones, tempting him to rise from the wooden veranda on which he sits.

The second paramedic is at the rear doors of the ambulance in front of the café. 'We can't wait,' he shouts up. 'We've a fella to get to the hospital.'

'For me,' says the girl. It is enough. Paul lets Emma pull him to his feet; assists more than he resists.

The ambulance man nearest puts an arm across Paul's shoulder. 'Watch the steps,' he says as he guides him.

When he has climbed up the rear footrest and gone inside, Paul Norton places a big hand on the head of the man lying on the gurney. On the scalp of ashen-faced Roderick Stone. 'Yes..s..s, my son.'

Rod Stone usually grins through this malarkey. This time around it draws a blank.

* * *

'I'm swimming,' says Rice. 'Mind my clobber, Jane.'

He removes his shirt and the vest he wears beneath it, shoes next, scuffed black brogues that he pushes onto the young mum's towel. He lowers his trousers, white legs, veined and sickly. The underpants and socks come off too. The two girls start to laugh, then stop when they observe the trance which has overtaken Rice. Oblivious to them, to his own nudity too, they must have spotted that.

'You're better off here than in Rochdale,' he says to Jane, as he turns and walks towards the sea. One or two people shout at him to cover up; as he walks, they clear a path. A naked man exerts a primal authority in the modern world. 'John the Baptist's cemetery,' he shouts back over his shoulder. 'There's no fun to be had there.'

Quickly, he makes his way into the water, pushes himself into the small incoming waves. Forward crawl. A strong swimmer, if no longer fast. His head goes under the water—one, two, out and breathe—taking himself further off into the deep. Some people on the beach are talking about him. A lady goes to find a lifeguard, without success. The station unmanned. His head is a speck in the water now. Off out to sea. Rice can swim and swim for hours.

* * *

It is not an end at all. They will surely go on and on, however dispersed they may become. And after them shall come others in their likeness, a surrendering army which otherwise forages away in the shadows of town and city, and on the frayed edge of every village and seaside resort. Lining the urinals of motorway service stations. The three we have seen are just ourselves in microcosm. There is an oaf who can but take drugs to obliterate what is barely there in the first place; then there is the poor landlord from fairyland, who has never spent a night in a mental hospital although—God knows—his presence there would not be out of keeping. It is a regular ward for him tonight, a cardiac ward. We must hope he recovers without truly knowing what difference such an upturn will make to the wider scheme of things. For we are all good people, are we not? Wishing for the best, a smoother passage, even for those we spend our lives avoiding.

And Rice 'Stickerhand' Bradford, swimming naked towards Teignmouth. He's unlikely to make it that far, will probably come ashore before he's half way. Scramble up onto the coastal path, scare some poor sod with his willy, although many a pair of trousers covers one. Way over fifty percent. A todger should not be a surprising thing, however much we kid ourselves to the contrary, or wish to avoid seeing the damned things for the sheer embarrassment every outing provokes. And surely some kindly police officer—or maybe an irritable and burnt-out one—will throw a coat or blanket over what the world has no need to see.

These three men, housemates if only for a short time—humanity gone to seed—are discernibly less pernicious than the usual, the enterprising, the procreating masses. Why it is that their actions should cause so much more offence than average is more than a mystery: it is a prejudice. If there is hope, it is a hope that their suffering will soon be over. A hope that will one day be fulfilled, sadly not without a little more tottering on the precipice of society. Rubbing of hand on scalp and shouting that phrase of their own devising. The only positivity in their lives. Could be there is an admission or two more into the Princess Margaret, where Varina will once more pick up the reins. She's good, always does whatever she can to help.

Printed in Great Britain
by Amazon

59372229R00106